PROFESSED

NICOLA RENDELL

PROFESSED

Cover Designer: Najla Qamber Designs
Interior Designer: The Write Assistants
Editing: Aquila Editing & Alexis Durbin from Indie Girl Proofs

For him, my love.

Dulce pomum quum abest custos.

Forbidden fruit is sweetest.

1

Naomi

He's all alone, in a gold half mask. Messy blond hair, killer jawline. Simple, thin, black tie. Lean like a rock climber and easy in his body. He lowers his glass of absinthe. His eyes slide up every inch of me, land on my face, and I see his mouth form a single word:

Damn.

I drag my eyes away from him. Above me, the roof of the crypt vaults up three stories, everything granite and dark marble, lit by nothing but church candles. On a scaffold platform, snaked with cords, the DJ is perched above the dance floor, where dancers grind against one another on top of gravestones. The DJ looks like a human blackbird with a strange beaked mask covering his face. Tux pants, a tight, black motorcycle jacket, each hand on a turntable. Below him, in the dancing crowd, I watch a guy in a phantom mask slide his hand right up a woman's dress. Her body arches backwards as he fingers her. The Whips, one of the secret societies, are here too. The Victoria's Secret Angels meet BDSM. Girls in black harnesses and body paint, snapping riding crops through the air towards astonished carved angels in the walls. Two girls writhe, chained to one another around a column, with two men on their knees in front of them.

One of the men lifts his mask and licks up one of the girl's thighs, and her hands tighten on her restraints. In the corner, two girls in nothing but nipple clamps sling darts at a board shaped like the Yale official crest. Above it all leer the faces of furious gargoyles and purposefully forgotten Civil War heroes.

He's still looking. I sweep my hair forward over my shoulder and adjust my mask. It's flexible plastic, but looks like lace, and one side has the eye of an ostrich feather. Etsy, of course, and borrowed. I feel a flush come to my face. That look he's giving me, it's the hottest thing in the room. Even hotter than the flaming metal trash can to my left.

It's a dinged, old, industrial thing, with fire licking up over the top. Into it, I drop my invitation, adding it to the already burnt dozens. The fire ignites the white ink before the black cardstock, and in the flaming letters I read one last time:

THE LUX ET VERITAS SECRET SOCIETY

INVITES YOU

TO

THE SECRETEM LUXURIA

MASKED. BLACK-AND-WHITE. NO UNDERWEAR.

11PM. TONIGHT

BURN UPON ENTRY

I grip the black satin ruched sides of my dress and yank it down for the seven-hundredth time, while the blond shamelessly lifts my hem from twenty feet away. The last time I wore this dress was three years ago at my high school prom. My date was a guy who smelled overwhelmingly of Axe body spray and preferred to dance at the edges of the crowd by moving his hands up and down his body like the gopher in *Caddyshack*. Back then, the dress was six inches longer and not nearly so tight as it is now. Either satin shrinks in the closet, or I've filled out a little. Tonight's hemline is the result of the fastest sewing alteration I've ever done in my life. I didn't think tea length was quite appropriate for a secret debauchery, but it's possible I might've over-hemmed. Maybe. Now instead of tea length, it's more *hussy length*.

The blond doesn't seem to mind, not a bit.

I straighten my legs over my white stilettos, also borrowed. Until

2

tonight, I'd only ever seen shoes like these on billboards next to the train on the way into Manhattan. I keep my knees together and notice something I'd missed. Between Blond and me, on the stone floor at the base of the staircase. I must have been standing right on top of it when I saw him for the first time.

A single word, written in chalk in neat, tight letters. Ominous. Delicious.

READY?

2
ben

one hour earlier.

I'm lying on my hotel bed doing the usual: eating Oreos, filling first, thinking about the philosophy of nothingness. Like how need and love are just nonsense ideas that humans invented to make sense of the infinite meaninglessness of life.

That's when I hear a noise at the door. I'm expecting the final bill, but I don't see a business envelope. This envelope, it's black with my name written in white on the front.

B. BECK

I fling open the door. This doesn't go entirely as I'd planned because when I yank it open, I yank it against the hotel lock first. Shut the door. Unlock the door. Open the door again. I see nobody in the hallway. There's not even a ding at the elevators. Dead silence except for the *whirrrrr* of the halogen bulbs above.

When I step back into the room, the door swings shut with a digital ding and a mechanical grind.

Just to be sure, I fling open the door one more time. Yeah. Bupkis. I open up the envelope. The card inside is hefty and black, with white dots down one side. I give it a read.

the lux et veritas secret society invites you…

Whoa, buddy. Talk about cloak and dagger. Talk about skull and bones. That dress code? The Latin? The secrecy? Holy shit.

If this were any other night, I'd toss it in the trash. Parties, they're not for me. I never have any idea what to say, because the minute you say you study *how nothing matters,* people clam up pretty damn quick. Tonight, though, it feels different. Tonight is different.

Tonight feels like my last night of freedom. Only I'm not getting married to a woman tomorrow. I'm getting married to a new job.

Tomorrow, shit gets real. Ivy League real.

In my small, black, rolling bag, all my clothes are packed, and I mean *all my clothes,* including my only suit. Which happens to be black. My only tie, which happens to be black. My three button-up shirts, which are all white.

I look down at my feet. Brown shoes. Nobody'll notice.

I turn the invite over in my hands. Last night of freedom. Nothing to lose.

Yeah. I'd like to know about this *secretem luxuria,* this secret debauchery. A whole hell of a lot.

••

When I step outside my hotel room, showered and adjusting my tie, I'm met by a long line of chalk dots on the carpet.
Clear enough, as spooky-ass signals go. I follow them all the way to the elevator and then into the lobby. But outside my hotel, I'm met with a chalk X on the ground.

Turning over the invitation, I read the back again. *You will be guided. Just wait.*

Yeah. That's not weird. At all.

What I'm waiting for, I don't even know. Straightening my collar, I watch a crow eat a cookie across the street. I mean, what could it even be? Uber? A cab? A guy in a white van? Fuck. Is this a good idea?

Probably not.

A young woman approaches from my left, talking on the phone. She's cute. Yoga pants, flip-flops because it's fall and still warm outside. I do have a thing for yoga pants. Flip-flops. Hoodies with thumbholes. She's not quite my type. Short blonde hair. I'm a raven-haired man. Preferably black hair. And blue eyes. That combination. Goddamn.

The blonde bumps straight into me, knocking me in the shoulder.

"Sorry," I say. I don't know why. She managed, against all odds, to slam into me on a totally empty sidewalk.

"Batell Chapel," she says.

"You're going the wrong way," I tell her. I haven't been here long, but I know that much at least. "It's down Elm."

She's already ten feet past me, and she says, "You heard me, Professor Beck. Batell Chapel."

Professor Beck? She knows me? Holy. Shit.

I pass under the big stone archway over High Street. I head down College and approach Batell from the back. It's a massive old thing right near the Green. One of those places it would never, ever cross my mind to go inside. Just as I'm about to make a left to circle around to the front, I see a chalk X on a tiny, old door. I hear the music and the noise of a serious, serious party somewhere behind that door.

Game. On.

I walk up a narrow, ancient stairway, hardly big enough for my shoulders across, and there's another door. On it, in chalk, the word READY?

Bring it.

As soon as I come out of the tiny stairway, a guy grabs my arm and pulls me aside. Tuxedo, high-necked collar, like he's in the wrong century. On his face, he wears a clear plastic mask that warps his features completely. "Dr. Beck," he yells over the music, and doesn't wait for an answer. "Welcome to the Luxuria. Dress code?" he says.

So yeah, I'm wearing boxers, because I'm a lot of things, but a guy who goes commando isn't one of them. Either he can tell that by looking, or this is the drill. "Sorry, man. Too weird," I yell into his ear. "Who the hell are you?"

He pitches his head back in a laugh and slaps me on the shoulder, acting like I should know him. A girl approaches, carrying a tray and dressed entirely in strips of electrical tape. The tape crosses her curves, accentuates her breasts, making geometry of the human form. For one second, I think I'd like to peel that tape back myself. But she's not my type, and she's clearly a student. Something in her brashness just screams *senior year.* So that's a mess I don't want to get involved in.

"What the hell am I doing here?" I ask the stranger.

He hands me a mask. A simple gold mask, designed to cover my forehead, eyes, and just one cheek.

"Put it on," the stranger says. It looks ancient, but as I take it from him, I realize it's not. It's plastic. Hardly weighs an ounce. I position it on my face while he says, "You're here because you're a big fucking deal." He nods at the girl as she lowers a tray between us. "This is our red carpet."

On it there's now one thick-stemmed, low-slung glass, ready with a slotted silver knife over the top, with a sugar cube balanced on that. From a shaker, the girl in the tape pours down a slow trickle of green liquid, which eats away at the cube.

Absinthe. Ivy League serious, for real. Some kind of red carpet.

She hands it to me and turns away, the ripples of the tape showing the topography of her whole body, like the sexiest USGS map that was ever made.

The stranger puts one hand on my shoulder, leans in and says, "Enjoy yourself, Professor."

Then she walks off, into the thumping crowd of masks, tuxedoes, and girls in collars. Masks on every face, and it's all black and white, everywhere.

Except for one thing.

A girl is coming down the staircase opposite me. Black-haired, blue-eyed, in a sexy little black dress and black lace mask. She's a fucking vision. She makes it hard to breathe. But that's not all. From where I'm standing, now slightly below her, I can see up her dress. There's a line of red lace showing off the curve of an absolutely perfect ass.

A gorgeous blue-eyed, raven-haired woman. A rebel in red lace panties.

That's not a student.

That's trouble. Just my kind of trouble.

"Damn."

3
Naomi

I feel a million butterflies landing on me, and I hardly feel like myself, neither in this place nor this dress. My normal Saturday night consists of falling asleep over a book in my dorm room and startling myself awake with drool coming down my chin. My normal wardrobe consists of an exquisitely well-worn array of hoodies and soft yoga pants with inexplicable black stains—you know the ones, they stay black while the pants fade to a soft gray? But here I am, in satin and $600 shoes. With an absolute hunk giving me the eye.

I'm hit with a familiar wave of *not belonging*. It feels like the opposite of nostalgia. But I'm here. This is happening. To the breach, like my dad always says. To the goddamned breach. So I take one step towards him and raise my eyes to his. A girl passes in front of me, dressed only in undulating stripes of black electric tape, curving over her breasts and her hips. Her body is utterly stunning. Beautiful and sensuous, with creamy white skin and swimsuit-model legs.

She wears a simple black mask that covers her whole face. But wait. I recognize that blonde fishtail braid. I recognize that collarbone. That belongs to my best friend.

"Lucy!" I whisper and lean down to hug her.

It's all starting to make sense, I think. If Lucy's part of the Lux et Veritas secret society, then she invited me. Why? I have no idea. A lobsterman's daughter would never really belong in a place like this.

My eyes dart back to the blond. I can't stop looking at him. I'm almost sure I see his lips form into a slow whistle, as he stares at my breasts. Astonishingly, he's not looking at Lucy. He's still looking at me. A rush of embarrassment warms cheeks. I press my fingers to my mask like I'm adjusting it, but really I'm just checking on what I knew already. I'm bright red all over.

Lucy swoops past, and then pinches me on the ass before disappearing back into the crowd.

The blond is a now approaching me, making his way around the edge of the crypt. He's got such a presence, one of those guys that you just can't take your eyes off of, not for love nor money. That hair is honestly messy, I can tell, not arranged to look that way. That scruff is real scruff. The sex appeal? Truth. And the way he's looking at me? The kind of guy who knows what he wants and is going to take it. What he wants is me.

And what I want is him.

Suddenly, another man comes into my line of sight, blocking out the blond. This one is wearing a Guy Fawkes mask, but I'd know that body anywhere, those shoulders and the way he looks in a suit.

It's Isaac. My ex-boyfriend, of course. Right on cue.

"Hey, beautiful," he says, putting his hand to my waist. I swiftly remove it.

The blond stops cold, but he's still watching. I can see him in my periphery. Peeling my underwear from my body.

Isaac tries to pull me close, but I resist again. He dwarfs me and has me by a hundred and fifty pounds. He rows crew and looks like a J. Crew model, which would be because he is. He actually models for J. Crew part time. I saw that they put him in a pink polo for their Spring/Summer line. He's not man enough to wear pink.

And he's an insufferable, jealous ass. We haven't talked since the end of spring term. He sends me Facebook messages whenever he gets drunk, and I see red every damn time. And typos. *So* many typos.

"I missed you," he says.

"I saw you in Spring/Summer," I yell up towards his ear.

"Fuck you."

"Pink isn't your color!"

"Let me teach you the ropes," Isaac says, trying to pull me to the dance floor. I smell the nose-pinching richness of his cologne, and like scents do, it thrusts me back in time. To meeting him, to being in bed with him. To him screaming at me in the streets, asking who else I was fucking.

Charming, just charming.

Now I dig in my heels, quite literally. I wobble a little in my shoes, but by bending my knees I get leverage against him.

He lets go of my wrists and gives me *what the fuck* hands.

In return, I thrust a *stop* hand at him. That's when Lucy swoops back in, like some aggressive rare zebra. She hands me an absinthe and a bottle of water and positions herself between us. Isaac is terrified of her. She said she'd gouge out his eyes with the blunt end of one of his complimentary J. Crew pens if he ever talked to me again. I look at Isaac over Lucy's head, like, *Remember? She wasn't kidding.*

I'm fairly sure Lucy flips Isaac the finger because he flips it back.

I let my anger and the sting of that Armani cologne subside. Lucy takes an absinthe for herself from a passing tray and toasts me. She raises her mask, and I see her cheeks are sweaty and flushed. She gives me that polished, coy, Greenwich debutante smile of hers and winks. I feel the clink of our glasses but can't hear it over the thumping music. Absinthe, it tastes like liquid licorice, but not like Good & Plenty. More like that really good Australian "soft eating" licorice, like somewhere between salty, bitter, and sweet. It's strong, super strong. As soon as it hits my stomach, I can feel this isn't your ordinary 80 proof. I like it, quite a lot, and the sweet green sludge at the bottom of my glass slides down my throat in a minute.

Meanwhile, Isaac and his over-amped testosterone levels have become distracted by a girl with orderly hot-roller curls, a D-cup, and a spray tan. That's more his type. God bless.

Slowly, I let my eyes slide back over to the blond, who's now unhooking my bra from twenty feet away. "Who is he?" I ask Lucy, into her ear.

She shrugs. "Don't know. But so sexy!"

No kidding. *So* sexy. I feel the heat come up into my cheeks as he starts approaching again. Lucy takes this as her cue to slip away, and my pulse picks up immediately. The way he looks at me, it's paralyzing. It's so steamy, it's so greedy. So determined.

The music drops down a bit, and he comes up alongside me. The air between us thickens somehow. He doesn't say anything, not out loud, but the way his pants brush against my leg, the way his thigh presses against my hip, it says everything. It says *I want you. Bad.*

I look up at him and say, "You've been watching me."

"Yeah," he says, breaking into a big, sincere, contagious smile. A dimple on his right cheek. Mercy. "I can't stop."

My vision seems to wobble when I look into his eyes. I have an irresistible urge to reach up and touch that jawline, the only part of his face that's exposed, to see what his skin feels like, to see how rough that stubble is, to feel each whisker pass under my fingertips.

So.

That's exactly what I do.

As if my hand isn't mine, I watch it move through the air, and find my palm against that sharp jaw and my thumb resting on his cheek.

Holy God! Naomi! Steady on! I snatch my hand away. What is happening? No wonder everybody lost their minds drinking absinthe. I turn away horrified. Next thing I know, I'll go insane and end up talking to empty swimming pools in the middle of winter. Absolutely zero impulse control! I press my hand to my side and say, "God, sorry. I don't know…"

His eyes seem sad. I can see he's a good bit older than I am, and I become absolutely sure he must be a professor. But a young one. Or maybe a grad student? I know I don't know him, though. I'd never forget those eyes.

He gives me another smile. I see that he's got a slight chin dimple too. I feel my heart constrict.

"I'm Ben," he says.

"Naomi." I extend my hand to shake his.

What does he do then? Lowers his head to my hand and kisses it.

My other hand instinctively moves to my chest, and I gasp. He presses his fingers to the inside of my palm and lets them linger there about three seconds past what would be acceptable in any situation but this one. "Are you a professor here?" I ask.

He shakes his head. "Not exactly." And that's when he puts one hand on the small of my back, sliding it along the satin to hook his fingers around my waist.

Exhaling, I try to regroup. I can't. His stomach is perfectly flat, not an ounce of fat on him at all. I've got an urge just to slide my fingers along that place between belt and shirt.

Inhaling deeply, I try to place that smell. It's familiar, it's clean. It's Irish Spring.

Mayday, mayday!

The music is still low, and we're close enough and deep enough into cloisters not to have to yell.

"What about you? A professor?" he asks. He's leaning down towards me, and I'm momentarily held hostage by the way his neck looks, so lovely and suntanned next to his crisp white shirt.

"Law student!" I say.

Why did I say that? Absinthe, has to be the absinthe. Or the fact that if I'd said, *Just a junior!* he'd step away from me like I have a rampant infectious disease.

He knits fingers deeper into the ruches in the fabric at my side. His hand is strong and firm, and his thumb nestles just perfectly along the curve of my back. The heat of his legs passes through his pants against my thigh. I want to share that heat. I want to know that heat.

The shudder starts just above my belly button and ends at the tips of my fingers.

Maybe it's the absinthe, maybe it's the Irish Spring, I just don't know, but that's when I grab his hand and lead him to the dance floor. At first, he resists me. Not a natural on the dance floor, which I like. Tentative, not too cocky. But I slip my fingers between his and squeeze. *Please.*

"I'm shit at dancing," he says.

I get up on my tiptoes and whisper in his ear, "I'll show you."

I feel his throat quiver against my cheek as he groans. "You will, huh?"

I nod. "I'll show you just what I like."

And with that, he's mine. He pulls me close to his body. I can see him studying my face, just as I'm studying him. I place my hand on the back of his neck, hanging on tight. Above us, the DJ's got one hand up, telling us, *Hold, Hold, Hold.* He's spinning two records at once: one, this mind-blurring backbeat, maddening, industrial, and the other Gregorian chants, now on a tight loop: *Spiritus sancti spiritus sancti spiritus sancti.*

Keeping it low, keeping it fierce. Keeping us on the edge.

Sanctiiiiiiiii...

Whump, whump, whump.

The DJ lowers his hand, lowers his head. The beat is just about to drop.

I get close to his ear. The bottom drops out of everything, it gets dead silent. My stomach presses against his belt, and I whisper, "Ready?"

He yanks me close… "Fuck yes."

And we're off. He keeps his head lowered to keep his face near mine. Immediately, everything in me is rushing for him. So much desire in those eyes, so focused here in the middle of all the chaos. The DJ, he sets that beat where all the magic happens. A sweet spot, the right speed to move your hips and be human in a way nothing else lets you be. Sex right through the air.

Ben and I start out close and only get closer, every second learning each other through touch and feel. Satin, suiting, belt loops, hems. Buttons, zippers. Seams. Fingers, jaw, thumbs, ribs.

I've never danced with anybody like this in my life. He doesn't let go, and neither do I. I've never felt anything so sensuous, so connected. There are a hundred people on this floor, but minute by minute they all fall away. Beat to beat, we get closer. I get the feeling that the DJ is playing just for us, we're that couple that people move aside for. I've never been part of that couple before. But I am now.

When the DJ breaks between songs, Ben grabs two absinthes off a passing tray.

"Careful," he says, even as he hands me one.

"Or what," I say in his ear, "we'll go insane?"

He tips his head, like maybe it's already too late.

"You're a fantastic dancer," I tell him.

"You are. I'm just hanging on for dear life."

Whump. Whump. Whump. A new, slower beat starts. Ben puts the glasses on a stone ledge behind me and grabs me again.

That's when Isaac reappears, trying to cut in. All squared shoulders and slim-cut trousers, puffed up with protein shakes and too many B vitamins. I feel the hot bile in my throat.

But Ben hangs on to me. Into my ear, he asks, "Want me to get rid of him?"

"I can handle it," I say.

Ben nods. "Just checking."

Apparently, however, I can't handle it because it's not about me, suddenly. Isaac puts his hands on Ben's shoulders, gripping the suit fabric

13

in his fingers. Isaac is the perpetual brawler. Too much liquor, hair-trigger temper, always ready to throw a punch. In my arms, I feel Ben stiffen.

Isaac actually takes off his mask, all alpha male nonsense, "That's my girl."

I wave a finger at him, *Not your girl!*

That's when Ben reaches up and puts one hand on Isaac's shoulder. Not aggressive. Just firm, solid, confident. He leans away from me, into Isaac's ear. I can feel Ben's voice under my fingertips on his chest, but I can't hear him. Isaac's eyes are right on me at first, hot and mean, but then they move to the floor. Like the game has changed. Everything seems to slow down. It's like watching a rutting moose get stopped in his tracks. Isaac relents, raising his hands to say, *Take her.* And then he steps away.

Ben seizes me tight in his arms and spins me off in another direction, candlelight streaking behind him.

When the music drops down again, I get up on my tiptoes and ask, "What did say to him?"

But he just smiles, like I really, really don't want to know.

"What did you say?"

I see his eyes narrow behind that mask. Just a little. He pulls me right to him, fingers moving past the small of my back in a possessive grab of my ass. As he shifts my panties an inch, I feel the wetness begin to rush out of me. It would be inappropriate it if wasn't so exactly right.

His fingertips press into my bare flesh. "I said I want you, and I don't fuck around. So that was that."

Now this here? Is a man. "That's mutual."

"I get the feeling you don't fuck around either."

"Never ever."

He pulls me to the corner, where it's quieter and more still. I try to catch my breath, but being so close to him isn't making it easy. I gather my damp hair in my hand and pull it off to the side, letting the cool air hit my neck.

From a waiter he grabs a fresh bottle of water and pours some into his palm. Then he lifts his mask and splashes it on his face. It's then that I get my first good look at him. He's just gorgeous. Sparkling eyes, rugged cheekbones. Dark blond eyebrows. With that water on his face, it's like he's just stepped out of the pool. Too late for mayday. This ship is sinking fast.

After placing the mask back on, he drizzles a little more water into his hand. With his palm cupped, he presses his palm to my neck and the water spills down my chest.

Shit. *Oh shit.*

Now he's pushing my hair away from my ear slightly. His lips just brush my skin, making my eyes flutter shut. Into my ear now, he says, "I'm going to kiss you. I don't think you could stop me if you tried."

With his lips on mine, his stubble grates against my cheek. At first, the kiss is warm and gentle and respectful but then increasingly searching and urgent. When I kiss harder, he takes it as permission to go further and further. Hot breath from his nose warms my cheek. I hold on to his neck, feeling his hairline under my fingertips and his jaw with my thumbs. The music goes silent in my head. I try to keep up with him, try to kiss him back and he lets me in, but he's overwhelming me.

Grabbing me by the ass again, he presses me up against the wall kissing me harder. He hoists me up against the stone, causing me to cinch his waist with my legs. He's hard and massive, and the base of his cock compresses my clit right through my panties and his fly, making me groan. I hang on to those sexy shoulders. But it's then I realize we're not against the wall. We're against an emergency exit door. The handle is just below my ass.

"Do you want to get out of here?" I ask.

"Fuck yeah I do," he tells me.

And that's when I thrust my hips backwards against the handle, both of us laughing into a new kiss, through the ear-splitting screech.

4
ben

She's a five-alarm fire. The emergency exit swings open, and I drive her into a stone stairwell. The stones are damp from rain, and warm air blows through a vent at my feet.. I taste her mouth again. Absinthe, whiskey and Everclear have nothing on this woman. Nothing. She's 1000 proof, and she's ruining me.

"I have *always* wanted to do that," she says. Her eyes are shining, even down here in the dark with only the street lamps way above us. Those eyes. Dark blue with a black rim around the edge.

"Yeah? Fuck the rules."

"Fuck them every which way," she says, more serious now. Eyes narrower.

"You've got a mouth on you."

"Sailor's daughter," she says, laughing just a little again.

I press her to the wall, pulling her into my hardness more and more each time. I need her to fucking feel it. I need her to know it. She's making me reckless, she's making me wild. She's making me *want* in a way that I'd forgotten I could or ever did.

"Why do you taste like heaven?" Like lemonade on a hot day.

"Do you like it?"

Do I like it? I'm so hungry for her I can't even think. There is no time. There is no philosophy. There's just *being*. There's just her and me right here together.

She slides her mask off, and I see her whole face for the first time. Those cheeks, the way her long black eyelashes graze them when she blinks. She's got this lovely, adorable nose, and a splash of freckles across her face. Her lips are a perfect natural pink. She doesn't take her mask all the way off. Instead, she just leaves it on her forehead, her hair a messy tangle to one side.

Now she slides my mask off. When she exhales, staring at me, her cleavage catches the light of the street lamps above. "Hello."

Her breathing is heavy. So is mine. I explore that face I hadn't gotten to see. She is so much hotter than she was before. That face seals the deal. A body is a body, but beauty is the whole. I want to see what beauty like this looks like in ecstasy. I want to see that beauty roar.

I force her to the other side of the stairwell, against a wrought iron door. The iron thumps against the stone, as I slide my hands down her legs. I hoist her up higher, and I press her to the door spreading her thighs. The smell of her now, the part of her I want so bad it makes me ache. Not just lemons. Honey and warmth and ocean water.

"I know this is a dirty thing to say." My voice is raspy and hoarse. "But I want to get inside you. I need to feel you."

"The cops will catch us," she says. She's laughing a little again. She's full of cute giggles.

I grind my hips hard against her pelvis. I hold her there with my hands, my thumbs digging into her hipbones. I watch her eyes. I'm lost in her and I'm not even inside her yet. I slide my fingers alongside those panties and feel her lips. So hot and already slick. I start to dry-fuck her right there in the stairwell. It's like I'm possessed. Me. In there. I have to have it. I have to have her.

She's after something in her purse. I hear a click and a rattle. "They'll give us a ticket for screwing in public and ignoring emergency signage." I watch her tear open a condom wrapper with her teeth. God *damn it*.

"Don't fucking matter," I say, unzipping my pants.

She slides it on, and I make sure it's all the way to the base. I'm going to need it that way, the way I'm planning to take her. Slowly, I press into her, finally getting as close as I need to be. Her gritted-teeth moans just make me want her more. The way she thrusts her head back drives me

17

deeper and deeper.

At first, I've got a fighting chance of hanging on, of finding my rhythm with her. But then she rakes her nails down my hairline, onto my neck. She unbuttons my shirt and claws my chest. She pinches my nipple hard, all the time with her head back and her eyes closed. She whispers a slow, steady stream of *fucks*.

"You're going to make me come," I tell her.

"Won't be the last time," she says.

Boom, I'm gone. Just gone. Busted apart in the rush of lemon, her whispers of *yes yes yes*, and her soft black hair.

5

Naomi

Even before he's finished coming, he begins massaging the edge of my clit with the pad of his thumb. Not touching it directly, but easing me into it, working me up and up.

"I'm close," I whisper, because I was turned on the minute I saw him, and that was hours ago. And oh God, does he ever know what he's doing, holy man alive. I press my head into the iron door behind me, hanging onto it with one hand and onto his neck with another. I'm on the brink of tumbling down into my orgasm when he slows.

Whimpering. That's the only word for the sound I'm making.

"Listen, come back to my hotel with me. I want to do this right." His face is impossibly sexy in this dark light, those eyes not even gleaming, just shadows under the far-above streetlights. "What do you say?"

Oh yes, yes, God, yes please. I nod—I can hardly do anything else. He lowers me down, pulling his still-hard cock from me as he does. He lets his length slide along my clit, and my body actually buckles with desire for more of him. I have to steady myself on the iron door behind me. Then I slide the condom off with one hand. He takes it from me and slips it in a dumpster.

As we begin to walk up the stone steps to the street, I realize my feet are absolutely killing me. I hadn't realized before, and I hiss as the edge of Lucy's shoes cut into a new blister.

"Sorry," I say, stepping out of them on the sidewalk.

He runs a hand down my arm. There's a sheen of sweat all over me, and he must be able to feel the goose bumps. He takes off his jacket, puts it on me, and then lowers down into a crouch, facing away from me.

"Everything okay?" I ask him. Somehow I think he must be looking for a contact or a dropped wallet.

He turns over his shoulder smiling and pats his back with one hand. "Hop on."

"Piggyback!" I whisper.

"Giddy up, beautiful."

I hesitate for one second exactly, and then use a stone planter as a stepstool.

There is something intensely erotic about the feeling of my legs around his waist, about the way his hipbones support my knees, the width of his shoulders in front of mine, the way he carries me so effortlessly along, the way his coat feels on the skin of my arms. I position my face right next to his, and I find he's smiling.

"Alright?" he asks.

"Oh yes," I whisper, into his ear. "We're perfect."

And we're off. He carries me down College, and takes a right on Chapel. I use the opportunity to explore the edges of his ears, his neck, the place where his shirt meets his skin. He smells not just like Irish Spring, but also like clean laundry and hair gel and all the most delicious things. No fancy cologne assaulting my nose, just rugged, real masculine yumminess. Every time I run my tongue over a particular spot on his right ear, he grabs my ass a little tighter and makes this perfect dark moan.

When we get to his hotel—it's called the Study, the nicest place in town—he carries me right through the lobby on his back. The lady at the front desk stares and then smiles.

"Hi!" I say, bouncing along through the foyer.

"Have a good night," she says and grins down at her laptop on the concierge's desk.

I cling on tighter to him as he bends to press the button for the elevator. Inside, it's mirrored. He stares at my reflection and digs his fingers into my thighs a little harder.

The vision of him making love to me on the floor of this elevator is outrageously tempting. Hitting the emergency stop and making the security guards blush? Oh yes, that sounds just *lovely*.

"Keycard is in the left front pocket," he says. He's shaking his head at me in the mirror. He knows what I'm thinking. "No way am I taking you right here."

"Why not?" It comes out as a whisper. "Because we need space."

"And time," I add, widening my eyes at him.

"Exactly," he says. "I need to lay you down and make you come the right way."

The only sound is my breath, coming out in a rush, and the sound of the elevator taking us up. I wonder if he can feel how wet I am through the back of his shirt.

Then the elevator dings, shocking me back into the world. I feel around in his suit coat for the keycard. I feel his wallet beside it, soft and worn leather. I take the keycard in my fingers as we head down the hall.

"Well done," he says, squeezing my ass. We make our way down the hallway, past a handful of rooms, and then he stops in front of one of the suites. He tips forward to let me put the key in the reader. With a beep and a click, we're inside. He drops me and turns around, pressing me up against the door. With one hand he pulls up my dress, and I reach up and slide the lock closed.

I'm undoing his tie. His jacket falls from my shoulders, and I draw his belt through the loops, filling the front entryway with a zipping *whoosh*. His big hands deftly undo the zipper on the side of my dress. It gets caught on the waistline, and then it too falls to the floor.

There I am. Exposed. Naked. My very least favorite way to be. *Please, God, don't say anything about the scar. Please, please, please.*

He notices it, I can see he does, because he has eyes and it's impossible to miss, but instead of mentioning it, he says, "You're fucking gorgeous. Fucking," his eyes trip up my body, "unspeakable."

My swallow is audible, a clicking gulp. I feel a flush run up to my face, hot and instantaneous as he hoists me back up into his arms, face to face. Who's touching what gets all mixed up in my head. We are hands and skin and need. As we smash into the minibar, the Keurig and all the little tiny K-Cups go flying.

I slip off his tie, but keep it in my hands, using it to leverage his head

21

as close to me as I can. He moves down my neck, sucking and biting all the way to my collarbone. He undoes my bra. As my breasts come free, he shakes his head, the way people do when they just can't believe what they're seeing.

Placing me on the bed, he finishes undoing his buttons, takes off his shirt, and stands over me a minute. He is unbelievable. Not an ounce of fat on him and a summertime tan to die for. He's got this tattoo on one shoulder, small tight black letters, *Illegitimi Non Carborundum*.

Don't let the bastards get you down.

Oh, this guy. *This guy.* He's perfect. I've still got his tie in my hands, tight in my fists in anticipation.

Carefully, he holds my wrists together in one of his hands. Then he loops the end of his tie around a finger.

I think I know what he's thinking. I sure hope I do. So I nod. "Yes please."

He puts my wrists one over the other, and then runs the tie around and around, finally knotting it at the top.

"That good?" he asks.

I clench and unclench my wrists under that silk rope. "Perfect."

With one hand on my chest, he pushes me back and pulls down my panties. He kneels on the floor and slides me by my knees into his mouth.

"Shit, holy, holy shit," I say. All my experience with oral sex has been a bit awkward and clumsy. This? This is *not* those things. This is artful, careful, patient, but also so deliberate I don't know if my pussy is dripping more or if it's him salivating.

He pulls away from me for one second to say, "You taste incredible," and then plunges back in. I pull my dress up a little higher to get a better look at him between my legs. His thumbs just come over my thighs, and his fingers grip my ass.

As he works me with his tongue, I feel my eyes start to roll backwards a little, that tense feeling on either side of my eyes. I grip his hair. "I'm close…" Of course I am. I was right on the edge in that stairwell. Now, I can feel my clit swollen and needy under his hands. So close. Right, right there…

With one finger followed by a second, he hooks his hand inside me. The noise I make is outrageous, vulgar and surprised. Then, I think, he introduces a third finger. I'm not entirely sure because everything begins to shimmer around the edges.

I grind my hips into his mouth. I feel my clit give that undeniable flicker.

He must have felt it, because he pulls away just long enough to say, "Let go, beautiful. Let me feel you let go," his breath warming my clit all the while.

When he touches his tongue back to me, the orgasm comes immediately. Everything turning to gray and then bright white. He's groaning into me as I come, and I pull so hard on the bedspread that I undo two hotel sheet corners at once.

6
ben

I need to drink whiskey from that belly button. Screw every other idea I've ever had. Jack Daniels. Belly button. Naomi. That's the only fucking philosophical logic I will ever need.

She's still on the heels of her orgasm, and I want to leave her there just like she is, but I have to take her with me. I have to keep her close. I hook my head under her bound wrists and take her off the bed to bring her with me as we kiss—because I cannot stop kissing her, *will not stop* kissing her. With my hand behind me, I fling open the minibar and fumble around blind. Chips, nuts, pretzels, what is that, a roll of Mentos?

Jack Daniels, where the hell are you?

Grabbing what feels like the right little bottle, I turn to look down. Gin. I toss it towards the desk. Second try, and bingo. I've got it.

But I'm going to have to let go of her to open this damned bottle. Proof that the world is an unfair and unkind place. It'll have to be done. I let go of her face, and it makes her moan, but she doesn't pull away. Instead, she grips onto the back of my neck with my tie and hangs on even tighter through the kiss.

As I crack the lid, her eyes widen, inches from mine. I feel her cheeks rise as she smiles. With one last dip into her mouth, I force myself to break the kiss, ducking down to get my head out from under her bound arms.

We stand there staring at one another for an instant. Her pupils dilate, and that's when I press her to the bed. "Hope you're not ticklish."

Even as she lands with a cushy *thunk* on the mattress, she's giving me that all-trouble smile. She scoots back towards the pillows, her long black hair a gorgeous tangle behind her, the same color as my tie. There's a tan line at her stomach, and it's killing me.

"So ticklish. But I can take it."

I lie down at a right angle to her body, with my cheek to her stomach. I can smell her wetness in the air and on my fingers.

"Ready?" I ask. I sink my cheek deeper into her skin. God, this skin. God *damn*, this superfine skin. I tip the bottle towards her stomach.

"Ready," she says. I feel her whole body quiver. The ticklish before the tickle is the agony of agonies.

When the whiskey hits her, she grips my hair tight. For one second, I resist all temptation: I watch it all unfold. The whiskey shivers, her body shivers, and then the shivers come out as a jagged gasp.

I lick it off, and she squirms and sucks air through her teeth. I suck it from her and growl into her body. Her feet hook around my calves. I move to her nipples, dribble on a few drops and smear them around with my tongue. I move to that perfect little depression at the base of her neck. Straight-up Naomi. Fucking heaven. Her skin, that hair, her sounds, the way her body moves under my mouth? Lemonade, when it's too hot for anything else? I can still feel my first orgasm deep in my cock, but I'm hard again. She's not only wrecked all my philosophies. She's turned me into a goddamned teenager.

I grab a condom, from my wallet this time, and tear it open. "We're going to need more of these."

But she shakes her head into the pillows. She holds my stare as she slides her hands all over her body, red polish on porcelain. "Put it here. Put it everywhere."

Christ. It's official. I've been pussywhipped in record time.

And I don't even know her last name.

7

Naomi

Morning light wakes me up, and the first thought I have is that these sheets, they aren't mine. They're fancy and starchy and smell like hotel. There's this delicious, manly smell too. Warm, hot skin. I open my eyes. Ben.

Delicious, sexy Ben. He's a stomach sleeper, and I lift up the sheet to get another look at his back. Oh, yes. Just as gorgeous and rippling now as it was last night.

The room looks like a small natural disaster blew through here. There are K-Cups everywhere, a condom on the floor. The sheets are a wreck, lampshades crooked, a chair overturned. I remember colliding with the chair as he carried me across the room. I remember it all like the sweetest sucker punch to the face.

It went on for hours. I have no idea when we fell asleep together, but I know I was in his arms. Just like I am now.

My ass is still sore from the spanks. Over his shoulder, I see his tie is still knotted around the bedpost. The whiskey, the belly button, the way he came. We'd said all sorts of things. Best. Need. Fuck. Mercy. Yes. More. Now. Please, please, please.

Beg me to come. Beg me.

Whiskey bottle overturned on the nightstand, my clothes strewn around under his.

Some of his cum is still there on my belly, white and dry like spilled milk. I stare at him next to me, his hair all messy, his eyelashes touching his cheeks.

They say a woman who does what I just did is a whore, a slut, a sinner. Let them say it. I don't believe that at all. Never have, never will. Screw the world that sees only whores and virgins, bad girls and good. I'm all of it. And proud.

And yet, I don't feel much like trekking across campus in my evening wear while everybody's heading to breakfast. If I hustle, I won't be spotted walking across the quad in this tiny dress and carrying my shoes while the rest of my residential college puts syrup over their Eggos.

So very carefully, I maneuver out from under his arm. I'm trying to be quiet as I shift the sheets, but the starch doesn't make it easy. I creep across the room and grab my dress and underwear. Pulling myself together quickly in the bathroom, I rub the mascara out from under my eyes.

I'm just about to go, but I can't. Not like this. I pad back to the bed. I scrawl my number on the notepad by the phone, with a heart next to it. And then I lean down and kiss him on the cheek. As I pull myself away, I quietly untie his tie from the bedpost and his mask from the dresser. There's no way I'm leaving without these.

On my way out the door, I see the hotel bill on the floor.

Another sucker punch, and this one not so sweet. He's leaving today. So this was a fleeting thing, a chance collision. One in a million. But even as I hit the button on the elevator, I'm wishing lightning would strike twice.

••
•

I live on the fourth floor of Yale's Durham College, in a tiny Dickensian room barely wide enough for my bed, with four mullioned windows that don't close all the way so that rain and leaves and the occasional ladybug come right on in. The windows are open now, and the shifting of the leaves outside reminds me of the sound of his necktie. I smell the whiskey and Irish Spring, somehow caught in my hair.

My independent study swirls in front of me on my computer screen like an amateur crossword puzzle.

His hands on me, the way he laughed and smiled. The dancing. The way he sent Isaac packing. The way we set off that alarm, the way he tangled his fingers into mine. His face when he came.

Oh God. God, God, God.

From the squeals emanating from open window on the other side of the courtyard, I'm fairly sure I hear a game of strip poker getting started. I look out my window into the grassy quad. Durham looks like it's three hundred years old, but it isn't. Cinderblock walls made to look like old plaster, new brass aged with industrial acids. Still, it's awfully pretty. We have a reputation for being wild with, and I quote, "no discernable intellectual tradition whatsoever." That is *not* our fault. Nor is it our fault that our dean is utterly, unbelievably, painfully dreadful... He's got this toupee that's always shifting positions, and he's made a career out of studying a single rare moth found only in Burma. Dean Osgood is his name. He's the weird old uncle nobody wants to talk to but shows up everywhere. *Not* our fault. Nor is it our fault that our Master of College got himself fired at the end of spring term and they still haven't replaced him. If they did, things would be more tame. He'd be like the stepdad who puts everybody back in line. But for now, Durham is an uncaptained ship on the very edge of a mutiny. I watch a pair of boxers fly from a third-floor window and go back to my desk.

The day ticks past, and I try to forget about Ben. He's probably flying back to Santa Barbara or something—he had that kind of tan. But I keep checking my phone anyway. I clean my room, I listen to Spotify. I try to focus, but I can't.

That stairwell. The growls. Every last thing. I open my underwear drawer, where I've hidden his mask, and run my fingertips over the curve where his cheekbone used to be.

Lucy, she hasn't said anything, but she keeps coming down the hall and looking through my door at me. I'm sure she saw me dancing with him, I'm even sure she saw me leave with him. But she doesn't come right out and ask. That's not her style at all. She's genteel, polite. Her family is the stuff of coming-out balls, ongoing SEC investigations, and a library on south campus with her family's name on the door. All day, she watches me like I'm keeping some enormous secret, like I'm pregnant or getting married or getting kicked out of school. Every half-hour she pokes her head into my room to spy on me. I keep telling her to stop, but she just shifts her head to the side and twirls her braid and wiggles her nose, like suspicious a rabbit, saying, "Mmmmm."

"Oh my God," I say finally, really trying to be serious but totally unable to keep from bursting into a smile, "Yes. I went home with him. Yes, it was ahhhmazing. And yes, I know his name."

"First and last?" she asks.

I shake my head. "First only."

She wags her finger at me. "Haven't I taught you anything?"

"We weren't exactly exchanging business cards, Lucy," I say.

She puts the finishing touches on a five-strand braid and smacks her lip gloss. She's painfully pretty, with eyes shockingly big, the color of honey. "I'm just saying, first and last really facilitates stalking. So, for future reference…"

Duly noted. "It was you that invited me, wasn't it?" I ask her.

She purses her lips. "Maybe." She's got cagey down to an art.

"Why, in God's name?"

She shoves me a little, then starts counting on her fingers, thumb first: "Because you're fucking brilliant. A shitload of fun. My bestie. You can dance. Fearless. Should I keep going?" She sticks out the thumb on her other hand and stares at me.

I hold my hand to my forehead, so freaking embarrassed. "No. That's plenty."

"So welcome to Lux et Veritas," she beams. "The worst-kept secret on campus. And the most freaking fun you'll ever have."

At five, I shower, reluctantly washing his smell and cum off of me. I do my hair and makeup and get ready to work the Durham Fellows' Dinner. This is the first one of the school year, and it'll be busy. A lot of shuttling sad hors d'oeuvres around, a lot of plates of poached chicken and nondescript gravy.

To make ends meet, I work as many extra jobs as I can. I work at the library, but mainly I work events at the college, like Fellows' dinners and Master's teas.

As I slather my body with lotion, I realize that tonight, I'm pretty sure, I'll get to meet our new Master. I know he's some kind of big deal, but I can't remember why. On one hand, I should care: The Master of College is a weirdly important job at Yale. Captain of the collegiate ship, surrogate father figure. Advisor. Boss. At least for me, as a Master's Aide. Everything, really. But provided I keep my nose down, even as his aide, I won't have all that much to do with him.

The last Master of Durham went down in a rather inglorious blaze after a mid-semester "reply-all" email snafu in which he revealed himself to be a raving lunatic He detailed his feelings on an assortment of things including, but not limited to, Israel, nuclear proliferation, the Second Amendment, and his pervasive distaste for every single person in the Yale Provost's office. The administration snatched him out of his job faster than you could say *Huffington Post.*

I pull out my black skirt and my tights from my closet and put on my battered second-hand Danskos. They're part of my required uniform. *The shoes* from last night are still right there. *Wouldn't it be amazing, if, by some astronomically ludicrous chance, he happened to be at the dinner tonight?* Maybe he's a guest lecturer, maybe we could have a torrid romance and fall in love and then he'd whizz me off to wherever he's from.

Nope, Naomi. Nope, nope, nope. Danskos and footie socks. That's reality now and always. I take my white work shirt from the hanger, slip it on, and button it up. As I do, I remember how he sucked on my nipples, gazing up at me with such utter, lovely admiration. They still ache. There are bite marks on my stomach, still tender to the touch.

Looking at myself in the mirror, I button the top button and feel grateful he didn't leave any visible hickeys. Ruthless *and* considerate. My kind of guy exactly.

I have a few ties for these events. A super boring crimson one with the college shield on it. A blue one I had to wear when I worked a fancy place in Bal Harbor two summers back. But I can't help myself, and I take out of my purse the black tie I stole.

I poke my head in Lucy's door. I return the shoes and say, "Iron?"

She holds up a finger and drags a Tupperware bin out from under her bed.

Her room is like a tiny Target. She has literally everything a person could need crammed inside it, from $600 shoes to top-of-the-line irons. She's from huge new money, and she says her parents show their love by giving gifts. I once said that sounds lovely, and she'd said, "Not when *I love you* sounds like cash coming out of a wallet."

What I don't do is iron the damned tie right there in front of her. Think of the questions! So I take the iron back to my room. I lay out the tie, nice and straight on the towel on my bed, and run my fingers over the creases, marking the spots where it had been around his neck, my wrists, my mouth.

Looking at myself in the mirror, I find the tie looks nice, actually. Way better than all the rest.

The iron returned and one more, "Mmmmm," from Lucy, I head out my door and clomp down the 72 steps to the quad. I hustle over the grass to the Master's House. It's on the far end of the courtyard and takes up two massive floors. In the kitchen, I grab my waitressing apron from the closet.

"Nice to see you, Miss Costa," says Dean Osgood. The toupee tonight is sort of kitty-corner on his head.

"Hello, Dean. How's the moth?"

"Elusive, Miss Costa. Very elusive."

I mean, why do I even ask? I could say the answer right along with him, word for word.

Dean Osgood adjusts his hair. I sometimes wonder about toupee care. Does he bring it in the shower? Put it in with the delicates? Hand wash? Is there a special soap?

"Be on your toes tonight, Miss Costa," Osgood says. Whenever he speaks, it's vaguely menacing. I sometimes wonder if he was in Vietnam, maybe. He's that kind of intense.

Osgood is right, though. It's time to get serious about Durham, finally. We've got a scandal to recover from, and Osgood is hell-bent on recovering our reputation.

"You'll meet the new Master tonight," Osgood says, straightening out his tie.

"What's his name again?" I ask as I make a bow of my apron strings around my waist.

Osgood stares off into vacancy and sniffs. "Dr. Benjamin Beck."

31

8
ben

I put on a tweed jacket with leather elbow patches, which I bought an hour ago at J. Crew a block from campus. I stare at myself in the mirror. Which is in the master bathroom. Of my new house.

What the hell am I doing?

I'm 38-years old. I'm the guy who believes in nothing. Who needs nothing. In tweed. In a big stone house with two fireplaces, a garage, two sets of matching wingback chairs, a mahogany dining table, and a staff. Me. Who grew up with nothing. I don't even know what I'm doing here.

I do know it's been such a fucking whirlwind.

Last year, I wrote a book. I called it *In The Ashes of Planets*. Nobody read it. The running joke had always been that I write books for nobody. Totally fine with me. But my old colleagues, back at UCLA, they didn't find that so fine. There were two of them, two old crotchety guys who hung on to their Aristotle and Socrates so tight you could see their knucklebones. They said, "Beck. We don't get what you're doing. What's all this nihilism? Who cares? Time to move on." Which was when they convened a quorum of two and rejected my application for tenure. *Poof.* Gone. Nothing again. My theory of nothingness? Proved. They gave me one semester to get my shit together and hit the road.

After the initial momentary shock, I found it didn't really bother me. Life just throws some punches, and you throw back. You roll or you fall. Either way, it's fine. It has to be fine, because there's no other option. So I said, "Alright," and thought about maybe taking a road trip into the desert. Like an old-school mystic. Maybe take all my books in a secondhand trailer and go off to someplace in Arizona. It didn't sound too bad. I could live off whiskey, Oreos, ramen, and bananas. Pretty awesome idea, actually. Except then it got weird.

The night after tenure went up in flames, I was sitting on my couch. I lived in a little place in LA with a leaky faucet and a rattling fridge. I had one cup, one plate, one fork. I slept on a mattress on the floor. I needed nothing. I wanted nothing. I was free of all the tethers of the world. That's how I like it.

But so I sat down that night, on the couch that the last tenant left behind. I didn't feel like reading, so I pulled out my laptop and decided on *True Detective*. I liked the vibe. Kind of Cajun apocalyptic. Then there's Matthew McConaughey in the car, talking to Woody Harrelson. And pretty quick he starts sounding…

Like me.

Wait. Say again?

Right. Like me, and not just a *little* like me. But *a lot* like me.

I grabbed my book off my cinderblock bookshelf. Then holy hell, I realize, as he's saying, "*The real question is not whether or not the world will end, but that this horizon of thought can be thought at all…*"

That Matthew McConaughey, as Rust Cohle? He's quoting *me*. Benjamin Beck. Nihilist. Nobody. Me.

I slapped the book shut. I paused the episode. I looked online to see if anybody other than me had noticed what was going on here. Yeah, they sure had. The writer himself, Nic Pizzolatto, he'd been reading *my book* while he was working on the screenplay. Holy. Fucking. Shit.

So back at work, I tell Aristotle and Socrates. They said, "Sue him!"

I said, "Yeah? Why? Doesn't matter, guys. Doesn't matter at all. Rust Cohle talks like me. He's a badass. And as everybody knows, nihilism is philosophical badassery."

Aristotle and Socrates weren't particularly amused.

Got weirder still. When I started the new term, the very last one I ever planned to teach, enrollment in my mysticism seminar skyrocketed. The semester before, I had two students. Two. But in the new term, the

33

numbers were climbing so fast I thought there was a glitch in the system. I even went to the registrar to say, "You know, they're signing up for *my* class, right?"

The registrar said, "Oh yes, Professor Beck. We know. We're moving you to the 500-person lecture hall."

"The what?"

"And giving you 20 TAs."

Because why?

Because the cover of my book, my nihilistic pessimistic fuck-it-all-ya'll book? The one that talks about the end of the world and the emptiness of life? The one with the cover I designed with Photoshop? That cover? My cover?

Boom. It was on Jay-Z's jacket in a video he did with Beyoncé. It had dropped earlier that week. Jay-Z, sitting on a motorcycle in the desert, holding a gun, pointing it at the sun. With *In The Ashes of Planets* on his leather jacket. So just like *that*, I became the hottest car in the academic parking lot.

The thing hit the Amazon bestsellers, and not just in "Philosophy Methodology," of which there are literally five books in the world. No. *The actual* bestsellers. I hit #3. I got interviewed on NPR. I had to hire an assistant.

Aristotle and Socrates didn't offer me my job back. They still didn't understand it. Of course. But someone else did. Yale.

Yale called me up and said, and I'm not quoting here, but just the gist: "Beck. Come teach here. Design your own courses, go look at ancient texts in our vaults. We'll give you carte blanche. Come teach about nothing. We'll even give you a house. We dig what you're doing. For real. You. Here. Us. What do you say?"

I thought about it for a while. Reasoned various ways through it. Compared it to wandering through the desert with my Oreos and whiskey. Then decided, for the sake of knowledge, learning, understanding, for the sake of teaching, for the sake of students and mystics and ideas?

I'd do it. I couldn't pass it up.

So now here I am.

Shit has officially gotten real. The job has started. The tweed is on.

But I cannot get my mind off Naomi. I found her number when I woke up and texted her a sleepy *Hey* right away. Then I stared at my phone for ten minutes waiting for a reply but got none. Since then I've texted her three times…

I missed you this morning.
Sent 9:56am

Last night was incredible.
Sent 1:03pm

Can I see you again?
Sent 3:28pm

    … with no response. At all.

    I jam my phone in my pocket. I stare at myself in the mirror. I hear the staff downstairs clattering dishes. I look like a guy who slept for four hours and has never worn tweed until right now, and has no idea whatsoever what the fuck he's doing. Which is all true.

    But last night I knew what I was doing. Her moans. Her fingernails. The way I fit inside her.

    I might believe in nothing. But Naomi, she didn't feel like nothing. She felt like something else completely.

9

Naomi

I carry a tray with Costco quiches and cut-up veggies through the fellows. They're an assorted group, almost all of them over 70. There's the anomalous young female professor, always in pencil skirts and the most gorgeous riding boots. Also, there's a young, tall, super-awkward scientist who lingers in the corner, watching everybody from above, like an endangered stork.

Some Master's Aides hate working the dinners. I actually love it, because I get to scoot by all manner of conversations without having to add anything. I get to be a perpetual unseen fly on the wall. Secret introvert paradise.

I often ask myself what I'm doing here. The answer is that I don't exactly know. I often feel vulnerable, lost, and like the girl who doesn't belong. Like I'll never be smart enough or quick enough. Like I'm here by accident. Which is actually true, in a way.

Four years ago this fall, I was a week away from marrying my high school sweetheart. Joe Riley was—is, I mean—his name. Copper-red hair, big hands, the same age as me. He came from a family of herringmen, and since we were kids everybody in my hometown in Maine said we'd get married, that we should get married, and wouldn't it be nice if a Costa and a Riley married, just think of the sea in that bloodstock. Seriously. Like Cutler, Maine, is actually Nantucket or ancient Greece. Only worse because we weren't royalty, we weren't sea-faring nobility, we were just fishermen's children, stuck in that crab-filled bucket. I felt so trapped by that idea, ending up a mom to four kids and all my still-unknown dreams gone. But back then—I say it like it was ages ago, because that's exactly how it feels—I really hadn't known what else was out there in the world for me. I said yes, because I really had no idea what else to do. I had no idea there *was* anything else to do.

Fast forward to that November. The wedding was planned for January, and I remember feeling such dread when I'd see the countdown calendar on my phone. To escape the dread, maybe, I went out to work the boats with my dad. There's nothing in the world for forgetting your problems like working a lobster glut, getting cold to the bone and so exhausted you can barely speak.

The wave came from nowhere, right at us from astern. I'd been slightly off balance, pushing traps off the boat, and my feet got tangled in the rope on the deck. I remember the squeak of my galoshes and clambering for the sheerline, then falling and falling for so long, it might as well have been off a cruise ship than portside of the Lady Francesca.

As I sank down into the water, trying to kick off my boots for no reason other than pure panic, I had one single thought. It was a horrible thing to think, but it's what swirled up into my head: *I wish I could have done something other than become a wife.* That was one of those come-to-Jesus moments, I think. Except I didn't see Jesus. I saw the propeller. And that was when I lost consciousness.

It changed everything. Recovering in the hospital, with hundreds of stitches lining my side, I realized there was so much more I wanted to do. I felt ancient, I still do. So a year out of high school, having thought for all the world I was going to get married and become a fisherman's wife, raise kids, with barely enough money to put food on the table, and grow old and gray with only a high school education, I realized *no*. Not me. For Naomi Costa, there'd be something different. Something *more*.

From the hospital, I told Joe I wanted to call off the wedding. He cried at my bedside, and big tears fell off his red lashes, turning the edges of his eyelids red too, and making his green eyes seem glazed and far away. I stayed strong. I knew I would suffocate in that town. I knew that if I ever fell overboard again, I'd have done something to be proud of. So within a year, I was a Yale freshman. It was magic, putting my hands on the dream, studying philosophy to make sense of thoughts and the world.

But dreams aren't easy. Here, sometimes, I also feel like I'm drowning, in a way. Surrounded by all this brilliance, I'll always be well under the water line. Never enough.

Hardly anybody knows my story. Lucy does, and also the little man standing just in front of me now, with his arms open for a hug. I set down my hors d'oeuvre tray on a side table. His name is Professor Sarka, and I have a feeling he was grandfatherly even as a little boy. He's the world's authority on maritime literature, and always talks like he's on a ship. Once, we had lunch, and the only thing we talked about was lobster pots. Another time, he drilled me on the best paint for boats. Once, we had coffee, and I showed him how to tie a rolling hitch knot with a shoelace he had in his pocket.

"Hello, skipper!" Professor Sarka says into the hug. I kiss him on the cheek, and he smells like cedar. "How are conditions?"

He's so adorable, it actually hurts. Ever since his wife died, his wardrobe has been a heartbreaking gamble. He's colorblind, he confided in me. Today it's three clashing tweeds and a plaid shirt underneath. He's about five feet tall and has enormous sailing hands. Somehow, he reminds me of a plump little bear.

"Conditions, Professor, are good," I tell him, picking up my tray again.

"Favorable for progress?" He selects a baby carrot.

"Mostly." I give him a cocktail napkin from my apron.

"Wind in the east?"

"Definitely."

"Found yourself a boyfriend yet?" He always asks me that, ever since his wife died. Love is on his mind, and he's missing her. Lowering his head, he says, "Love, Naomi. It's a good thing."

Self-consciously, I smooth my tie. "Not yet. I think they're all out of my league."

Sarka shuts his eyes. "You are out of *their* league, my dear." He grins delightfully at me, but then he begins lowering himself behind his whiskey, peering out over the glass. "Broadside, incoming."

I slap a smile on my face and turn around.

38

The broadside is none other than Osgood again. "Miss Costa. Too much canoodling. Work the room, move those finger foods."

Oh, you go canoodle, you fuzzy caterpillar. "Sorry, Dean."

But move those finger foods, I do. Everybody is abuzz, waiting for the new Master. Everything smells new, like fresh paint. They've done renovations upstairs in his private rooms. Everybody is excited for this Professor Beck. All the ladies are gathered in clumps. They remind me of women waiting to catch a bouquet at a wedding.

Vague details about our new Master come back to me in fits and starts. I know he wrote some book that got everybody's panties in a twist, and they offered him a job and the Master's position. That's right, now I remember... He's in philosophy. A notorious nihilist. Great. Nothing better than someone who believes in absolutely nothing. What *fun.* I also remember he's the only unmarried Master we've ever had—not even a widower, just a flat-out bachelor. All the girls who've stalked him online say he's adorable, and use the word *adorbs,* so I know they really mean it. But I haven't searched for him. Provided he doesn't fire me, try to convert me into believing in nothingness, or tell me I should go back to Maine to work the boats, I'm pretty sure we're going to get along fine.

I return to the kitchen and load up with more finger foods and toothpicks.

The circulating continues. I bring around a tray of tiny artichoke things in puff pastry that go like hotcakes. I always think about grabbing one for myself but never do.

As I'm trying to move the last two artichoke puffs, things fall to a hush.

Bing, bing, bing, goes a fork on a glass. That'll be Osgood.

I pass between fellows, and they politely decline my offer of the artichoke puffs. All the attention off me, I turn towards the window and snag one at last, sticking it into my mouth. It's utterly delicious. Creamy and salty and the pastry both crunchy and soft.

Dean Osgood's voice fills the room. He always talks too loud for the space, always. I notice it's getting hot in here, and a little stuffy. Late August, and all the linen and sports jackets and menopausal hot flashes.

Everybody's eyes still off of me, I grab the second puff and jam it in my mouth.

"Just wanted to say a few words to welcome our new Master," Osgood says. Compulsory pause. Hand to God, he must practice this stuff in front of a mirror. "So I present to you all, with greatest delight and excitement, Professor Benjamin Beck."

I pay no attention. I turn away so nobody sees me chewing while I pretend to gather up napkins from the coffee table. That's when I hear a voice, his voice, *that voice,* saying, "Please, Dean, call me Ben."

I freeze. Slowly, with little shuffles of my Danskos, I turn around and stop chewing.

It's him.

It's Ben. He's in a tweed jacket with leather elbow patches.

It's Ben. Ben is the Master.

I fucked the Master.

No, the Master fucked me.

Hard.

Perfectly.

Oh shit. Oh shit!

He hasn't seen me yet. Oh, sweet Jesus, God above. What if I just ran out the French doors right now, just bolted across the quad and locked myself in my room? Lucy could bring me food. I could say I'm in quarantine. My professors could send me everything by email! I'd never have to face him. He'd never have to know.

Except I can't. I can't take my eyes off him. And there's nowhere to go. My mouth is full of artichoke cream. I'm in the crush of bodies, pinned next to the curve of the grand piano. I'm stuck, staring. At Ben.

Just the sight of him makes my whole body tighten, and I can feel myself getting wet. *Let me feel you, beautiful. Let me feel it.*

Osgood raises his glass and says, "Join me in our traditional Durham toast…"

At that moment, Ben's eyes fall right on me.

His face says, *Holy shit.*

I clutch my cocktail tray. *Oh God. What have we done?*

All the fellows echo back, "Welcome, Master Beck!"

Ohhhhh. No.

10
ben

When I see her, I can't even move. I've got my glass halfway up for the toast, but I'm frozen. She's got her hair in a lovely braid off to the side, with some of her curls spilling towards her face. Her face shifts from horror, to terror, to surprise, into a kind of soft *Uh-oh!* face.

What is she *doing* here? What the hell is going on?

The room roars alive with conversation, and she vanishes into the fellows.

I can't follow. There's a throng of people, so much white hair it's dizzying, so many smiles and handshakes it's exhausting. I'm also overheating under my jacket. I don't even know what I'm saying to these people. Something about Radiolab and NPR and the book, everybody wants to know about the book. They ask me where I grew up, I say Las Vegas, they say the usual, *Las Vegas!* like it's so exciting. It wasn't. It was awful and poor and dismal. I don't say my dad walked out on us, and I grew up in a trailer, a block away from the public library where all but the philosophy books had been stolen, lucky for me because I loved them. Or do I? I have exactly zero idea what words are coming out of my mouth. All I can do is search for her, search everywhere for that black hair, that body, those cornflower-blue eyes.

My throat feels tight, and I'm suddenly absolutely pouring sweat, like I have some sort of disorder or a fever. I take off my jacket and put it over a wingback chair by the fireplace. That's *my* chair. *My* fireplace. My new house. Jesus Christ.

Vaguely, I hear the noise of that emergency door sounding in my memory. I have to get out of here. I cannot do this. What am I doing here? Fellows' dinners and gold-rimmed champagne glasses?

Naomi. Must find Naomi.

I have this compulsion to find her, grab her by the hand, and make a break for it. So once the throng eases up slightly, I navigate through the masses of people, looking busy, brushing past white heads and horn-rimmed glasses, and conversations about things that I only barely understand.

Where is she? Where *is she*?

The Dean sidles up to me. "First order of business, Beck. Learn to mingle." The guy acts like an eccentric, but I'm beginning to suspect he's actually a profound asshole. He sat me down earlier today to warn me, of all things, about "avoiding scandal." *No scandals, Beck. No scandals. You hear me? No scandals.*

"I have to… Have you seen? Is there a girl named Naomi working here?"

The Dean's eyes flash, and he adjusts his ridiculous hair. "Miss Costa," he corrects me. "Miss Costa is her name."

"Right, right, sorry. Miss Costa." What a beautiful name. Naomi Costa. That puts *cellar door* right out of the running for sweetest-sounding words in the language.

"Miss Costa is probably in the butler's pantry. Getting snifters for after dinner. That's where I sent her anyway…"

I go into the kitchen. I still don't feel comfortable here. I feel like a visitor in this vast bright room with black granite countertops and well-organized shelves. The trailer where I grew up had a barely functioning kitchen stove and a used mini fridge. I might as well be on Mars right now. Mars with a double sink, two dishwashers, and a huge cooktop. The fridge, it's about eight feet high and it purrs, like a Ferrari.

Fuck. I can smell her. I can smell that lemony deliciousness through everything else in the air.

Wait. What the hell is a butler's pantry? Is that like a *pantry* pantry? Or some kind of fancy, special pantry?

I have to find her. I have to find someone that makes sense. Who made sense yesterday and will help me make sense of today.

Now I'm like a wolf on the trail. That smell, I knew I'd never forget it. This morning, I woke up and she was gone. My heart just clenched when she wasn't next to me. It wasn't a one-night stand. It had been the earth flipping around on its axis. So I'd rolled over and pressed my fucking face into the pillow where she'd been sleeping. *Never forget that smell,* I'd thought. *Never fucking ever.*

There's a lady cooking at the stove, this thin black lady with short white hair. She pulls a wooden spoon out of a pan and turns to me. "What do you need, honey?"

I think I must look like a wild man. That's absolutely how I feel. "Did a girl…"

"Call me Letty," she says, smiling at the sauce, "And if you're looking for Naomi, she's through there." She points with her wooden spoon at a door.

••

I shut the door behind me. The pantry, it's small and full of even more kitchenware. There's a light above me, but it's dim in here. She's there in the corner, putting brandy glasses on her tray. When I come in, she doesn't turn around.

"What are you doing here?" I whisper. It sounds more like a bark. "How are you even…"

She wipes her hands on her apron and turns to me. "I didn't know. I swear to God, I had no idea who you were."

Who *I* am? Who the hell is she? "What, you work here?"

She nods her head. "And I *live* here." She's pointing up and over.

"And you stole my tie!" I grab it and give it a tug.

She reaches up and tugs it back. "I just…" And she claps her hands to her face.

"I love that tie," I tell her.

"Me too!" she says through her fingers.

But now I'm in trouble, because I'm about six inches from her, and it's literally electric. I'm burning for her. I think I can feel her burning for me, two coils on the stove. The passion I feel, it's fucking irrational. She makes me feel fucking…unscholarly. Eros the core. "You didn't answer my texts."

She peeks out from between her fingers. "What texts?"

"These!" I pull out my phone and show her.

She makes this sort of outraged huff. "You put a *four* instead of a *seven* at the end!"

I stare at my phone. I think back to the notepad. "What are you, European? Who makes sevens like that? With the little," I swipe my fingers through the air, "cross thing?"

"I do!" she gasps.

I take her by the shoulders, pulling myself together. "So let me get this straight. You're a student here," I say, trying to get my bearings. "At Yale. At Durham. An undergraduate."

She nods, with her palms to her beautiful cheeks. Her arms shift a little under my hands, and I squeeze tighter. I was pissed and now I'm melted.

"At least tell me you're a senior. God, tell me you're graduating early. Tell me you're almost not a student anymore…"

She peeks out from between her fingers. "I'm a junior."

"A junior!" I roar. "How old are you?"

"Shhhhh!" she says, putting her hand to my chest. "I'm *almost* 21!"

"Some law student!"

"You didn't say who you were either!" she whispers back.

God, see, now… Those lips, that mouth. I think of how hard I kissed her, of that feel of her tongue against mine, fuck, even her teeth on mine. The heat of her breath on my cheek as we kissed. The way she tasted. "You're hardly legal and we were throwing back absinthe!"

"It's fine," she says, pulling her hands from her face and sticking them at her sides. "Totally fine."

"Bullshit!"

"Aren't you some kind of nihilist?" she says. "Aren't you supposed to be unflappable?"

We're right against one another now. I've been moving towards her all the time, walking her back towards the cabinets. I'm pressing against her body, and she's gripping the countertop with one hand. She closes her eyes. I listen to her breathing. I watch her breathing. I put one hand just under her breast. The feel of her ribs under my fingers.

Then she reaches up, runs her hand along my neck, which she *knows* makes my whole body shiver, and says, "It didn't happen."

The fuck it didn't. I'm rock hard against her leg. I press into her to make sure she can feel it. "It happened."

The need for her, it takes over my entire body. I wish it didn't. I wish she was just some woman, some girl. But she isn't. The way she moves, the ways she looks up at me. The freckles. Her eyes widening. The hollow at the base of her throat.

We're just inches from each other. "I want you," I say to the place between her ear and the corner of her jaw.

She shudders. "What are we going to do..." It's a bare whisper, the air just slips from her mouth to make the words.

"This." I pull her face to mine and kiss her. We're back in that place again, in the stone stairwell, and the breath from her nose heats my cheek. My hand starts sliding down her body. She's gripping my neck hard, digging those beautiful fingers into me.

But then she pushes me away. "We can't," she says.

"Aren't we already?" I say. From where I'm standing, feeling what I'm feeling, I don't think there's any goddamned choice. "Naomi..."

She shakes her head. She fixes her hair. Totally unnecessary. But those painted nails, moving all over her naked body.

"I'm Miss Costa," she says with an audible swallow. "You're Master Beck."

And just like that, she slips out from my grasp. Leaving me alone in the butler's pantry, rock hard against the brandy glasses.

11

Naomi

These clogs make my escape an awkward and noisy one, especially because I'm about to burst into tears. It's a problem I have, getting teary. I've heard it's *cute*, but actually it's just *annoying*. I clap out of the butler's pantry like a Swiss milkmaid, and Letty has this look on her face like, *Oh, honey!*

"Oh, God," I say. Does she know? She saw us both go into that pantry. Ben roared, *"A junior!"* loud enough for the bell ringers to hear him in the Harkness Tower. Letty surely must have heard.

"Letty…" I brace myself on the countertop. Trying to focus on her, and yet absolutely sure Ben is going to pop out from behind me any moment, and I'll drizzle down onto the marble floor like a chocolate fountain.

"Mmmhmm!" Letty says and stirs her sauce with a particular kind of knowing flair.

"Letty," I say. "Please…"

But she just smiles and rolls her shoulders. "I know nothing. I say nothing. I just make my sauces and go home."

False! The truth is, she knows everything that goes on around here, absolutely everything. Her nickname is The Vault, and now she knows there's something going on between Ben and me. Master Beck. Master Beck! Not Ben. Never Ben.

Letty looks up. She winks. "You're safe with me."

God! I give Letty a squeeze. "Thank you, thank you. But it's nothing. Seriously. Nothing."

Again the eyebrows. "Oh, honey. The lady? She doth protest *way* too much."

Shit, shit, shit. I know. It's not nothing. It's something. Something like a road flare in an enclosed space.

I head out into the foyer, and I realize I'm shaking, trembling even. Dean Osgood blocks my way, needling me with those beady eyes. He's got dandruff on his shoulders. I have no idea how that is even possible. "Problem?"

"Nothing. I have a migraine. You know how I get them."

He cocks his head like this is the first he's heard of my migraines, which, of course, it is.

"Seriously. Dark room, two Excedrin, I'll be golden tomorrow." I press my fingers to my eyebrows like Lucy does when she's got a headache coming on.

"I find you highly suspect," he says. "You're always up to something. Philosophy is risqué, Miss Costa. You know I think so. It makes people act rashly. We cannot have people acting rashly, understood?"

Dean Osgood, he's the Darth to my Luke. He's the Senate to my House. Every step of the way he's giving me trouble and always has, like it's his duty. Like it's his obligation. Like it's good for me. Which, right now, it most definitely is not. "Please, Dean. I just need to lie down."

He nods, one curt gesture, and I'm out the door. I run diagonally across the grassy quad. But when I get to the big door that leads to my stairway, I realize yet another epic disaster: I'm locked out. I've left my keys and my ID behind. They're in my purse, which is hanging in the hall closet, in Master Beck's house.

"Shit! Shit, shit, shit," I say to the big locked door, yanking hard on the handle and rattling it. "Shit!" Oh now, look! He's reduced me to a single-word vocabulary. That's about right. Fan*ta*stic.

I grab some gravel from the nearest flower bed, from under the rhododendrons and the azaleas. I pitch it up at Lucy's room. I've got a terrible arm and totally botch it the first time, slinging it into the gutter with a clatter. I grab a bigger stone, this one about as big as a marshmallow, and throw it as hard as I can at her window, which is right next to mine. *Ping* goes the rock and ricochets off onto the slate roof.

Her little head pokes up and she opens the window. "Oh, hello."

"Let me in!" I say. "I left my ID."

"Shouldn't you be working?" She's hanging out the window now, braid first. There are hints of Rapunzel.

"Just let me in! This is no time for Q & A!" I hiss back to her.

"Please?"

"Please with sugar on top, and I'll even write your papers for English!"

"Deal!" she beams and vanishes back into the dormer.

I'm so exposed out there, and I'm going to have to wait a while. She's got to come down four stories of winding stone staircase to get me, and she plucks down them like a foal that's just learned to walk. The Master's House faces right out onto the quad I see the fellows inside moving around, getting ready to head to dinner, like they're inside a big fishbowl.

Suddenly, Ben's face appears at the French doors. He doesn't do anything, just watches me.

And then ever-so-gently places his forehead against the glass.

I'm going to die. My heart is breaking, and yet it's so overwhelmingly full. Everything is spinning, and my hands are getting clammy like I'm going to faint. Imagine, fainting, just because he looked at me. Unfortunately, I don't have to imagine it because I think it's about to happen.

I dart into the Japanese Zen garden. If I'm going to pass out, let it be in private. The garden is made into the little corner of the courtyard, donated by somebody or other. There are stone walls around it, high ones, so it closes out the world. In the middle is a Japanese elm. I sit down on the bench in the corner.

Call me Master, I need to be your Master, beautiful, I need to be everything to you.

And me. *Yes, Master. Please, please, please. Be everything.*

Oh. My. God. I stick my head between my legs in the imminent-car-crash position.

What am I going to do? *What am I going to do?* I'm so screwed. Being with him, it's like being on fire. Which means that now there's a fire on the first floor of Durham and I'm stuck in the attic.

"Well, this is romantic," says Lucy from the entrance of the garden.

I look up at her. I can feel my lips trembling. Just a friend in the world, that's what I need. "Lucy…"

If she gives me another *Mmmmm*, I just can't be held accountable. I'll tell everybody that she wears contacts and if she doesn't, she has to wear the world's thickest glasses, which make her look like a cartoon. But she doesn't.

She opens her arms right up and holds me tight. No questions asked.

12

Naomi

After spending the night shoving pretzels in my mouth, watching *Wuthering Heights* and muttering, "But they should be together! Why, why, why!" and flopping around on my bed, I am now in front of the Master's door, about to knock. It's 6:58 am. College is dead quiet. Without my ID, I can't even have breakfast. This has to be done. I have to face him.

Also, I'm burning up to see him.

The knocker is a weirdly misshapen lion's face. I lift it up and lightly tap the door three times.

Though I've showered and hope for some semblance of togetherness, I feel like a total mess. I regret so much that I walked out of that pantry. Regret that I didn't grab him, look him in the eye, and say, *Let's do this, because I can't help myself, and neither can you.* Regret that the man I want is the man I absolutely, positively cannot have.

I knock again. I count the number of stones under my feet. Up above me, a squirrel throws an acorn and it clunks off my forehead.

Of course, that's when he opens the door, when I'm pressing my hand to my head and whispering, "Asshole!" at the tree.

"Hi?" he says. He looks up. The offender is gone. The acorn ricocheted off into the flower beds. I probably look like a lunatic.

"Good morning," I say.

He looks sleepy and has his hair off to one side of his head. There are sheet marks on his face. "Naomi…"

"I left my purse." Has anybody, ever, looked more handsome in a 2011 Los Angeles Turkey Trot Fun-Run T-shirt? But I am determined to stay professional. Regret or no regret, this is an impossible situation.

"I know," he says, and produces it instantly from the hook by the door. "I didn't go through it."

"Thanks," I say. I try desperately not to look at the growing hard-on tenting his boxers.

His eyes dart around, bedroomy and so freaking sexy I just cannot *even*… "I meant what I said. I don't know what this thing is between us."

"It's insanity."

"Naomi…" Now his voice is gravelly.

My defenses are weakening. Retreat, retreat! "Thank you, Master Beck," I tell him, and turn around to go.

But he grabs my hand. "I'm here. I want you. You need to know that."

Oh Lord, oh Lord, oh my Lord, it would be so easy to step right inside. But I cannot. Bad plan, bad ending, bad everything. He's a riptide. I have to stay away from that current.

"Have a good day, Master," I say.

He actually groans right out loud and lets go of my hand.

And then I turn around to go.

But as I walk through the dining hall with my tray, pouring whole milk over my Raisin Bran because I'm that girl, I don't feel like a responsible adult. No. I feel like a coward.

I shove a cinnamon bun in my mouth. It's a day old and almost inedible.

A total, terrified coward. I want him. And I have no idea what the hell to do.

At my second job on campus, I try to focus on what I'm doing, which is proving really, really difficult. I work in acquisitions in the Beinecke Rare Books and Manuscript Library, which sounds a lot more romantic than it is.

Usually.

Usually, we acquire strange things in fairly musty books that I don't understand. I photograph them, index them, and hand them on to a specialized librarian. Usually, the stuff I see doesn't mean anything.

Except today, of course, because our newest manuscript is *The Four Loves* by C.S. Lewis.

Further proof of my ongoing theory that God, if there is one, is an utter and complete jerk.

I've got Spotify playing in my ears, Discover Weekly. I don't know how their algorithm knows I'm heartbroken and aching, but it does. They hit me with Billie Eilish's "Ocean Eyes."

"Oh come on!" I whisper at my earbuds.

I am a stream of alternating thoughts: Focus, Ben. Focus, Ben. Right now, I try to focus hard on these magical documents, a smattering of A4 and legal paper, tiny notes stuck to the edges with brittle and ancient Scotch tape.

With my white gloves, I touch C.S. Lewis' words on the page. "*Need-pleasures, like water for the thirsty…*"

And I'm looking at C.S. Lewis' words and thinking, *Hole in one, my friend, hole in one.*

I feel my phone buzz in my back pocket, not just once but the long buzzes of a ring, as Spotify goes silent, replaced by my ringer. It's going to be my dad. He's the only person I know who refuses to text and who calls at absolutely the most inopportune times.

A big sneeze bursts from me, and I narrowly avoid a C.S.-Lewis-snot catastrophe. Sneezy allergic people can't work down here. I can't even remember if I took my Claritin this morning, that's how mixed up I am.

For two rings, I consider not answering. But if I don't, he'll just keep calling and calling until he convinces himself that someone murdered me on the Green and threw my body in Long Island Sound. We almost got there once. He'd been about to file a police report. Not a nightmare I want to repeat.

So I press the little button on my headphones and answer. "Hi, Dad."

"Just checking on you." In the background, I can hear the clanking and seagulls. He must be out working. It's the start of lobster season, after all.

"How's everything?" I ask, tucking my chin close to the mic and speaking softly.

"Tired. How about you? How's…business?"

That's a jab. He's hates me being here. Thinks I'm *overstepping* and leaving *my people* behind. "Going through some papers," I say, as if it's nothing. As if I'm not looking at treasure chest, full of gold and pearls, while I feel my heart getting zipped open like my black dress.

"Just renewed the registration on the boat."

That's him saying he's got papers of his own. Papers of struggle and real life. He wouldn't know about C.S. Lewis if I told him, and wouldn't care even if he did. Philosophy and manuscripts and all the rest make shit for difference when you spend your entire life hauling angry crustaceans out of the Atlantic and your labor is valued by the pound.

"Season starts today…" I hear the strain in his voice, lifting something heavy. God. The guilt. The guilt is crippling. Stay strong, Naomi. Stay strong. You wanted something bigger, something more, and you've got to fight to keep it.

"I've got a lot going on campus. Classes start for me this afternoon."

"Sure could use you here," he says. A lobster pot clanks. "They've got an opening in the groundfishery program…"

That'd be at the community college. That, to my dad, is what is useful. Learning the patterns of crab and lobster movement on the ocean floor. What I do, what I want to learn, that's useless. That's thoughts and abstraction and foolishness. And he won't support foolishness. He's made that abundantly clear.

My fingers grace the word *Eros,* for erotic love.

"Dad, I don't want to go through this again. Every fall you do this to me."

"Every fall I need your help."

The problem is, when I'm anxious or tired or overwhelmed—which is a lot of the time, to be honest—what my dad says sounds logical. But I can't go back there. I just cannot.

"I need to go," I tell him. "Be careful out there."

"I'd be safer with you here."

"Love you."

End call.

Begin overpowering guilt.

I blink back some tears. My dad could say five words and crush me. Today he said maybe fifteen and I'm wrecked.

With my sweatshirt sleeve, I wipe my nose and focus on C.S. Lewis. *Need love. Gift love. Human happiness.*

I catalog the next page and hit play on Spotify. My phone buzzes again.

An alert from my bank.

"You have $3.21 remaining in your checking account. Reply YES for a cash advance from your credit card."

Jamming it back in my pocket, my head starts spinning faster than ever about impending bills for tuition and room and board and the little things known as "incidentals" that add up so fast, the small tiny things of life: hairbands, music subscription, phone bill, train ticket home for Thanksgiving, books, drugstore purchases for things like Advil and tampons. When they add up, under a heavy heart, they don't feel so incidental at all.

∙∙

I leave the bowels of the Beinecke to find campus bustling. I get a hot water from Blue State Coffee and use my own tea from my purse, which buoys me a little. Not much, but a little. It's a nice change, all these people around, all these distractions from the stream of thoughts in my head. On my way back to college, I stop at the bookstore, getting books for my English and History seminars. Walking down the steps towards the registrar, I'm held hostage by an end cap: Copies of *The Four Loves*. The acquisition was an exciting one, and the bookstore is making the best of it too. I grab one and head for the register, but at the next end cap, there it is: *In The Ashes of Planets* by Benjamin Beck. I press my fingers to the cover. Matte, black and white. Clean and smart. I can't afford it, but I can't help myself and add it to the stack. I put my whole tab on my credit card. At the register, I cross my fingers and just hope like hell I'm not maxed out.

Miraculously, I'm not, and I lug my books back to college with the plastic bag cutting into my fingers like huge pieces of floss.

Returning to my room, I sit down on my bed and look out my

dormer window. I open his book, my chest thundering as I read his words. *"So, while we can never experience the world-in-itself, we seem almost fatalistically drawn to it, perhaps as a limit that defines who we are as human beings."*

Brilliant and yet heartbreaking. I press the book to my chest and glance out my window.

Of course, there he is, walking across the quad. It's nearly lunch, and it makes sense, but seeing him there is like some cosmic hiccup, some impossible coincidence that screams out, "It's meant to be!" He's dressed casually, not in a tux or a tweed now, no. Now he's dressed like himself. Those chinos, that shirt, a simple blue plaid, short-sleeved. The way the muscles in his neck run down into his shoulders. Even wearing flip-flops. Old well-loved flip-flops?

Naomi. You have no chance of resisting this. None.

He looks like some surfer out of place. I will him to look over at me, like my thoughts could cut through air. He doesn't. He can't know that this is my window, this little funny slate dormer in the corner that looks like some craftsman tacked it on for a laugh. Completely rapt, I watch him walk across the quad, every single step making my heart beat faster. He strolls along. He looks at the trees. He pauses to look up at the sun, and I see him sigh. Halfway across, he runs into one of the admins from Dean's Office. It's old Mrs. Hillyard with blue-black hair, who carries all the keys to everywhere in her purse and is roughly a thousand years old. She's impossible to talk to because she whispers and yet can't hear anything anybody says. Talking to her, Ben is so easy in his body. He shakes her hand, and I can see her big smile from four floors away. She's undoubtedly saying something about how nice it is to have a handsome new Master in college.

Oh, Mrs. Hillyard. You don't even know!

She says something to him, and he leans in, not understanding, with one finger to his ear, and one hand gently on her arm. God. A sweetheart too. Patient with the odd little old lady who talks and talks. They make their goodbyes and he's off. Finally, he vanishes through the big oak door, into the dining hall.

I slump down onto my bed. If this goes on, I'm done. I'll never make through my classes. I'll never finish an assignment, I'll never write another paper. If I did? It'd be 2500 repetitions of the word *Ben*.

Opening up C.S. Lewis, I turn to the chapter on Eros. I see him telling me that those in the throes of erotic Eros-driven love are the *swoony-devout*.

God. Exactly. That's how I feel exactly. Swoony-devout.

C.S. Lewis fails to offer any remedy though. Which also makes sense to me right now. There is no logic of wanting. Only feelings that ache and ache.

My mask from the ball is hanging on the edge of my bed. I take the ostrich feather and put it inside the book to mark my place. Somehow, that just seems right. Somehow, it's the thing I need to do.

My laptop is somewhere under the covers, and I find it and boot it up. The old girl is dying a slow spinning-beach-ball death, but I coax her back to life. What I need to do now is pick the last class for my schedule. Registration for my Philosophy seminar has been locked until today. Majors only in Philosophy 3321: Mystics.

It occurs to me that possibly, just possibly, I'm in for another cosmic hiccup. My stomach kind of goes inside out. I widen my browser to reveal, letter by agonizing letter, that my suspicion was exactly right.

Instructor: Prof. Beck.

Frantically, I search for any other option. I mean, I'd be willing to take a seminar in Latin if it fit the bill. Virgil's farming manuals? An obscure class on ancient fish? Something, anything. Anything at all.

Except there isn't anything else. That's the class I've got to take. Without it, I can't move on to the next seminar. All the seminars are lined up like that in Philosophy. Like dominos. One after the other, logical and clean.

Which means that if I don't take Professor Beck's class, I can't graduate. I can see it's filling up fast, right before my eyes.

So I do it. I hit *Register*. And flop back on my bed. He's just become Dr. Benjamin Beck, Professor and Master.

Are you there, God? It's me, Naomi. Tips? Got any?

I put my own pillow over my face.

I'm drowning here. It's an awful sinking feeling. But then the truth of it all gets pretty simple: If I have to go back to Maine, if I can't hack it here, I'll kick myself forever for not taking a chance with him. For not seeing him, for not working my hardest, for not fighting as hard as I can for what I want. Because you only live once. And you never know what tomorrow will bring. A wave from astern that you didn't see coming.

If it's him I want, it's him I want.

I pull the pillow off my face and open my eyes wide.

His class. Me. I'll tell him then.

We're doing this thing. Yes, we are.

I look at my phone.

Class starts in 20 minutes.

In a frenzy, I leap out of bed and look at myself in the mirror. If I'm going to have to see him out in the world, I want to look good. He's not in his Turkey Trot T-shirt anymore, and I want to look my best. I flip through my bare closet. Aside from repurposing my waiting uniform, I'm short on college-girl chic.

I fling open my door and pound on Lucy's, which comes open under my fist.

She's in the middle of scrolling through Facebook. "Hello, lover," she says.

"I need clothes." Now her room is like Fashion Week exploded all over everything. She's walking with her toes up in the air to let her polish dry.

"Set the scene. Are we...what? Yachting? Attending a ceremony? Horse riding? Going to court?"

She's only half teasing. "Going to class, like you should be. But today a hoodie and yoga pants is just not going to cut it."

Lucy looks suspicious for one instant and then flies into action. She's flinging skirts and boots and cardigans through the air. God, what is that, a white strapless prom dress? It's all sorts coming from the closet, in streaks of color and fluttering fabric. A pair of red capri jeans thunks on her bed on top of the pile, followed by a striped boatneck tee. She pauses and points.

"More flirty!" I tell her. "Less clambake."

Rummage, rummage, rummage. She's so focused, she even lets her toes touch the ground. Then she emerges holding a lovely little sundress, dark blue with tiny pink flowers all over.

"You're the best," I say, taking it from its puffy hanger.

She waves that off. "Whoever you're after, they're damned lucky. Tell them not to forget it, or I'll come remind them."

My face flushes, I can feel my skin get hot, and I think, *If only she knew.*

I run back to my room and slip it on. It's a little snug in the waist but otherwise perfect. As fast as I can, I put on my eye shadow and my eyeliner—I wasn't born with it, it's definitely Maybelline—curl my eyelashes, and moisten my fingers to rub away any specks of make-up that landed on my cheeks in all this rushing around. As I do, the remnants of shadow on my skin make deep streaks under my eyes, making me look like a linebacker for the Patriots. Classy! What a hot mess. But I get it all cleaned up, give my legs a quick rub with my lotion, grab *The Four Loves* with the feather peeking from the pages, and run down the 72 steps.

13
ben

I haven't prepared at all for my first lecture because of Naomi Goddamned Costa.

Last night, once the fellows' dinner ended, things should have gone like this: Go for jog. Shower. Sit down with whiskey. Open books. Write notes. Open more books, write more notes. Close books because fuck that noise, and write new notes. Go back to old lecture from last term. Realize I can just use old notes. More whiskey. Make new syllabus. Fight with Word over formatting, the asshole. Finish syllabus. Bed.

Instead, last night went like this: Whiskey. Think of her belly button. Think of that soft skin. Think of being inside her. Think of needing to be inside her again. Think of that scar, that laugh, that hair. Think of her coming. Put face in hands. Adjust pants. Go to registrar's portal. Begin typing in Naomi's name. Realize that's fucking suspicious because I'm on the campus wireless and that might be as bad as the NSA. Type in different Durham student's name. Pretend to be looking at different student. Type in another Durham student's name. Pretend to read about other student. More whiskey. Repeat ten times. Eat twelve Oreos. Finally, type in "Naomi Costa," and find out the following:

- Full name: Naomi Francesca Costa (God. Even that middle name.)
- Cell phone: 509-591-9517 (Thump, thump.)
- College: Durham (Heart pounds in spite of knowing this already.)
- Year: Junior (See above.)
- Declared major, Philosophy. (Fuck. Fuck. Fuck! Yes! No! I don't know! And also fuck all those assholes who say it's not useful.)
- From Cutler, Maine. (Tiny fishing village, pop. 507.)
- Father, alive. Profession: lobsterman. (Holy shit. Best profession ever.)
- Mother, deceased. (Oh God, no. Anything but that. Anything at all but that.)

Print above. Save above, hide above in sock drawer. Advil. Shower. Bed.

Then this morning, I find her purse and she comes by, like magic. I could barely choke down my coffee after that.

So now here I am, completely unprepared for what's coming. Literally, zero idea what I'm going to talk about for my first lecture at Yale. Then it hits me, as well, as I unpack my stuff on the table in front of the whiteboard, that this isn't UCLA. These kids, there has to be 200 of them, are staring at me like small carnivorous animals who want to eat whatever I have to say, and then chew and chew it until it's gone. Digest it. Pick it over. Tear it up. They're like little predatory walking brains, the way they're looking at me. At UCLA, it was so chill. These Yale kids? They're on the hunt. And one of them is even wearing the shirt with my book jacket on it.

I'll never live that shit down, ever.

I checked the roster early this morning before breakfast and didn't see Naomi's name on it. Believe me, I looked. But now, as I get ready to speak, I see her. In the last seat, front row, in a little summer dress. Pink flowers, navy blue. I can see the tan lines on her shoulders. Simple black flip-flops. Hair down. Just enough cleavage to make me forget every fucking thing I've ever known.

I might as well just set fire to this whole place and peace out.

So I wing it. I'm good at winging it. Kind of.

Class goes by, I think I might be talking sense or possibly not. At some point, I write the word *NOTHINGNESS* on the board, because that's the nihilist mantra. I talk about *The Big Lebowski* and Turgenev. I talk about papers for the term. I have everybody introduce themselves, tell us what they want to do with their Philosophy degree. Classic icebreaker, but there's only one answer I'm waiting to hear. So I start with her. "Go ahead," I hold out my hand to her, pretending I don't know every inch of her and her name too. "Miss…"

She stands up and turns slightly towards the class. I watch the hem of her dress slide down her thigh, and lean against the lectern for help. Then she says, "I'm Naomi Costa." Soft but confident. "I'm a junior at Durham. And as for what I want to do with my degree?" She looks up at the ceiling, gets this cheek-pinching smile, and look straight at me, "I'd like to have your job one day, Professor Beck."

Fuck.

Everybody else introduces themselves. I don't remember a single name, a single answer. Her, it's all her. Finally, icebreaker finished, I say, "Welcome to all of you. Thanks for taking my class. And please, come to my office hours." I manage not to look directly at her. I say I'm the Master at Durham, and I'd love to see you there, anytime, for lunch, for dinner.

I do glance at her, for just one second, and say, "For anything at all."

Then I ask, "Any questions before I let you go?"

Small pause. Her beautiful arm rises. I'm stuck looking at that curve between her shoulder and her chest. "Yes, Miss Costa?"

"Professor Beck. Is it really true that you believe in *nothing*? Do you really talk like Matthew McConaughey all the time?"

I can see she's about to giggle. I love that. It must be a defense mechanism. It has the secondary effect of wrecking my self-composure.

Alright. Bring it, beautiful.

I clear my throat, and looking right into those sea-blue eyes, I do my best McConaughey impression, get that vocal fry going super strong. "We're nothing. We're the dust of nothing. Nothing."

Roar of laughter. I see her snort. My chest feels like it's going to burst.

And it's over. They're off to their next thing, the room filled with the clatter and thumps of 200 brains on overdrive.

After class, a few students stay behind. I actually sign my damned autograph for one, which is pretty much mind-blowing and kind of awesome in the way that super weird things are awesome. But at the end of the line is Naomi. Smiling.

At last, it's just the two of us. It's everything I can do not to flip the fucking table over and take her right here.

"Hi," she says.

The dress is cut just low enough that I can see the very curve of her breasts as they come together. She loved how hard I sucked on them, all the while pinning her down with my body. What I wouldn't do to carry her back to Durham and do that right now, all over again. "Hello, Miss Costa."

She slides a book across the table. C.S. Lewis. *The Four Loves.* "Sorry I was a little rude this morning. That's for you." She keeps her fingers on the cover and doesn't step away.

I've read it, but years ago. I remember doubting him, marking up the pages of some library copy with question marks. Lewis trying to make logic of love. Love. The thing that doesn't really exist. Love is nothing but a chain of coincidence and a mess of thoughts. It's the confusion of need and lust. It's nothing. Every pessimist agrees.

Riiiight.

Now, because of her and the way she's making me feel, I'm interested. I'm fairly sure she could have handed me *The Joy of Cooking* and I would have been interested, but I like this much better. I see a bookmark poking out. It gives me rush because it's the ostrich feather. She's stealthy. Secretive. Symbolic. I take it and put it in my bag with my laptop, my fingers just brushing hers. "Thanks." Now I make a show of grabbing my bag and getting closer to her, walking out with her. But we're alone in that huge lecture hall, and I get as close as I can to her without touching her. I'm 6'3". She's got to be, what, 5'6"? So perfect. So fucking perfect.

We're so close, I can feel the heat of her bare arm on mine. I glance back and there's nobody there, but shit. "I want to touch you. I need to touch you."

She exhales, a slow, deep calm breath. "I wanted you to say that."

"You won't get out of my head."

"You won't get out of mine."

"I can't believe you're in this class," I trail one finger down her hand.

"I need you. I can't stand this," and then that exhale again. So deep, it makes her rib cage slip down into her breasts.

It's then that the big door at the back creaks and I step away. She does the same, and we act like normal people. Professor and student, heading up the steps. Try to, anyway. I happen to have a nearly painful hard-on against my computer bag.

She flips her hair aside, revealing the curve of her neck to me as she puts her bag on her other shoulder. I see these red marks where it was, depressions in her skin from the pressure above. Everything inside me wants to go to Home Depot and buy all the rope they sell.

"Do you have office hours today?" she asks.

Fucking right I do. I'll make all the office hours that ever were for her. "Name it."

"Three o'clock? Your house?"

Done.

The next few hours pass like I am locked in a time warp. The first thing I do is open up the book she gave me. I was right. She's marked the page with the feather from her mask. I emit an audible groan, walking down College. Fortunately, nobody notices.

I read page after page as I walk. I'm utterly engrossed. Everything he's saying, I'm feeling. I actually nod a few times because everything he's telling me, I feel I somehow already know. Because of her.

After that, every minute is a whole hour. I try to stay as long as I can in the dining hall for lunch; I talk so much, I feel hoarse. I go for a jog around campus to get my bearings a little better. It takes exactly 19 minutes. Fucking, fuck, fuck. All I want is to see her, to hold her to see what happens next. I want to get sweet and filthy with her. I want to make her shiver and whimper and say my name. I think back to when I'd spanked her, leaving a handprint right across her ass, as she moaned into the pillow, "More. Please."

This girl. This woman. Let the walls come right on down.

In the shower after my jog, I imagine her there with me, on her knees. I lean against the tiled wall, absolutely throbbing for her from inside out. I let the water rain down over me, thinking of her skin on my tongue, the whiskey welling in her belly button. I need to find out what she's made of. That bite mark she gave me on my thigh, it's still there. The impression of her teeth, deep and purple. She's on her knees in front of

63

me, taking me into her throat, as deep as she can. As deep as I tell her. I come like a fucking river, whispering her name.

At 2:55 pm, there's a knock at my back door. I have an instant raging hard-on. My heart pounds through in my balls. I open the door.

It's Dean Osgood. "Good afternoon."

My hard-on withers with tragic speed.

He looks different. He's lost the toupee. "Haircut?"

Touching his head, self-conscious now. "It flew away, if you must know."

Do not laugh, Ben. Do not laugh. "I have an appointment with a student at three," I say, scanning the quad for Naomi.

"Alright, Beck," Osgood says, suddenly dead serious and no longer ridiculous looking either. "Here's the deal. I don't think you're a good fit for this college."

"I'm here, aren't I?" Good work, buddy. Way to be combative to your superior.

"For now. I wanted a professor and his wife from Harvard, one of the housemasters there. Nice people. Married for twenty years. She studies plants and he talks about Edgar Allen Poe. *Those* are the kind of people this college needs, and I fought like hell to get them. I was overruled because of you and," he grits his teeth, "that bizarre burnt planets book."

Now that's why he's so weird with me. He thinks I'm an outsider, which of course, I most definitely am. I'm betting he grew up somewhere like Cambridge, like his dad is some law professor at Harvard still. All locked into the establishment, they can't stand anybody else inside it. "So much for Welcome Master."

"You've got that right. So just know this: I've got my eye on you. I'm watching you. Any misstep, any shenanigans, you're out. If Durham gets hit with another scandal, we're dissolved. They rename us like fraternity and we vanish from the scene. You lose your job, I lose mine. Fucking…" His face turns red as he searches for the word. "…*Disaster.*"

"Have I given any indication of a guy who likes scandal?"

He rubs his mouth hard. "The problem with a bachelor Master, see, is this whole place is full to the brim with beautiful young girls. That's why I don't want you here."

"Buddy, you're a bachelor."

"I'm a widower and seventy years old."

He has a point. "I'm in Philosophy. I don't do shenanigans." The image of her tied to my hotel bed flashes into my head. "I want to be here. I'm not going to get involved with a student." That's a lie. I know I am. But she's not just "a student" anyway.

"I saw you leaving the butler's pantry, right after Miss Costa."

Damn it. He's put something together. Even a little connecting of the dots, that'd be a huge mess. Keep it cool. Channel your inner Kant, Ben. Breathe right through it. "You've made yourself understood," I tell him.

"Consider this: You get involved with her?" he snaps. "*Her* whole fucking academic career? Gone. It won't even be in our hands. If anybody sees you, it'll leak from the Provost's office and be all over the internet in an hour. So she's done for and *you?* Never mind *your* superstardom," he snaps again.

Now I just don't say anything. Even Kant would've hit this bastard in the face by now. Holding her over me. Dickhead.

"This is your only warning," he says, glowering at me. "One fuck up, and you're out. And remember," he says, doing that two-fingered pointing asshole move from his eyes to mine and back again. "I'm watching."

I close the door. God damn it. He knows. He'll see us. We're doomed. Right now, and from now on always, surely always, the need to protect her is greater than the need to fuck her. I'm so goddamned furious, I want to break something.

I let loose a hard, straight jab into the wall. As my fist is flying, I think *this is gonna be a mess*. Drywall everywhere. But the impact of the punch rolls immediately back up my hand, straight through my bones, into my elbow.

"Fuck!" I snarl. Cinderblock made to look like plaster? Are you *kidding me?*

That's when I hear the noise of footsteps approaching. I hold my knuckles, throbbing and bleeding a little. God damn it. God damn it, Beck.

A soft, gentle, knock. Not with the knocker this time.

I swallow hard. I wince. I'm pretty sure my knuckles are broken.

I wonder what she's doing out there. Moving her hair aside. Breathing. Just being. Fuuuuuuuck.

A second knock. A little more urgent this time. Five taps.

There's no way I can open this door. No way. I've never felt so sorry about anything in my entire life.

One more patter of knocks. This time, more spread out. If knocks could be sad, these are.

"Master Beck?" she says on the other side of the door. That beautiful, kind voice. I say nothing. Fucking nothing. If I open this door, Osgood is going to see her come in and we're both completely through. It's that simple. That kind of catastrophe. I have to keep her out. I have to keep her away. For her sake. Give a shit about me.

And then finally, the most beautiful girl in the world walks away from my door.

As a drop of blood splatters from my fist onto the floor.

14
Naomi

For the second time that week, Lucy's got her arms around me. "Little lamb," she says. "What is going on with you? I know you cry at Hallmark ads but not like *this*."

Somehow, against all the odds, I managed to get up the 72 steps and crumple against her doorway. Instead of replying, I sniffle hard and wipe my nose on my sweatshirt again.

"Are you going to tell me what's going on?" She smooths my hair. I feel her get her finger tangled in my mess of curls.

I lower myself all the way to the floor of her room. I grab a bag of almonds. She's always got almonds. I shove a whole big handful in my hand. "Oh God," I say.

"Wasabi. Sorry. Listen," Lucy says, sort of on her tiptoes like she always is when she's thinking up something devilish. "Jack and Coke, they're having a party."

I manage to swallow the hot ball of almond fire. I can feel it up into my eyes. It's better than crying over Master Beck, who wouldn't even answer the door. I don't understand it. He wanted me— he said he wanted me—today in the lecture hall. There was absolutely no mistaking it. But then three hours later, he wouldn't open the door. I know he was home because I'd heard some kind of racket before I knocked.

Asshole. Asshat. Asseverything.

"Jack and Coke, huh?" I say, and suck down a big gulp of water. Thursday at Yale is the big night for parties. Jack and Coke is an old-school secret society, all boys. Most of them are crew guys, but some just pretend to row crew and instead wear loafers and faded-out red shorts every day. Those guys. Also, there's a chance Isaac will be there. Normally this would have made me give her a *no thanks*, but my defenses are decidedly compromised.

She nods. "At the Yacht Club."

I almost spit my water out of my nose. "That's in Branford. What? You and me on a bus?"

Now she's got that *you're so cute* look on her face. "Uber, baby. My treat."

Behind shut eyes, I listen to my thoughts. I want to be alone. I want to yank the covers right up to my eyes and watch the fifth season of *Girls* until I fall asleep. I want to eat microwave popcorn and wallow. I want to write sad status updates on Facebook that make my friends leave comments that read only, "?" I want to go to the gym and make the elliptical clatter at full speed. But I can't bear being here. I just can't. I'd have my nose pressed up to my windows watching for him until I fell asleep. Time for a change, Naomi. It's true. Time to cheer the fuck up, buttercup. "Dinner first?"

"Now you're talking," she says.

And as I open my eyes a polka-dotted navy mini skirt flutters through the air and lands on my head.

We go to dinner at Shake Shack, and I get a smokehouse burger with extra peppers. Lucy, normally the kind of girl that really would prefer her dressing on the side, positively astounds me by ordering the same thing as I do.

"It's got cheese. And some kind of mayonnaise," I whisper.

She grinds her elbow between my ribs.

"Two large fries," I tell the guy at the counter.

"And a beer," she says. She pulls out her ID. She's 21 already. She told me she started a year late due to an unfortunate scandal after her senior year in high school that may or may not have ended up with her on that kidnapped-to-rehab-camp show.

Lucy swivels on one leg, cute as a button. "I mean, unless you'd give us two beers. I'm awfully thirsty…"

Deadpan stare in return. "I'll get my ass fired, girls. No way."

"Fair enough," Lucy says, and pays with her parents' American Express.

While we're sitting at our table waiting for our food, she's watching the line anxiously. I can't figure it out. Either she's planning on getting a milkshake to eat with her fries, or she's up to no good. I bet on the latter, Lucy being Lucy. Without a word, she gets up and gets back in line. Then it hits me. There's been a shift change and there's a new guy at the register. She's going to get another beer, this one for me. Lucy. She'll either become president or a notorious felon.

I busy myself with my phone. I don't know why. Nothing is happening. I look at the weather. I look at the news. Nothing registers. My head, it's with him. I take a deep breath, a sigh. *Damn* it. Leave it to me to fall for the first guy that I'll never get to have. The desire to see him, it makes this weight inside me. I'm not even sure I could eat. I'm hungry for him and him alone.

Then my phone buzzes. Number and name blocked.

You like cheeseburgers. You're perfect.

Ummm. What?

I don't answer. The face of this weird guy who I met during my one and only foray into Tinder jumps into my head. God, no. The last freaking thing I need right now is a stalker.

Within just a few seconds, another message.

"The lover desires the Beloved herself."

Oh my God. That's from C.S. Lewis. That's from the book I gave him today. My eyes scan every single table. Where is he, where is he? Holy hell. Corner bar table, all alone, not even looking at me. I steel myself. I'm somewhere between freaking out and furious.

I was at your door.

Just as I hit send, I stare at him to see his response to my reply. His eyes close, sadly. His thumbs are still. Until finally he replies with a simple:

We're fucked.

I feel a flush come up to my cheeks and tears in my eyes. Stupid, stupid, stupid.

I know.

And then what does he do?

He replies with the broken-heart emoji.

My whole body rolls in frustration and sadness, which is when Lucy sets down a beer in front of me. I glance over and watch him stand up, and pocket his phone. Tossing his garbage in the bin, he heads toward the door without a glance back at me.

The Uber ride takes about twenty minutes. Ahmed is our driver, 4.9 stars, and he's got a cluster of about thirty pineapple air fresheners on the rearview mirror.

Ahmed is now undergoing the barrage of Lucy's barked orders about driving directions. "Don't take Chapel, okay, Ahmed? Copy that? We'll get all jammed up there by the hospital. Elm, Elm all the way. Ahmed? Got it?"

"Lucy, he's got a damned GPS," I tell her. I want to clap my hand over her mouth. Poor guy, just trying to make a living, and then he picks us up only to get verbally assaulted by little Lucy Burchett.

"No problem!" Ahmed says. "I like a lady who knows what she wants!" And within minutes, we're zooming towards I-95 and the Quinnipiac Bridge. Out the window, I see IKEA flash past. Part of me wishes I was there, eating chicken fingers and drinking lingonberry soda all by myself. But I'm not. Probably for the best. Brooding sadly over display furniture and flopping down onto mattresses isn't exactly the sort of thing I'd call healing, even if it does feel really, really good. No. The thing to do is be with people now. To keep myself busy and distracted.

Lucy sits back contentedly, backseat driving well done. I clutch my purse in my hands and try desperately not to look at my phone every 30 seconds.

"Fess up. What's going on with you?" Lucy says. "No tricks." She taps her temple. "Lucy knows all of them."

Ben's body flashes into my head. I used to wonder who in the world those people were who thought about sex every however-many-second seconds.

I am now one of those people.

"Classes. They're stressful."

Lucy shakes her head slowly, wagging her finger at me in an *oh-no-you-don't* way. "Not for you. And I know it's not dad problems."

I groan and press my head against the headrest behind me. "He called the other day. Almost dropped tears on C.S. Lewis."

Lucy has no interest in manuscripts at all unless they're mostly lurid. "It's not him because you haven't been obsessively cleaning your room. When your dad pisses you off, I smell Pledge next door and hear lots of rattling. So that's out."

Here's the thing. Stonewalling your best friend when she's a girl like Lucy, it's impossible. I feel like this is how it must feel to get interrogated by the CIA. They know every last fucking thing about you and won't let you off the hook until you crumple.

Lucy wiggles her nose. "I mean, obviously you met a guy. Summer dress? Please. I saw you dancing with that stud at Lux. Ever since then you've been all…" She makes a big circle with both her hands, pinching up her face in my general direction. "…*whatever* is going with you."

God. She's right. What Ben and I did that night, it's like it unleashed my inner Naomi. This sexy, fearsome girl inside me that I never knew existed. A girl who asked to be hurt and who did some hurting back. I wonder if the bite mark I left on his thigh has healed yet. "So what if I did?"

She claps. "Knew it!"

"Why did you invite me anyway?" I ask. If she hadn't, none of this would have ever happened. Probably.

"I didn't. The society did." She lifts her shoulder. "They agreed on you.

Nothing makes any sense whatsoever. I might as well just resign myself to that. "Anyway, it's just…" My breath catches at my words. "A guy."

"Riiiiight. You don't wear your eyeliner like that for *just a guy.*"

She notices everything. Everything! "A professor," I whisper, as far under my breath as I possibly can. Not far enough through because I see

71

Ahmed's eyebrows shoot up in the rearview mirror.

Lucy has exactly no reaction to this at all. Her eyes are wide, her mouth open, and she's just frozen like that, as if she's waiting for a surprise party to yell her name. "And?"

"And! It's a mess!"

"Married?"

I shake my head.

She lifts her shoulders. "So? What's the problem?"

I groan. "We don't all have your hereditary disregard for ethics."

"I can teach you, sister. It can be learned."

My phone buzzes. I yank it out of my bag. It's a thunderstorm alert. Fuck it. Suddenly, a rush of emotion comes flooding up to my face. Disappointment, sadness, breakage. My nose stings, my vision gets blurry. It's not just the usual Naomi eye-mist. It's real tears. Stupid, stupid, heart on my sleeve. Giving me away always. I clutch my freaking phone to my chest. In the rearview, I can see poor Ahmed looking at me sadly.

Even though I want to tell Lucy all about him, every last thing, what happened today in front of his door was so deeply humiliating, I don't have the words at all. I want this to be my own private failure. My own secret broken-hearted mistake.

"Whoa," Lucy says. "This is serious."

She's right about that. It is serious. And I just want to forget about it for tonight.

∴

As we arrive at the Yacht Club, the sun is just slipping past the horizon. The boathouse itself is an old wooden gray building on the Connecticut River, with crew boats moored for a hundred yards either way. I've been out here just once, for a party with Lucy and her parents. It looks a whole lot different now than it did then. The Jack and Coke guys have hung up incongruous Japanese lanterns. They're sort of milling around, leaning on things, looking loose and cocky in their boat shorts and loafers. Just as Ahmed drops us off, someone hooks up their phone to a big set of speakers perched on the back of a truck. Out comes "Cake by the Ocean." And that's when I spot Isaac.

I saw the J. Crew catalog for Fall/Winter. They've got him in a corduroy slim-fit blazer available in pewter and coffee in both regular and tall sizes. He was helping a small child in a yellow dress organize her blocks.

The feeling I get when I see him is somewhere between excitement, dread, and relief. Isaac is an ass, but at least he'd answer the door if I knocked.

Being with him, though, it all seems so long ago. The stuff of kids, almost.

As we enter the milling crowd of guys, two Jack and Cokes hoist Lucy up on their shoulders like she's a cheerleader and hustle her down to the river. I lose sight of her but hear a delighted squeal and then a splash. Isaac sidles on up, gazing down at me like he's not sure if I'm going to attack him. We broke up after he followed me after class and then gave me the third degree on why I was "having coffee with some other guy." The "other guy" was my TA and we were talking about my paper. That's when I gave old Isaac the heave-ho. I gaze up at him. Time to be nice. "You looked handsome in that blazer."

He looks stunned. "I feel like you actually mean that."

All my fight is drained out of me. "Lovely lining."

"Thanks," he says. "For Winter/Spring, I just learned they've got me wearing a light pink cashmere turtleneck. Assholes."

I snort. "You actually don't look that bad in pink. Sorry about that."

"Yes, I do. Don't lie." Isaac hands me a drink. Clear plastic cup, ice, slightly fizzy. Lime. Definitely a gin and tonic. This is that kind of party anyway, and the Jack and Cokes don't *just* drink Jack and Coke.

I take a sip and am utterly flattened. "Whoa Nelly, what *is* this?"

"Naval gin," Isaac says. He pulls out a little bottle from his pocket. The label is rudimentary and seemingly hand-drawn.

"Where'd you get that, a seventeenth-century schooner?"

"It's legal now," he says, triumphant. Apparently, all the illegal liquors are now in Yale's liquor cabinets. We're all going to end up with Swiss cheese for brains and be institutionalized before we turn forty. But at least we'll have fun going crazy.

I take another drink and cough a little as it goes down. I lick the tonic off my lips. That bitter deliciousness. "If we don't drink all of it, we should donate it to the hospital so they can use it to clean their syringes."

Isaac laughs. This big, bold laugh, like all of him is in it, through and through. The laugh of a guy who knows that when he laughs, everybody else will follow. A congressman's laugh, really. He's just arrogant enough to become one.

"How was your summer?" he asks. He slips his arm through mine. At first, I stiffen. I don't want him touching me. I don't want anything to do with him. But seriously, Naomi, it's an arm against an arm. Calm down.

Except his warm arm immediately sends me back to the way Ben pinned me down on the bed. The feel of his hands on my forearms, so beautiful and gentle, but then getting stronger and more possessive as the night went on until we had our hands knitted together while he fucked me, staring me right in the eyes.

"Naomi?" Isaac says, waving a hand in front of my face. "Hello?"

"Sorry. This gin!"

"Who was that guy at the ball?" he asks. He's trying to be casual. He has on his casual face. I've seen it before. He was wearing a merino sweater vest while carving a turkey in the special Thanksgiving issue.

"My TA," I say. "Same guy who I had coffee with. You were right all along. We're having a torrid romance, conducted in secret after our Philosophy seminars." Jesus, Naomi. Humor can get way too close to the truth. Careful. Batten down the hatches with this gin in your hand.

"Sorry about that, Naomi. I just…" Isaac says, running his hand through his hair, "I really like you, *liked* you. I guess I got a little possessive."

Weirdly, this seems absolutely inappropriate from Isaac; at the same time, if Ben were to say that, to get all possessive, I'd be absolutely flattered. Desire, it makes all the difference.

"Friends?" Isaac says.

"Friends."

And his face lights up in that all-American smile.

He leads me to the dock and sits down with his legs dangling off. He pats the dock, and I sit down beside him. "I saw you in Mysticism. I hope it's good."

Cue sad violin music. I nod. I sip my rubbing alcohol and tonic. "Lots of hype."

He shrugs. "I guess. Have you started the reading?"

"Jesus, no. I haven't even started. How bad is it?" Somehow I can just see Ben assigning, like, 2000 pages a week, I don't know why. Because he writes philosophy books, that's why. Because *he* probably reads a thousand pages *a day*. That kind of smart. Scary smart.

"Just… weird," he says, pulling up his phone and showing me the syllabus. The standard mystical philosophy texts I'd expected to see… only there at the bottom?

I grab his phone. The world is slightly woozy. Could be the gin, or the fact that *The Four Loves* is now on the reading list.

For the love of all that is sane in the world, why, oh why, oh why? I don't know if I'm going to cry or laugh uncontrollably or both. I gulp down the rest of my gin and tonic all at once.

"Ahoy, sailor," Isaac says, smiling at me, slipping his phone into his pocket.

"Rough day," I tell him.

And as if in some kind of secret camaraderie, he bottoms out his G & T too. He sucks air through his teeth, with the final swallow. Perfect teeth. Perfect face, perfect body, and yet not even close to what I need and want.

"Wait," I say, "Why are you drinking? Isn't it rugby season? I remember last fall you wouldn't even eat the cookies in the dining hall because you needed to stay... what was it?" I try to remember. "In fighting condition?"

Now he looks like mischief, glancing from side to side. "I'm having neck problems. Like Peyton Manning."

"Oh shit," I say. "I'm so sorry." Instinctively, I touch my neck.

"Nerve compression."

Internally, I recoil. I know that pain from the propeller accident. Absolutely nothing like it in the world. "Are you okay?"

"I mean, it's fine." He stretches his neck from side to side, as if that'll make a difference. "Rugby, it's not life. But upshot." He pulls a white pen from his pocket. "I got a medical marijuana license."

I stare at the pen. It's not a pen. It's an e-cigarette with a tiny pot leaf on the end.

Dropping my voice, I whisper, "Is that..."

He nods. Nice and slow. "Top grade. It'll blow your mind." And then he inhales smoothly from the vaporizer. He holds his breath, and just a little steam, barely noticeable, passes through his nose.

"That's it?" I ask.

He nods again, *super* slow now, his eyes just a little sheened over. "Try it."

"I've never..."

"Why not now?"

Shit. I try to get out of my haze of gin. Why not now? Thursday night, no class tomorrow until the afternoon. I'm upset and furious. Why not now? Why not?

"Come on, Naomi. Get a little crazy with me."

He's so gorgeous. My heart is aching so hard. He might be Isaac, he might be generally an asshole, but he likes me, and he's warm and delectable and *right here.*

He hands me the pen. "C'mon. I want to get stoned with you. Not marry you. You'll be so fun stoned. You're hilarious already."

The pen is light, weighted at one end. That must be where the battery is. "Am I?"

"Fuck yes! That joke about the syringes? The schooner? Pffffft," he laughs, just a little bit harder and bigger than normal. "Come on. It's no fun to get stoned with stupid girls. I should know."

I cannot help but smile. In my head I see them all lined up like pretty paper dolls around him.

"I'll shotgun you a hit," he says, leaning into my shoulder, "How about that?"

Lord. There was a time when that very sentence would have melted me. But thinking of kissing him now, it just makes me feel guilty. And gross. And then guilty again. "No shotgun. I'll do it," I say.

Putting my lips to the end, I inhale slowly. It's pepperminty and a little like inhaling steam from a humidifier. I have no idea how hard to inhale. After about a second, Isaac's eyes flash. He says, "That's good. Hold it."

My brain is already spinning. He takes the pen away, as I hold the inhale. After another second, he nods, and I let it go.

Immediately, and I mean immediately, my pussy rushes with wetness. An absolutely instantaneous turn on, uncontrollable desire, throbbing clit. "Holy shiiiiit," I say.

Isaac nods again. *Told you so.*

I see he's got a hard-on himself. Whoa. Whoooaahhh.

When he looks at me again, his eyes are heavy. A little red around the edge and the lids almost puffy. Stonnnned.

The music gets louder, the river starts to get farther away. The leaves are, weirdly, rustling louder than I've ever noticed leaves rustling before. There's a bird across the bank which is, without a doubt, the most beautiful bird that ever was, ever, in this history of birds.

Hollllyyyy shit. I take off my sandals and lie back on the dock, looking up at the barely visible stars. My toes just dip into the water. Isaac lies back with me and does the same.

My brain whooshes backwards in time. *The walls of my pussy part for him, and I groan. He's thick, he's so fucking hard. I feel his balls just brushing my ass. "I want to see what you're all about." Yeah, I say. "Tied down, this how'll you get to know me?" Yeah. I'll take you that way, take you apart. What do you say to that? Then he thrusts into me, I slide up the sheets. I say yes. Take me apart, Ben. Take me apart. Please.*

My sense of balance, even lying down, is completely askew. I have a brief flash of panic that I've been roofied. Not entirely false as I've effectively roofied myself. I look at Isaac, pressing my cheek to the rough old dock boards. "I'm super screwed up."

"Right?"

There's a freckle on his ear I never noticed. It's quite nice. He's quite nice.

The whole world is rolling around. I shut my eyes to find my center and it's nowhere. We listen to Vampire Weekend a while, and then something that sounds sort of like U2 on another planet.

"Seriously, Naomi. I'm sorry. I miss you. I wonder if we could…"

Everything goes quiet. My thoughts drift back to Ben. The way I felt when he came into the butler's pantry. The way I was horrified at what I'd done when first I realized who he was, but then absolutely thrilled in the same instant that he wasn't gone forever. The way the words in his book shot off the page and made me want to march down to his house and say, "How can you believe in *nothing*? Isn't what you feel right now *something*?" How this all, most definitely, unequivocally, insane as it is, doesn't feel like just some crazy fling.

I fumble for my phone and sit up. This takes me a second because I have no idea what's happened to my true north, but then I find it again. Kind of. Maybe. Who the hell knows. Only one thing matters. I open up the text from Unknown. I stare at the broken heart emoji and magically, in my head, the two halves of the heart come back together. Without thinking at all, I tap off a message and hit send.

where are you?

It could be a minute or possibly an hour that passes. I'm that screwed up. Next to me, Isaac is talking about his plans for after graduation. Flat-front chinos, Milan, MBA? L.L. Bean? I don't even care.

Then I see those little shimmery dots in the corner. Oh my God, he's typing. I clutch my phone. Far in the distance, thunder rumbles, and there's a flash of faraway lightning.

Master's house. My house. Weird.

Where are you?

I glance around. Where in the world am I? Why does my mouth taste weird? Oh shit. Right.

parted.
part.
PARTY.

Be careful.

Time to get to the point, skipper. Time to get down to business.

why didn't you open the door?

Osgood came. He warned me.
Believe me, I wanted to. I wanted to open that door.
I heard you there.
I'm so sorry, Naomi.

That, at least, makes sense. Osgood's favorite topic at the moment is avoiding scandal. It's verging on obsession. So I can imagine how that conversation might've gone down.

does he know?

No. Suspects, maybe.

I take a deep breath. There's this expression in sailing, from Lord Nelson back in the Royal Navy. *Never mind the maneuvers. Go straight at them.* I've always found it a pretty damned good motto, so…

i can't stop thinking about you.
i need what we did again.

As I send that second message, it occurs to me I might have gone at it a little high there. Pun intended. But nothing I can do now. Message received.

Fuck.

My heart pounds. The lanterns go around me in a huge circle time and time again. Isaac babbles. Girls squeal, the music thumps.

i need to see you.

This is madness. I'm begging the Master, a guy twice my age, by unknown text. I've officially lost my mind. Completely. And yet I know what I'm doing. I'm not an idiot. I'm not naïve. I want him. I aim to get him. All he can do is push me away, and if he does it again—right now—I'll give it all up. I'm not going to push and push and be that girl who gets what she wants by being as annoying as a thumbtack stuck in a shoe.

So whatever he says next, that'll tell me where we're headed. To tell me if I should let go of Ben and grab Isaac by the perfectly square jaw and kiss him, or plunge into Ben completely.

Do you know the half-door in the stairway...

My heart leaps right out of me. I'd once seen it and giggled because it was like an enormous dog door. Do I know the door? I can see it in my head right this very minute.

yes.

It's open.

Oh my God, oh my God.

Coming. I'm coming.

Twice? Good girl.

Annnnnd toe curl.

79

15
ben

The secret door is behind my water heater. This afternoon, after Naomi walked away and I pressed my head to the door like an abandoned chocolate lab for roughly twenty minutes, I decided there was no way I could let her go.

Here's the thing about nihilism. It's all about letting go. It's about believing that nothing matters so much you want to hurt over it. It's like Buddhism without the peace. Just let that shit go. I believe in it because I've had to let everybody go. My dad. My mom. Our dogs. My little brother. Jobs. Money. Life is one long series of losses. The one constant in life isn't death or taxes. It's loss. And if you believe nothing matters, loss doesn't hurt nearly so bad. Attachment is nothing but pain.

But I want her so fucking badly, I can actually feel the burn in my muscles when I think about her face. Everything she does makes it worse and slays me a little harder. The book, the question in class, the way she looks at me. The fury of her desire. The scar. But the small things too: I saw her at Shake Shack, where she'd only go if she was going to have a burger, so that really sealed the deal, a girl as beautiful as she is who studies philosophy and who *also* eats burgers. So as I'd sent that broken-heart emoji, I knew that if she came back to me, if she could understand what happened with Osgood earlier and decided she still wanted this as much as I did, I needed to be ready: I needed to find her a secret way inside.

I want to let her in.

I need to let her in.

For an hour, I ran around my own house like a burglar. I flung open doors and moved furniture. I rattled all the built-in bookshelves in the library to see if one of them opened as a secret door. I found exactly nothing.

So then I went outside and went up the stairwell running parallel to my house. It's a crazy medieval winding thing, brick and stucco. Durham is full of them, like a rabbit warren. But there on the second floor, there's a little door. Half-sized and strange. I tried to get the lay of the architecture. If this is the second floor and the wall is facing the quad...Shit! Shit. It went into my house, somewhere, someplace. So then I ran back down the stairs like a madman and attempted to look casual walking down the side of the quad by my garden, my barbeque, and my lawn furniture, which is so weird I cannot even get my head around it. All the things I don't need and don't know how to enjoy, even though I have them.

Back inside my house, up the steps two at a time, I raced down the hall, past the empty guest room and the empty office, and then to the closet with the washer and dryer. Bingo. Behind the water heater, next to the washing machine, the little Lilliputian-sized door.

Fuck yes!

Then I got involved in a complex Tetris-like engagement with the washer and dryer, which are packed in there so tight they have one inch of clearance on either side. I'd tried to shift the washer first, and then the dryer, edging them out just enough to get a look behind. No doorknob on the tiny door, just locks. Keyed deadbolt on this side, same as the other. Not a door that was ever really meant to be opened, unless there was a plumbing disaster.

So I'd gone down to the kitchen. Nobody was there, which was almost unbelievable. This house, it's like living in the White House or something, staff coming and going all the time it seems. But for that moment, I was alone. I dug through the drawer with all the manuals for the appliances and the spare keys. So many damned keys. Why would anybody ever need so many keys? Because this house is a mansion, that's why. I put them all in a coffee cup, bolted back upstairs. With my torso slung over the washer and my feet dangling, I tried every one. Until I found it.

So now here I am, waiting for some magic doorway to open behind my fancy washer-dryer set. The rain has started lashing the windows, and the rumbles of thunder echo around in the sky. The thunder sounds different here than in California. Deeper and longer.

I'm all wound up and ready to spring. Seeing her. Feeling her. Touching her. Being inside that perfect thing that is Naomi. God *damn it*.

I hear footsteps outside the stairwell. I freeze. But then they go past me. A student, heading back to their room.

This is risky, but it doesn't matter to me right now. If she's willing to risk it, I'm willing to do the same.

I have never wanted anything more than this. Ever. I try to move the dryer a little more.

More footsteps, these thumping and heavy. A guy's footfalls. Not her.

Suddenly, the door opens. I see her waist, and a navy polka-dot skirt. Even her knees are lovely. She bends down and pokes her head in. Smiling.

In a crouch, she shuffles in, and then she stands in the tiny triangular space I've made behind the dryer. I take her bag from her and then grab her body, hoisting her right up over the energy-efficient Maytags.

She's in my arms. Fuck. She's here. I'm frozen.

"Door!" she whispers.

Door. Door, God damn it. I lunge over the dryer and then carefully draw it closed without a bang. I lock it. Now, we're face to face.

What I should feel, as the man in charge of her well-being and education and all the rest, is an immediate desire to stop this insanity. I should snap out of it. I should tell her to leave. I should tell her this is dangerous. I should say that once we get in deep, I've got a feeling there will be no undoing us. Until we're both undone.

Maybe a better man would have.

But I don't.

My hands meet her ass immediately, and I lift her up on the dryer, her legs spread around me. I'm rock hard and pressing against my pants. Our lips still haven't touched. I smell that lemon sweetness all over her. I smell gin and weed. Her legs are smooth and silky under my hands, the muscles of her thighs giving way to the pressure of my fingers and thumbs.

"Are we really doing this?" she whispers.

"Is this what you want?"

No hesitation and she nods. "Yes. I want to feel you inside me again. I want what we did again."

"It's going to be a lot more than that," I tell her, my voice coming out gruff now. That darker part of me is emerging. All her fault.

"This has to be our secret," I tell her, shifting her hair behind her ear. It's so damned beautiful. Wild and untamed, almost. She's wearing little pearl earrings that glisten against her skin.

"I won't tell anybody. Never," she says. She's got her arms over my shoulders, and I feel her fingers pressing into my neck.

Contrary to every last impulse inside me, I'm still trying to be reasonable. Wise. Sensible. Her fingers on my skin, though, it's making it damn near impossible. "We need to be careful."

"I know," she says, her tongue sliding over my earlobe, "But don't be careful with me."

Ka*pow*.

With that, I carry her right out of the washing machine closet. She wraps her legs around my waist and hangs on to my neck. One of her flip-flops slides off as I carry her down the hallway. "What'd you do to your hand," she asks.

"You don't wanna know."

"Yes, I do."

"Punched the wall. Cinderblocks."

"Because of me?"

Carefully I maneuver us through the bedroom door, painstakingly aware of her body and the hard surfaces everywhere that could hurt it, scrape it, bruise it. The only bruising she's going to get will be because of me, if that's what she wants. "Because of you."

She clings to my neck. "Sorry."

I lay her down on the bed and fold at the waist with her. Our foreheads are pressed together, our noses side by side. "You should be," I say, smiling and running my tongue over her ear's curved edge. My hands are all over her now, taking her in, enjoying the fabric on her skin. She kisses me, and then nips my bottom lip as she pulls away. That little flash of pain, it makes a fuse blow in my head. The pistol at the starting gates.

I flip her over on the bed and lift up her skirt. She's wearing these perfect pink panties that hug the curve of her ass just right.

Seeing her like that, thinking of her in lace for anybody but me… "Listen," I say, crawling up her body. She turns to face me. "The other night, things got pretty rough."

"I know," she says. Her makeup is a little smudged, and she looks twenty times more sinful than I remember. "How's your thigh?"

"Do you want it rough again?"

Those eyes, they widen. "Oh yeah. You know I fucking do."

A growl shoots out of my mouth. She's this elegant creature, but when she talks dirty, when she gets filthy, I've got this impulse to clean that filthy mouth. "I don't want you wearing panties like this for anybody but me."

Her tongue slides out from her mouth, and she holds it between her teeth, smiling. "You want me to be yours like that. All yours."

"All fucking mine," I say. "That's the deal. Mine. Nobody else's. I can't stand it."

Those eyes move up my body and finally land on my face. "Don't be jealous, Master," she says, "There's no need for that."

"Good girl," I say as I begin peeling her panties off of her, inching them down that perfect body. I can see she's been wet for a while, her panties soaked right through. I bite the perfect curve of her ass.

I want to devour her. I want to ruin her.

I want to fucking vandalize her.

For just one second, I get that pure, distilled scent of her. The desire of her body, sieved through the lace. Holy fuck. I want to keep these panties forever. I take them off of her completely and hold them on my finger in the air. "You don't get these back."

She rolls over and shifts her hair to one side of her head so it lies in a long, curly trail down one shoulder. "They're yours…"

"Say it again."

"They're yours, Master."

"Fuck." It was hot before we knew what I was. That word was loaded long before Yale. But now. Now it's way better.

The smell of her is still heavy in the air. I need to taste her again. With my thumbs I part those tight, prettily groomed lips. She is, quite literally, good enough to eat. Her taste is unlike any woman's I've ever known. Her wetness thicker, her moans better. She's all the superlatives.

Every stroke of my tongue on her clit brings her closer and closer, every adjustment of my speed makes her writhe. I like seeing her suffer. Just a little. I love having that power over her, because she sure as shit already has it over me.

I reach between her tight lips, feeling her muscles fight me and then pull me in further. As I hook my fingers inside her, her back arches and she lets out a sigh, her head rolling back into the pillows and her body rearing off the sheets. I touch her swollen clit, and then add my tongue, just pressing down on its edge. I'm trying to bring her back to me, but she stays gone and moans, "Please, please get inside me. Please, Master Beck. Please."

I pull her off the bed by her ankles and make her stand. With her body in my hands, I walk her back against the closet and force her against the door with a thud. I pull her shirt off, and she starts pulling mine off me. As she does, I'm undoing my fly, releasing my cock. I keep her bra on and take her breasts in my hands, slipping them between lace and nipple. They get hard under my touch.

One hand between her breasts and one on her hip, I swing her back around and throw on the bed, making her squeal with delight.

"Get on your knees," I say into her ear. "All fours, edge of the bed."

She not only does it, but tucks her feet beneath her when she does. How can anybody be this fucking perfect? How can anybody know what I need before I do?

I am so ragingly hard I'm not even thinking as I separate those lips again, this time with my cock. A wave of contractions shoots up my abs and into my chest. Then I realize. Holy fuck.

"Naomi. Condom."

She swings her head to face me, and one bra strap falls down. "We're good. I'm good."

This is absolutely insane, yet also so unbelievably right. "Me too… but fuck."

For a moment, we just stay there, staring. Me with my cock in my hand, her with her chin on her shoulder. Every health class, every ad stuck to a side of a bus, every warning in the doctor's office has said this is the worst thing to do. It's all I can do not to press myself all the way in, but this is a precipice somehow. A reckless moment of no return.

"Promise."

It's insanity, but I trust her. And she trusts me. Barebacked, I press inside her. Instantly, instinctively, my neck rolls backwards. Jesus Christ, I'm 38 years old. I should be stronger than this, but I can feel that pre-orgasmic rush tearing through me already. "Why do you feel. *So. Fucking. Good?*"

Her whimpering moan tells me she's got no answer either.

I undo her bra, and it watch it slip down to her hands. Hands on her hips, I overtake her, as I pump myself into her. Over and over again. She gets me so close so fast. It's almost fucking unfair.

"Keep squeezing me like that," I tell her, "And you're going to make me…"

"I can't help it," she says, and I see her toes curl under her body.

I move my hands to her breasts and get as far into her as I possibly can, until all of me is gone inside her. The tip of my cock compresses against her cervix, and her head lashes back towards me.

"Where do you want it?"

"Inside me. Please…"

Holy shit above. That's what I needed her to say. It's just about to happen. I'm about to come inside her, flooding her with me.

"You're sure?"

She nods, and her hair slides up and down her back.

The orgasm is coming.

But that's when there's a knock at the door.

We both freeze. I'm so close to releasing in her, I'm almost deafened and blinded by need and desire. I don't pull out. I'm convinced we can wait it out. We have to wait it out. I've only just gotten my hands on her, and I'm not about to let go now.

Another knock. And then the goddamned doorbell, with its irritating midi Mozart ringtone.

It'll go on and on forever. God damn it. She groans in disappointment as I pull out of her. "Did you come?" she asks.

"Not yet, and stay there," I say, fumbling for my clothes. Pants. Shirt. I try to wipe her taste off my lips, like that'll give me away. "Don't you move, beautiful. Not an inch."

Barefoot, I run downstairs, trying to get myself together. Pants, shirt, hair. We're good. I pause in front of the door, sniff, and turn the handle.

Guess who. Standing there like a bloodhound.

Dean Motherfucking Osgood.

16
ben

"I heard a squeal," Osgood says.

"Jesus Christ," I say. I wonder if that's the face he has when he's chasing his moth around the Burmese jungles with a butterfly net in hand. "Dean. Seriously. This is ridiculous."

"From your house, a squeal."

I cannot even believe this guy. "No you didn't." I put my hands in my pockets. "I was just setting up my direct deposit."

But he charges past me heading for the stairs.

"What the fuck are you doing?" I race past him, getting in his way, raising my voice so she'll hear me. "You can't just walk into my house."

"Beck. It isn't your house. It's the college's house!"

I put my hands on his shoulders. "Seriously, Dean. What is wrong with you?" I'm keeping my voice raised. It's not inappropriate, though. I'd be a whole lot angrier if I wasn't trying to keep her safe. "If you want me out of here so bad, go to the Provost. Otherwise, get out of my house."

I'm this close to punching him. I don't care if I break another knuckle.

He relents. He glares at me. I step back.

Then the bastard tears past me into my bedroom.

Holy shit. Impending disaster. Tsunami incoming... Naomi in bed, undressed. It's all about to explode. But when we get to the bedroom, she's gone. Not a trace. Not her underwear, not her bag, not her bra, not even the flip-flop that fell off as I brought her in here. Just an unmade bed, same as any bachelor would have. Except that's when I realize two things:

I've still got the key to that stupid door in my pocket...which means...

Naomi is still in here somewhere.

The doors to the washer and dryer are closed. She'd got to be in there. I lean up against the laundry closet with my arms crossed.

"Doesn't seem to be anything untoward going on in here..."

"What did I tell you?"

Osgood huffs.

Now he's off the trail he's more reasonable. I cannot for the life of me understand this maddening pursuit of my private life. "Am I not allowed to have women in here?"

"Women!" he booms. "You're the moral center of this whole operation, Beck. This is *exactly* what I was afraid of. Women!" And then he squats down and looks under the bed.

"Do you see any? Do I seem like the kind of guy who'd turn into some kind of sex maniac overnight?" The irony of this is totally out of hand since that's just exactly what Naomi has done to me. Turned me into a sex-hungry testosterone-laden beast. But I manage to keep a straight face.

"You dodged a bullet this time," Osgood says, slowing coming up from the floor. I hear some creaking joints. "But I'll tell you something. If one of your conquests is that Costa girl like I suspect? You know how she affords tuition?" He points at his chest. "Durham Dean's scholarship. My chaired position. So..."

He doesn't need to say the rest of it. I get it. He wasn't kidding when he said he could ruin both of us. My gut churns at the thought. That's the real deal. That's tangible.

"Nothing. Is. Happening," I say. "Now, I've got to get back to work. Don't you have a butterfly to pin or something?"

He stomps off down the hallway, but I stay with him, pressing my hand to his meaty, slightly pudgy back. I'm not a violent guy—situation with the wall excepted, and sexual kinks aside—but I am seriously tempted to shove him down the stairs. But I don't. I just imagine it in my head.

"Thanks a bunch for stopping by," I tell him as I guide him out the door.

"Don't forget. I'm watch—"

I slam the door in his face, lock the deadbolt, and hustle up the stairs. I fling open the closet. She's there, in a ball on the dryer. Petrified. Instinctively I hold her close. Into my shirt, her voice comes out muffled and extra quiet, "Ben. I shouldn't have come here. This was a mistake."

Her hair smells so good, her body feels so good, she's such a drug. "I know. It's risky. But when I see you, when I think about you, and all my reason just vanishes."

She swallows hard. She doesn't reach out to hold me, but stays in that tight ball, before finally unraveling and sliding off the dryer. "I should go," she says, putting her clothes back on in some semblance of order. She's having a tough time with her flip-flop, her toes keep getting tangled in the straps. I get down on one knee and fix it for her.

Gazing up at her, terrified and so young, I'd do anything she wanted. I'm not going to keep her here. No matter what I want, it's less important than what she needs. A parallel universe streams through my head, where we met somewhere else and things were different. Where we collided like planets and were allowed to stay in each other's orbit. But that isn't this universe. That isn't this world. The cosmos is nasty. I've always said so. A vengeful, soulless bastard of a place.

Still on my knee, I lean my forehead on her shin. My stubble rustles against her smooth skin. I hang on to that leg with both arms, clutching at her for a long moment. I close my eyes. I breathe her in.

And then fish the key from my pocket. Because I know I have to let her go.

17
Naomi

Days slide into weeks, and I immerse myself in the grind, digging down right into my core to stay away from him. It was a stupid, immature, ridiculous idea in the first place. Who falls in love after a one-night stand? Nobody, Naomi, nobody.

But it becomes increasingly clear, day by day, that it wasn't just a one-night stand. Nope. Not a fling, not fading. Just getting so, so much worse. Every Thursday, the Lux et Veritas initiates go out and party. Sometimes Lucy convinces me to go, but most Thursdays I find myself just staring down at his house hoping to see him. One glimpse of him passing the French doors or standing in his kitchen.

The fellows' dinners are agony. Whether on purpose or by chance, we end up bumping into each other about six hundred times each night. Like we're magnets, but our poles are all out of order. In the kitchen, in the foyer. At the table where I lay out the nametags.

"I miss you," he whispers one night when the main speaker is a lady with an expertise in rare beetles. Osgood, he organized that one. Obviously.

My whole body stiffens. He's standing next to me, facing the other way.

"Are you okay?" he asks in a hush. "I want to look after you. Even if I can't have you."

I think that if I begin to talk to him, I'll never stop. I'll tell him that I want him and I miss him and how stupid it is because I have only been with him twice, just twice, and it was nothing, really nothing, and that we barely know each other, right?

Except that isn't true. Because of his class. I have come to know him, deeply know him, through what he says and how he says it.

That happens twice a week, three beautiful hours of my life every week, I sit there and listen to the man I am hopelessly, helplessly, stupidly in love with. Every hour is more wonderful and gut-wrenching than the last. But I never miss a lecture. Not once. Because he talks of mystics, and love, and sadness. He talks about things that make sense to me for the first time ever. And I'm completely and utterly hypnotized. When he shows us films or clips from YouTube, he dims the lights and comes to stand near me. Just standing nearby, crossing his arms. Letting me feel him standing near me.

He talks about infinity and the end of the world. He talks about the days when people believed if they saw the saints in a painting, they were real. Like spirits in their house.

Then he pulls out *The Four Loves*.

He talks about mystical worship and hope, and how Lewis exactly expresses the nothingness of losing love, once found.

And he looks right at me when he says that, holding my stare as he dismisses class. But I'm the one to lower my eyes first, and I don't look back.

A month into the semester, on the first really cold day of fall, Lucy sneaks a bottle of wine into our room.

"We can't have this here."

"Shhhh," she says, and works the cork out halfway with an opener and the rest with her teeth.

We crawl in her bed together. Her windows shut tighter than mine so it's nice and warm. She's got this downy mattress cover that makes it feel like we're in an ad for toilet paper, falling into the clouds. I bring my own pillow and wear my favorite hoodie. This old gray thing with a rainbow on the front.

We look for something to watch. My penchant for period dramas gets resoundingly rejected. I try to talk her into *Wuthering Heights*, saying it's actually about a neighborhood in Orange County. "Like *Real Housewives*."

"I'm not *that* stupid," she says, and flicks along on her iPad as HBO GO predicts what we might like.

Upon the screen pops *True Detective*.

"God. That Matthew, he's so fucking dreamy. Have you seen him in those bizarre Lincoln ads?" Lucy says.

My stomach turns. There's no question that Ben's book is the inspiration for those ads. I can't even stand this. The world is out to get me. "Oh look," I say, flipping along, "A documentary on poisoners. That sounds fun."

She shakes her head. "*True Detective*."

I sigh. I don't have the will to resist. And I stick my hand in the bag of almonds—these are sort of a smoky paprika, where does she find these things?—and resign myself to my fate with a Solo cup of chardonnay in hand.

It hurts. The whole thing hurts. But again, I'm mesmerized. It's him, but not him. It's a dream. We binge-watch the whole thing over one weekend, and for the next two days, every single time I close my eyes I see that introductory montage, but see Ben's face instead of Matthew's.

Upstanding righteous proper conduct. It's wearing me out.

I want to get my hands on him. I need to get my hands on him.

The other place we bump into each other, every day, is in the dining hall. I'd go to another college to eat, but my allegiance to Durham keeps me coming back here. And the knowledge that I will invariably see him. I even know when he eats breakfast, lunch, and dinner. Sometimes I purposely stay away. But not usually.

Usually it happens over the dessert trays. They always have lemon bars. I love lemon bars.

"These remind me of you," he says one day, picking one out of the case.

"I don't even have the verb for what I feel for you," I say as our fingers brush on the tongs.

"It's fucking killing me, Naomi," he says, pretending to look busy deciding now about fudge or possibly a cookie.

"What do we do?" I say. Now I'm considering fudge too.

"That's completely up to you," he says.

I look up at him.

"I'm right here," he says. "Just say the word."

And I stick my lemon bar in my mouth, the whole thing, so I don't have to answer.

18

Naomi

It's October 10. I wake up to a shocking thunderstorm battering the windows with rain, a real old-fashioned Atlantic squall. I just lie there, listening to the wind whistle eerily in the Harkness Tower way above me. My phone shows me the fingers of a hurricane over Connecticut, and the water is lit up red with small craft warnings. I pinch my fingers on the map and see it's not going to hit Maine, thank God.

Exactly a month since I snuck into Master Beck's house. Exactly a month since I lost my nerve and left.

Lying on my bed, I watch the water outside. I even actually feel the water inside because a little spews in from where the window doesn't quite meet the frame. I've lived in this room for two years. I don't even know why because it's nothing but trouble. I think if weren't for me, they'd stick an extra water heater in here or something. Yet it's all mine and quiet and weirdly old-fashioned and romantic, which is why I love it so much. Three times, facilities have tried to fix the windows, and three times they've been air- and water-tight for about a week. But then the building shifts, like a stretching old woman, and they crack open again.

I take a roll of packing tape from my bottom drawer and cut off a length, sticking it to the frame and pressing it down hard and tight with my fingers.

Out my window, through the driving rain, I see Professor Beck inside his house, passing the French windows that he once pressed his face up against, looking at me. My stomach somersaults when I see his silhouette. Professor Beck. I'm calling him Professor Beck now exclusively. That incident with the lemon bars is proving about as sticky as the lemon bars themselves.

Just say the word.

My history with guys isn't insanely long, but nothing to whine over either. The usual smattering of ups and downs at college, most of them giggle-worthy after all the tears fell. A boy freshman year told me he loved me the first day I met him and then cried for an hour for no discernable reason. A boy I slept with later freshman year, he was a smotherer, and he smelled so much like Gain laundry detergent I began suspecting he kept dryer sheets in his pockets. I dated a football player sophomore year who told me not to pretend to be too smart in front of his friends. Then there was Isaac, who loved me senseless and scared the shit out of me too.

Before that, of course, there was Joe Riley. My fiancé. The fact that I was engaged to him, not even Lucy knows. I only call him my high school ex if I ever have to mention him. Which, I make sure, is hardly ever. Somehow it's embarrassing to me that I was once that girl. But I wouldn't mind telling Ben, I realize. I'd like to tell him. Somehow I think he'd understand. I don't even know why. Maybe because he understands the dream of something bigger. I can see it in his eyes.

But *the dream,* it's awfully glamorous from the outside looking in. With the dream came responsibilities and worries, things I just have no idea how to deal with sometimes. Call me foolish. Call me not quite 21. But it does get to be a little heavy, the grind through a world that never feels like I belong. I know I'm not the only one that feels this way. I see it in everybody aching for something bigger.

I wake up my computer and see in the corner what I'd forgotten: October 10th. Yesterday was fishing quota day. I grab my phone to call Dad to see how it went.

The seagulls squawk at me before he even says hello. "I got my IFQ. It's a big one."

"That's great news," I say.

Clang, clang, clang goes a rope on one of the sheerlines. I'll bet the water is high today, up there north of the storm. I can hear it on my dad's end, the spray a little louder than normal. I imagine the lobsters with their banded claws flopping around in their crates while the waves batter the hull. Unconsciously, my hand travels to my scar. I haven't been on the boats since the day I went over the side.

Yet for just one second, I get a profound, aching pang of homesickness. That smell, the sounds, that place.

"I think we're coming up on a glut," he says. "So Thanksgiving. Promise me, Naomi. You'll give me a hand. I can't run this ship solo in the ice."

Dread overcomes me, and it feels like I've eaten a dozen bad oysters. That clammy, panicky, half-faint feeling. "Dad…"

"There's nobody else. You know that. Times are goddamned tough. So promise?"

"I'll try," I say. I actually mean it. I do want to help, but I'm also scared shitless.

A seagull squawks, and he ends the call without saying goodbye.

My schedule pops up on the screen. Google Calendar tells me what I know but had willfully forgotten.

Paper due for Professor Beck. Today. 7:59pm.

I flip over to V2 to see the prompt.

Tell the story of a mystic. Try to channel the medieval scribes. Have fun with it.

I listen to the hurricane on the windows.

I think about going down under the water and just wanting to wring every last ounce that I could get out of life. Wishing, just wishing that I had seen what was right in front of me.

The thing is, I still feel that way. Wring it right out. Life is so short. A month without him, that's been more than I can stand.

Just say the word.

I work all day. I skip my classes, making excuses about "the strep that's going around." I run on tea and apples alone.

19

ben

Two things nobody prepared me for before I took this job.

First. Falling for a girl with hair the color of black lacquer and the sweetest eyes in the world, who sits in my lecture staring at me, never even blinking, and jotting everything down without looking at the words on her page. And who lives four floors away.

Second. The weather, the rain that'll come right up from the ground and soak you through so you give serious consideration to investing in a wetsuit to walk even one block at all.

I'm sitting in my house, in front of an actual fireplace. One of the staff guys had to show me how to light it and seemed to take a kind of delighted pride in showing the Master of College how to light a fire.

"Your dad never taught you?"

"California, man. We never needed one."

And he laughs, like Connecticut weather is a curse, but like we're all in it together, and that makes it not so bad.

But now warm and safe in my house, I don't mind it. That noise, that rain. It reminds me of throwing water balloons off the roof of our trailer, trying to hit my brother on the asphalt down below.

I haven't stopped thinking of her, not for one second, not in the

29 days since she was in my bed. It's verging on obsession, one of those obsessions that settles in so deep it feels like it might be chronic.

Naomi Costa. My chronic illness.

I open up my laptop, anxious to see the term papers. It's not quite 7:30 pm and they're still rolling in, fast and furious before the deadline.

This class is so big that the TAs have the grading covered, but I can see everything. There's only one I care about, of course. Only one paper that really want to read.

Hers still isn't there. I get up and pour myself a whiskey and a grab stack of Oreos from the pack. Then I sit back down. The roster says:

Carlisle: Submitted
Cohen: Submitted
Connelly-Armstrong: Submitted
Costa: NOT SUBMITTED

But then that vanishes, the red letters peel back from the screen.
Costa: Uploading…

I shove four Oreos in my mouth at once. Holy hell. This blows every single sporting event right out of the goddamned water. Screw Hail Mary touchdown passes. *This* is where it's at.

Costa: SUBMITTED.

Fuck! I clutch my whiskey and hit *Read submission.*

In 1959, Francesca Newham was born on a beach in Maine. Her mother was a fisherwoman, and her mother's mother before her, and for all the generations going back to the beginning of time, the fisherwomen felt the labor pains and moored their boats, and then squatted down in the water like women do even now in birthing pools. It was the way things had always been done. So that's how she was born, right there into the water on the stony shore. When Francesca was born, the first thing all the fishermen on the wharf said was that she looked like an angel because she had the right cheeks and she never cried. She grew up on her boats, and was proud to say she'd never lived on a house that didn't rock all the time. At age five, she got her first job on her mother's boat, putting rubber bands on claws. They say she talked to the lobsters, and when she did, they settled down. She wore a tiny rain jacket and loved to hang her head over into the spray. At 18, she became the first female greenhorn to work the Arctic routes. At 20, she had saved up enough to buy her own boat and hire her own crew. She was that kind of woman. It was the 1970s, and when she wasn't fishing she read books by Betty Friedan and marked up the pages with arrows and hearts.

Decades passed, and every year is chronicled in a slim little journal, marked with the year on the side in white ship's paint, applied with a toothpick. Every day, Francesca kept a journal like all the good captains in the world have, going back to when they wrote it on whale bones. Like any good captain's journal, hers detail the weather and the magic of the sea and also her feelings about life and the world.

> *June 4, weather fair, wind from the southeast.*
> *June 5, perhaps I want a child and no husband.*
> *June 10, wind at 10 knots from the sou'sou'east. Maybe I*
> *want a husband and no child.*

In other entries, in bits and pieces, she wrote about dreams about far-off places, fishing for flounder in the sun, which she took as a sign because in these dreams she wasn't alone. She had a second mate who looked just like her and who was even more fearless, who'd stand on the bow laughing. She dreamed that dream over and over, and eventually she threw her birth control pills overboard, because she could just feel that it meant there was a baby somewhere out there in the air. After all, she was almost forty, she wrote. If she was going to take that journey, it was time to get started.

It was an October hurricane. She was far out at sea. The hurricane came up from the Cuba, angry and fast. The radio said caution, all small crafts, caution, warning, caution. She wrote that she listened to the radio and smiled, and then harangued the dispatcher, saying she was sure he was warm and dry, but being out there in the disaster, that was really living, she said, "Do something that scares you every day, boys," and captains all over the radio said, "Francie Newham, you've got bigger balls than the lot of us."

The hurricane became gigantic, slowed down and got meaner. For days she spun like a toy in a drain. Then, one night, her ship bumped up against something. She felt the bump and woke up and looked outside, only to see another boat right alongside her. On the boat was a man. She wrote that when he looked at her, she felt lust in her veins and she couldn't resist. His name was Captain Charles Costa, and he drew her to him like he was a living storm. Even as he helped her across from her boat to his, she knew that the baby in the air was closer than ever. For three days, the hurricane spun and ripped beaches right off the land, and ruined buildings and flooded worlds, while the two of them spun and spun, playing cards and drinking rum and telling lies to one another and knowing it.

For the next nine months, she wrote that she became a soothsayer of the sea. It was inexplicable but true. Old fishermen still remember it. They say from the day she got pregnant she could reach her hand out over the water and count the lobsters on the ground. For the next nine months she and her baby made fortunes and brought in pots so full that lobster claws poked out, stuffed solid with lobster and seaweed, and she credited the baby. She said she'd dreamt it, and her second mate was the one with all the magic. Together, she dreamed, they would sail all over the world.

Like her grandmother before her and her mother after that, Francie was out to sea when she felt the labor pains of her second mate coming into the world. She wrote in an unsteady hand that these pains didn't seem like normal birthing pains because they went on and on with no baby coming. She said she saw her second mate's fist pressing into her belly, the full shape of a hand, and she laid her hand down over it, palm to palm, like prisoners across the wall of a cell.

She began bleeding, she wrote, and marked a course for shore. She anchored her boat in the cove and walked to the beach, barefoot and wearing nothing but a shirt she'd stolen from Captain Costa nine months before. They say she came to the shore pale white and not speaking. When they saw her, the fishermen came running to help her, and some of them toasted her, but she said, "Don't toast yet. Not yet." The fishermen tried to help her, but she wouldn't let them, and she knelt down into the water as her second mate came to life, floating for a while in salt water until one of the fishermen pulled her out of the water and said, she's a fighter this one, she'll never get tangled in a net. And as the fisherman held up the baby into the sky, like an offering, Francie Newham slumped into the sand and the waves. She looked up at the sky while the water lapped at her ears. They say when she closed her eyes for the last time she was smiling. And with her last breath, she said to name her girl Naomi. "Beautiful in every tongue."

I finish reading. The Oreos have dissolved in my mouth. I swallow. I go back over it again and again, even whispering the words aloud like someone just learning to read. It's one thing to love someone in person. It's one thing to love their flesh. It's one thing to admire their eyes from across a lectern and pray to a god you don't believe in that you'll see her at the dining hall. But to want to know and love a mind, too? To have some whisper of that hidden land?

Now more than ever, reading her words, feeling that most intimate part of her here, I know one thing is true. I need to be with her. I have to get to her. I need to get to know her, really and truly know her. Love her, lust after her, understand her, embrace her.

Fuck the rules.

Hear that sound? That's the academic code of ethics going up in flames.

She's in my heart, and I'm withering away without her. A man cannot exist on Oreos and whiskey alone.

Naomi. She's the only salve.

I open up my email. I make like the upright professor rather than a guy with shaking hands and his head in the fog. This is the first time I've written an email to her, and staring at her name in the address field, even that rattles me and makes my biceps tighten up with anticipation. Still. Keep your shit together, Beck. Don't start gushing here on the Yale email server, you ass.

Dear Naomi:
Please come talk to me about your paper. I am available this evening at my house.
Prof. Beck

20
ben

I wish I could say I stare into the fire and sip my whiskey and ease into my wingback chair like a legendary nihilist. I wish I could say I contemplate my awesomeness and the certain knowledge of what will happen next like some kind of entitled ass that knows the girl is going to come to him because that's how assholes think. But I don't. I reread the message I sent to her about sixty times, then I run upstairs to my bedroom. I wash my face. I wet my hair and put in some gel. I change out of my sweatpants into chinos and a sweater—the first real thick, woolen sweater I've ever owned.

I jog downstairs. To wait. Because maybe, just maybe, she'll come to me.

Because of the weather and the time, the house is empty. Nobody milling through, nobody anywhere. Thanks, universe. Thanks for that.

Through the kitchen window, I see a flash of red. An umbrella popping open.

I clutch the countertop. It's her. Holy fuck alive, it's her. She's in yellow galoshes and black leggings. She's wearing a gray hoodie. I loved her in that satin dress, I loved her in that summer dress, I've loved her in every damn thing she's worn, all of it cataloged in my head, but this, *this* is what I'd been craving. Her, just her, worn out and soft.

In a hoodie with fucking thumbholes.

I slap the counter like a gambler folding his cards. I'm done. D-O-N-E, done.

I clap my hands to my head. Play it cool, Beck. Never know who's watching.

As she approaches, I open the door. "Hi, Miss Costa."

She looks petrified. "Did I screw up the assignment? Was it late?"

Oh, Jesus Christ, of course that's what she'd think. What an idiot. Why didn't I put a smiley face or something on that email? Idiot. "No, no," I say, "Not at all."

Holding the door open for her with one arm, I step aside to let her in. I take her umbrella from her and have gallant plans to close it, but it gets wedged in the doorway and I can't get it unstuck.

I hear her giggle a little, and she slips back under my arm and presses some series of buttons to make the thing close.

"Nice sweater," she says, shaking off her umbrella and hanging it on the hook next to the door. The fact is, she's more at home here than I am. I'm still a stranger in this place. Aside from everything else, I could also just use someone at my side to help me find my way. Umbrellas and fellows and sheeting rain. She knows what she's doing, and I most definitely do not.

"Thank you," I say. I touch my chest with my palm and run my hand down my stomach.

She gives an approving nod. "It really looks good on you. Some professors wear sweaters like that and they just…look kinda…" She shrugs.

"Assholeish?"

Her face lights up. *Yeah!*

"I felt like the leather elbow patches were a gamble, but I decided to go all in."

We're making pleasant conversation, but all the while she's getting closer to me and I'm getting closer to her. All awareness of personal space is going out the window; all sense of the outside world is zooming out of my head at warp goddamned-speed.

"What did you want to talk about?" she asks. She's standing there on the front rug, her boots still dripping. It's all coming together now that I've read that essay. Those are fishing boots. Those aren't for show. She's not for show. She's the real deal. Authentic Naomi Costa, through and through.

"Come in," I say. "Have an Oreo."

She looks puzzled. "An…?"

I swallow. "You've reduced me to eating Oreos alone. Whiskey and Oreos. I can't stomach anything else."

Her breath catches in her lungs as she inhales and closes her eyes. I'm just inches from her face. Not touching her though.

"Your essay was fucking amazing."

"Is that the grade?" she says, her eyes not coming up to meet mine but instead moving down to her boots. "Fucking amazing?"

I nod and give her a rasped *mmm-hmmm*. "It's above an A+. Very rare."

"Is that all you wanted to say?" she says. Now she looks up at me. There's a prickle in my hands. There's a light in her eyes and a flush in her cheeks.

What I should do is step away. But I just can't. She's so gentle, so tender, so lovely. No artifice, no bullshit, just this beautiful woman with a mind that wanders and whips every direction. "Is it true, what you wrote…"

Her nostrils flare a little, and she's got her eyes closed again. I place my hand to her cheek. It's cool under my fingers.

"That was my mom. Nobody knows that story."

Her eyes are damp, glittery with tears. "I don't know why I wanted to spill it all to you, but it was like I had to, almost. Like I had to let you know." She smiles. "I don't think I answered the prompt."

"Fuck the prompt." I place my forehead to hers, and my thumb on her cheekbone. It's like it makes her forget her thoughts, because the next thing she says is:

"When I think of you," she says, "I feel like I'm drowning."

"This whole month has been agony. I thought it would get easier, but it's not."

Her head presses against mine, it almost feels like surrender, the way she breathes and slumps towards me.

"Remember what you said over the lemon bars?" she asks

"Yes," I say. My voice sounds as deep as if I just woke up. Every single thing inside me, it's aching for her to say *Yes. Yes. Just yes.* Against all reason, against all rules. To fucking rebel with me, to stage a secret revolution, just the two of us against the world.

She raises her face to mine. She's wearing no makeup. She's never,

ever been more beautiful

"I want you to devour me, Ben." Then she does it. She kisses me, softly at first, but then getting more and more passionate, gripping at my sweater with her hand, pressing her body against mine.

Fuck, holy fuck. She's saying yes. She's saying yes.

I pull her close to my hips, I'm hard for her, I'm always hard for her, and kiss her back. Violently, wildly, aggressively, just unleashing one fraction of what I feel inside.

Finally, I force myself to pull away. I can taste her lip gloss on my mouth, and for a second I'm lost. I hang on to her ass and don't let go. "Not here," I say.

"Then where?"

I've had the place picked out for weeks. Every last step of this fantasy has played out in my head a hundred times.

"Come to the side window of the Guest Suite," I say, "Fifteen minutes."

21
Naomi

I march out of his house like a furious student, like my paper just got horribly critiqued, not wanting anybody to suspect a thing. I slog across the quad to my stairway. Once inside, I take the stairs three at a time with my boots squeaking every time I pivot on the curve. At my floor, I bolt down the hallway shaking so hard now I can barely get my key into the door. Lucy pops her head out and said, "Want to go get some frozen yogurt?"

Gulp. "I'm fine," I say. "I think the mystery fish last night at dinner was off." I make a sort of nauseated about-to-gag face.

She shifts her nose and cocks her head to one side. Without taking her eyes off me, she reties the bow on her pajama pants. Tonight her hair is down and almost mermaid-like, the curls from the braid now a long string of *s* shapes.

"I've got a study session," I tell her.

"Since when?"

"Since now. It'll probably go late."

God, I hope it goes late. I hope it goes forever and ever. Once in my room I lock the door behind me and stand for a moment with my hands pressed to the wood. There's no time for a fancy outfit, but I put some makeup on. Not a lot. Just so I feel put together. I dust blush on my already flushed cheeks and take a deep breath to steady myself. I feather my eyelashes with mascara, roll on a little lemon sugar, and then take off down the steps again, so anxious to get close to the suite it aches. I know it's raining, but I don't care. I'll stand in the middle of a hurricane for him. Without a second thought.

At the door to my stairway, I peek out. It's a lot like peeking out of a medieval prison cell, I imagine. That sort of teeny rippled glass window that I can see out of only on my tiptoes. Outside, I see nobody braving the storm. Dean Osgood's quarters are at a right angle to me. Peeking up and over, I see his curtains are closed, thank goodness. Still, it's risky, and I dart quickly from my stairway into the Zen garden, splashing and sloshing and gripping my umbrella with both hands as the leaves from the quad stick to my boots in clumps.

Inside the garden, the leaves from the Japanese elm are half-fallen. They're no bigger than minnows, and there are thousands of them on the damp ground. In the lamps from the quad, they're almost purple-black and as slippery as ice. My heart is pounding in my chest. But I'm neither going to cry or faint, and that's some serious progress on the toughen-up-buttercup front.

This is happening. *This is happening.*

Fifteen minutes is a lifetime. I count upwards from one to a hundred. Then back down again. I listen to the rain on my umbrella and then focus on how it comes out in gushes from the gutters and into the drains.

I don't dare sit down and get my pants all wet, so instead I stand under my umbrella, and try to settle my breathing, but I'm trembling. I breathe in and out slowly. I once heard that the difference between anxiety and excitement is breathing.

Doubtful. Very.

Finally, there's the noise of tapping on glass behind me. My fists clench around the umbrella, and I slowly turn around. He's there, opening the side window, eyes sparkling with the darkened suite behind him. The walls of the garden protect us from view here. Much safer than the front door. He presses the window open, and offers a hand to help me inside "My lady," he smiles.

Oh my God, yes.

However.

The window is just exactly the wrong height—it comes even with my belly button—so I have to sort of pitch myself through. I high center myself, and I begin to laugh silently, almost uncontrollably. He's trying to pull me through, and my jacket is coming off over my head.

"Oh no," he says. "Wait, wait, your arm…"

We dissolve into snickers.

Clutching the windowsill and squirming around the frame, I whisper, "Grab my leg."

He tries to be helpful. He paws at various parts of my body—my ass, my thighs, and not in a sexual way but, well, in a way of a man trying to help a woman through a window kind of way. I can feel him laughing against my body, and periodically, air shoots from his nose. "Move your foot!" he says.

"Where!" Now my face is smashed up against the radiator. "Aren't you impressed with my grace?"

"Other foot!"

Finally, something gives way, possibly part of the shutter outside, and I tumble inside in a somersault and land with a thump.

There I am, in a slippery wet Gore-Tex heap at his feet.

He helps me up and then shuts the window.

I'm struggling with my rain jacket, which has gotten dreadfully tangled over my head. It's inside out but my hands are still in the cuffs.

"Stop squirming," he says. I think he's trying to touch my head, but instead he palms my face. "Jesus, you're so adorable," he snorts. "Stop moving! Let me help you."

I hold still. I can't see him. All I can see is nothing and all I can feel is wet rain jacket all over. But my snickers die down and I hold my arms out like a scarecrow.

He unzips me somehow and finally I'm free. I smooth my hair. The world now is quiet and still. My jacket falls to the floor.

Being so close to him, all alone, it makes me speechless and breathless. I'm so nervous, the world is wobbling everywhere I look, and I hear white noise in my head. The chaos of the window gone, it's him and me and infinity now.

At my feet, he helps me take off my boots while I steady myself on the windowsill behind me. God, how I love him at my feet. It makes me feel invincible, immortal, worshiped. But I notice, as my second boot comes off, that my socks don't match, not even close. One is argyle, the other is striped. Well done, Naomi. Well done. "Laundry day."

"You're fucking perfect, you know that," he says, taking the striped one off first, and then the argyle.

He begins unzipping my hoodie. Underneath, I'm wearing a pink camisole. Under that? I can't even remember. My hoodie falls to the floor, and as he removes my tank from over my head, careful not to tangle my hair, I realize it's just an ordinary, somewhat sad, gray bralette. A favorite, but hardly sexy.

Using his fingers around my wrists, he pulls my hands away and places them at my sides. "This is how I needed to see you. You could give me all the lace in the world, and what I needed was unmatched socks and this." He runs his finger under the edge of my bra, just touching my nipple.

"You were a fan of those red panties."

"I'm always a fan of red panties." He leans down for a kiss. "But I'm a fan of you like this even more." His lips come to mine. They're smooth, and I taste just a hint of Burt's Bees. A little minty and soft. I can feel his smile against mine at first, but slowly, with my lips and tongue exploring his, he changes from polite, handsome, upright Benjamin Beck into the hungry, demanding, aggressive man that gave me the time of my life in that hotel room.

"Oh God, yes," I purr into his mouth, because I love this side of him, the Master I first met, before we knew what we were to each other. Before the back and forth and the maybe-maybe not. Back when it was simple and easy and two people on fire for one another.

Just as hungry as he is, I tug his sweater up his body and break our kiss with the snap of wooly static.

"We're going to go slow," he says, pushing some hair away from my face. "Yeah?"

"Yes, please." Such sweet agony, nibbling when we're both starving.

But we don't go slow, not at first, because we can't. It's the first glimpse of home in a month, and we have to get there together. My hands are all over him now. My thumb presses into his nipple, his fingers pinch mine, I hear his breath linger in his mouth. With my other hand, I explore that cock a little more. I touch his balls, and he pauses in the kiss, giving me a "*Fuck yeah*" into my mouth. I'm tempted to get down on my knees in front of him, but I want him to lead the way this time.

"I'm yours. All yours."

He has exactly no trouble interpreting what I mean. Gripping my hips, he walks me over to the couch in front of the cold fireplace. It's this big oxblood-red leather thing, button-tufted and studded with brass rivets. He turns me around and folds me over the arm, pressing the back of my head down to the seat with his hand. My cheek touches the leather cushion, cool and luxurious against my skin.

I expect him to pull my pants down fast and get inside me right away, but instead he slowly unpeels my leggings and panties. "Stretch out your arms," he whispers as he undoes my bra. Slowly, he traces every inch of me. Up and down my back, giving me goose bumps, finding that ticklish spot just below my ribs. Every inch, he savors, and I savor back. My muscles quiver as he learns that if he moves around the curve of my hips to my pelvis, my knees involuntarily weaken and drop from under me. The first time it happens, I brace myself, but then he says, "Just let go."

And so there I am, laid out like a cat on that sofa, literally purring and shivering as he explores all the secret places I've never told anybody about. He's careful and respectful of the scar, though, and especially tender on that side.

"It doesn't hurt, "I whisper.

"It hurts me."

The clatter of his belt comes shortly after, the unzipping of his fly. One hand firmly grips my stomach while I hang on to the sofa cushions. From the sounds behind me, though, I can tell he's taking off his socks, and I smile into the sofa. What a prince.

The skin of his cock is smooth and warm against my inner thigh. He dips himself into my wetness, but not all the way inside me.

"Shit, Naomi," he says. "Are you always..."

My cheek shifts against the leather as I nod. "For you."

With my fingertips on the cushion, I walk back into him, until I'm at a right angle to his body, holding on to that leather sofa arm with my hands. I arch my back the other direction. He lets out a low growl as my ass cheeks compress his cock. In response, he places one hand on that part of my hip that makes me literally weak in the knees and begins rubbing my clit with the other.

"I'm going to make you come," he says. "Just like this."

He wets his fingers inside me, but momentarily takes them away to taste me. His finger leaves his mouth with a tiny *pop*.

"Fuck, see. That," he says.

And then he goes after me, after my orgasm and need. His touch is expertly strong, but never overwhelming. He knows exactly how to take me to the point of insanity.

I dig my fingers into the arm of the couch. I get lost in his pelvis pressing against mine, his cock actually throbbing as I begin to come. He folds his body over mine, and his teeth sink into my shoulder.

"Shit, shit, shit," I say. His teeth sink in a little harder. And I'm a million ripples rolling out on still water.

22
ben

As she comes, a thick rush of her wetness spills out onto my fingers. If I was hard before, I don't know what I am now. That night in the hotel, I hadn't known her. And knowing her has only made me want to fuck her until she can see how she's made me feel.

Her orgasm still rolling, she almost drops back down, her knees weak, it seems. "I've got you," I say, pulling her tight to my body. With my cock bent down, pinned between her ass and my thigh, the need for her builds and builds. I walk her towards the bed, making a vice for her nipple between two fingers and keeping my other hand to the handle of her hip. I couldn't take my hands off of her now if I had to.

I spin her around and lay her on the bed. Her hair is a mess behind her, and so fucking beautiful, so devious yet angelic, it damn near knocks the wind out of me.

With my fist around the base, I press my cock into her lips. Her smell is on my mouth, my fingers, everywhere. Lemons and ocean and all the fucking wonders of the earth.

She's pawing for my cock too, my balls, her fingers begging me to get inside her. "If we get interrupted, I'm going to die," she says through heavy breaths.

"We won't." I'm pressing into her, my head just parting her walls.

Her back comes up off the bed, and I place my hand under her spine when it does.

"If someone bangs on the door, don't stop."

"Not this time," I tell her. The head of my cock opens her up further. "Never again."

"Promise," she gasps.

"Fucking promise."

Our eyes never separate, except for the periodic slow blink of bliss. When I pull my cock all the way out of her, she whimpers, *"Don't go."*

"How do you know what to say to me..."

"I need your cum inside me."

Fuck. That. Goddamn it, *that*.

One hand to her side, I shelter her with my body, elbow above her shoulder. Each of us keeps one hand to the other, my thumb to her cheek, her fingers to the back of my neck. Her other hand travels up and down my back, dragging along skin to skin. I feel the first wave of pre-cum, and I groan into the kiss. Her fingers come along the back of my head, spread out, and rake through my hair.

"Don't stop. Please, don't stop," she says. "Ever."

"There, there, there, fuuuuuuuuck," I say into the soft skin of her neck. My head drops to her shoulder. Everything tenses hard. "Fuck, Naomi. Holy fuck." This orgasm, it isn't three good pumps. It's one long ferocious spill. Finally, drained of everything, I collapse on top of her, my face next to hers. She feels so fucking good. She smells so fucking good. She *is* so fucking good.

"Holy *shit*." My voice is muffled by her hair and the sheets.

Her ankles find their way to the top of my ass and stay there.

I grip her as tight as I can.

Her fingertips on the edge of my ear, her lips on my temple. I'm the broken man. I surrender. I'm all hers.

For a long while, we stay just like that. The rain keeps pouring down on the windows.

I let go of her for only a moment to draw the big comforter up over us. I press my head to her breasts and close my eyes, feeling the cool cotton on my back, and her warm, soft body everywhere else.

23
Naomi

Fingers trailing down my forearm wakes me up. I don't open my eyes. I just lie still, wondering how long he's been watching me sleep, how long we've been here at all. I love the way he touches me, the way he goes from gentle to ruthless in an instant.

"I can tell you're awake, pretty girl," he says.

I open one eye.

He's smiling at me. "You're beautiful when you sleep."

Rolling over in his arms, I get my wits about me. It's not easy. I'm melted into the feel of his skin on mine, the way the trail of hair on his stomach is tickling the base of my spine.

Into my hair he says, "It's snowing."

I sit up a little in his arms, and sure enough, he's opened the drapes a few inches and I see big flakes falling outside, golden in the slightly yellow lamplight. Snow globe flakes. Movie scene flakes. "What time is it?"

"Eleven."

I roll over, putting my face against his chest and pulling the comforter up over our heads to make a fort.

"Let's just stay here. We can barricade ourselves in," I say.

"That would be fucking fantastic." He presses his chin to my head. His voice is extra sexy down here, with it echoing against his rib cage and the downy comforter all around us.

"Nobody will put it together," I say, snuggling in closer. He rises up on an elbow, making the tent a little roomier. "We'll just vanish. There's a place that makes awesome sandwiches down the street. They're super shady and they'll deliver to an open window. Nobody ever," I kiss his cheek, "has to bother us again."

As he lies back, the comforter falls on his face. "I don't want anything to mess this up. I was thinking about how to get in touch with you." He turns so we're nose to nose again, and I can't help but move my hand up to his jaw. His eyes follow my hand. He smiles, and then he looks back at me. "Even those texts are risky." He shifts his head slightly and gives me a kiss on my palm.

"Throw rocks at my window. It's the little one in the corner. Fourth floor," I say.

He snorts. "Can you imagine?"

I laugh a little. "Honestly? Yes. After you pulled me through that window, I think anything is possible."

"I've never seen someone so graceful get so jammed up."

"Says the guy on the other side of the window!" I giggle. "What about Skype? That could work. We could each make a new account." He looks to be contemplating it, and I admire the way his Adam's apple moves when he swallows. Let's face it. I admire everything about him. I want to take a painting class just so I can use him as a life model.

"I don't know. Would it be bizarre if I suggested something a little old-fashioned?"

I perk up. "I'm all for that. I've got a fixation with period drama."

He shakes his head at me like, *What a piece of work.*

"What! The costumes! The romance!" I say, feeling just a little defensive. "So great!"

He smiles. "I'm shaking my head because I do too, for God's sake."

"You do not."

"Yes, I do. Poldark? Fuuuuuuck."

Through my giggles, I cling on to him so tight, I feel like I'm going to break him right apart.

"What old-fashioned thing do you have in mind?" I have to say it twice because the first time is just a blubber of noise against his shoulder.

He shifts my hair back from my forehead. "Letters. Actual letters. We can hide them."

I pull back into the fort an inch. "How long have you been thinking about this?"

He shrugs. "Roughly since I met you. If you fold up a piece of paper into quarters, it fits right into a sandwich bag."

And so it's settled. We're going to write letters, old-fashioned letters, and hide them for each other. In the Zen garden.

We are those people.

We get dressed, piece by sad piece, and finally stand face to face against the locked door. My fist to his chest, I say, "Promise me this isn't the last time."

"This is only the beginning."

As we leave, under the gently falling snow, we agree on a gap between the stones, three rows up, four rows over, right behind the Japanese elm.

And just as I'm leaving the Zen garden, he whispers, "Thank you."

The snow falls softly between us, dampening our whispers a little. I answer, "See you tomorrow. At breakfast."

The next morning is icy, with ice pellets flying from the sky onto the granite sidewalks. One of those terrifying days that makes me wonder if the entire legal staff of Yale just sits around crossing their fingers and actually praying to Jesus that nobody slips on a staircase and splits their head open.

Lucy and I go to breakfast, arms out on either side of us and legs at awkward angles.

Once inside the dining hall, things are far less exciting, but at least we're warm. With our scarves and hats still on, we make our rounds through the dining area. Nothing seems good, not even cinnamon rolls. So I settle for my old childhood standby, slightly stale Raisin Bran. Dad was frugal, I'll give him that much. We sit down at a table by the window. It's got two advantages: It's only big enough for the two of us, and it has a direct line of sight to the Master's house. It's a little wavy through the old panes, but clear enough.

This morning, I realized I didn't even come home with underwear on. There's no way we left it in the suite, I'm sure of that, because I double-checked. He must have grabbed it for me. I love that idea, him grabbing something of mine. Something to keep and hold on to.

Lucy sits down across from me, and I pick up my spoon, pursuing a raisin through the milk.

"Some study session. I heard you come in and it was almost midnight," she says.

"Constitutional law, you know," I say. I stuff my mouth with an entire day's serving of fiber.

She purses her lips while she peels the wrapper off a tiny blueberry muffin. "You're glowing, you know," she says.

I put my finger to my cheek. "Windburn?"

And out comes a garbled "*Bullshit!*" from around the muffin she's just eaten whole.

I try to be serious about my Raisin Bran. Forget it. Every few seconds, I glance out the window. All I want to know is everything about him. How he takes his coffee, how he folds his shirts. How he looks standing buck naked in my room.

From the corner of my eye, I see movement. I freeze with Bran in my mouth. He's wearing chinos and those damned loafers—when will he accept that this weather is here to stay?—along with a new winter coat. I notice symmetrical folds on the chest, like it's just come out of a shipping box. Something about him shopping online for coats by himself kind of breaks my heart. He does put on this awesome beanie though, so at least he's got that.

First thing that happens after he steps out of his door? He takes a spectacular spill on the steps.

"Oh my God," Lucy says, chortling. "California never prepared him for this."

I have an impulse to run out the door and help him. He's lost his hat on the ice, rubbing his elbow. But he's a big boy. So damned cute besides. After a few slips and slides, he gets up and grips the railing like he's temporarily paralyzed.

Forcing myself to look away, I chase a soggy flake around the milk.

Lucy makes a long, "Hmmmmmm." I don't dare look up. I'm positive I've given myself away. But when I do look at her, she's tackling a banana and doing something on her phone. Now I see him cross the quad, talking on his cellphone. No gloves. I feel like we're going to get to full winter wear in stages. He makes some *yes I hear you*-type gestures and then sort of idly wanders into the Zen garden.

My heart wallops my rib cage.

Half a minute later, he emerges.

A rush of excitement fills my whole body. "I need to get back to work."

Lucy looks at me like I've lost my mind. "It's ten on a Sunday. What work? Let's go sit in the sauna at the gym."

I snatch up my tray and bolt. "Constitutional law. It's complicated!"

As I'm heading to dump my forks and plate, I intercept him in the front doorway. We don't look at each other, not even for an instant. But I swear to God, I can feel the weight of the air change as we pass one another.

However, as I'm shuffling straight-legged towards the Zen garden, I realize this was an idiot move. I can't go jaunting in there and running back out.

Naomi. This man is making mush of your brain.

So instead of getting his letter, I make the sensible choice and head up to my room. After the breakfast rush has passed and I've been pretending to be busy for forty minutes, Lucy leaves for her Pilates class, and I sneak back downstairs with my ancient Yaktrax on my boots now. In the designated place in the garden, I find a piece of folded paper encased in a sandwich bag.

It isn't Poldark. It's better.

I tell myself not to dilly-dally. I can't be standing there in the snow reading a love letter from the Master of Durham, can I?

Apparently I can because I am. With my back to the world, facing my stairway door, I open the letter as balls of snow roll of the page like sugar. His handwriting is lovely, strong and meaningful, no hesitation at all. It's the same as on the whiteboard in class, but tidier and steadier. Occasionally he'll slip an errant capital letter into his words, and it just makes it look all the more manly and confident. It doesn't have my name on it or his, but says:

Beautiful,
My only regret is that I didn't wake up with you in my arms. I looked for you in my bed but you weren't there. You need to be there. I refuse to wash your smell off me. Maybe I'll never shower again.
Yours,
B

I press the letter to my chest and raise my face to the snow. I'm smiling so hard, it pinches my cheeks. I take a deep stinging breath and wonder if it's possible to be so happy. But when I open my eyes, my happiness is doubled because standing behind the French doors of his house is Ben, smiling back at me.

I run up to my room, the 72 steps nothing at all right now. I slip his letter into my journal and then take a small stack of blank paper from my bottom drawer. My fingers are cold but not because of the weather. My heart has pulled all my blood to my chest.

It takes me three tries, but I think I do it. I hope. As I fold it up, I press my lips to it and inhale.

Back down the steps. Fortunately, Lucy isn't back yet. All this coming and going would most definitely not be covered by my Con Law excuses. I almost miss the last step, but cling on to the railing and make it unscathed. I feel like a burglar almost, sneaking around college and making sure nobody's watching me. I hide the bagged note, back under the stone. Part of me wants to wait here for him, but who knows how long it'll be, so back up I go.

24
ben

I watched her read my letter in the garden, so I can't do the same, but God knows I'd like to. From between the stones I take the sandwich bag. The anticipation of reading her words is so intense I can't even make it the fifty feet back to my house. So I step under a covered archway, dedicated to Samuel Morse of all people, and open the plastic bag and read:

B-
All night I dreamt of the way your hands fit around my hips, the way you feel inside me. I have never felt anything like you before. There's nothing like you. I woke up smiling and I'm still smiling now. I cannot believe you are real. I cannot believe I have you.
I'm yours too. Always,
N

Again and again, I read it. I've never seen her handwriting before now. She's seen mine, I realize, on the board. Her letters are so lovely, so elegant and orderly. She's written to me right in the middle of the page, almost centered, with white spaces in between the lines. Her p's and y's hang a little lower than any of her other letters. Shit, even her uppercase N is sexy.

I take a blank piece of paper from my jacket pocket, already folded, and a pen. I place it on a piece of smooth dry granite in the archway and write:

N
I'm the one that can't believe it. You're making me wish for impossible things. I wish I could slip into your room when nobody's watching. I want to see you in your space. I want to see how you live in your world
B

I place it in between the stones and head back into my house. I look up at her window, and I see her smiling back down at me. I tilt my head towards the Zen garden. Twenty minutes later I see her come back out and find my letter. She walks back to her stairway, but turns and walks backwards the last few steps, watching me the whole way. She isn't gone but a few minutes. She's just as anxious for more as I am. The idea of her standing in that stairwell, not even going back up to her room to write back to me, is driving me wild. But not as wild as her reply. Seven words of pure fucking glory:

The door will be unlocked for you.

I rub my hand over my hat, and the wool scratches my forehead. Fuck me. What if I did it? What if I snuck up there? Jesus Christ. What is she doing to me?

I know I'm supposed to be that guy who just lets go of shit. The guy for whom nothing matters. But this matters. The way I need her matters. She matters.

"Beck," says a voice.

I spin around. I drop the smile off my face.

Osgood is wearing a hat that's kind of the same color as his toupee used to be. A camel color.

"Hey there, Dean."

"What are you doing out here in the snow?" He gnaws on a dry piece of skin on his lip.

"Nice hat." I fold up the letter, trying not to look like I adore the very creases.

He glowers at me. "What's that in your hands?"

I play it cool and slip it into my inside pocket. I zip up my jacket to my neck. If he wants it, he's going to have to fight me for it, and I've got a feeling he didn't grow up throwing punches in Cambridge like I did in Vegas. "Just some mail."

"How's Miss Costa?"

The sensation is like getting pushed off a cliff. He can't know, I'm sure of that. But he's got a good poker face. I'll give him that.

Fortunately, mine is better. Vegas. It's got its fucking perks.

"I wouldn't know," I smile. "Sorry to cut this short. But I've got some work to do."

∴

3:17 am. I've lain in bed for two hours thinking about whether to do this. I can't stop thinking of her up there alone. Waiting. Finally, I get up and look out my window. Her light is still on, but every other window on her floor is dark. Fuck it. I can't resist. I can't stay away. I put on a pair of sweats, sneakers, a gray zip-up hoodie with a T-shirt, and a baseball hat. I look at myself in the mirror. I look like exactly what I am. A 38-year-old guy trying to pretend he's 22. But what the fuck can I do about that? Not one goddamned thing. I am what I am. Hers.

The endless steps burn my glutes, and my pulse bangs in my temples. At the door to the fourth floor, I put my hand on the knob and listen. No music, nobody laughing. But just before I open the door, I hear the noise of a flushing toilet and wait. I hear someone walk past in slippers, maybe, that soft-footed noise of someone returning to their room. I open the door again and listen. Nothing. I open the door with a brassy squeak from the hinges.

Inside the hallway, I get my bearings. Rooms 409 and 410 are to my left, so I go right and pull down the bill of my hat. Every door that passes makes my blood pressure rise higher and higher. I'm so fucking close to her, so fucking close.

I pass room 417. Two more to go on this side of the hall. The noise of a door creaking open behind me startles me, but I don't turn around. Can't turn back now. I slouch a little, making like a college senior heading to his girlfriend's room, and keep on going. To room 421. Where I pause and catch my breath, alone in the hallway.

On her door is taped a picture of Naomi and a girl I recognize. One of ours, a Durham student. Lucy is her name, I think. I've met her. Lucy Burchett, maybe. They're covered in dye and paint, holding on to one another giggling. They're at that Indian festival, what's it called. Holi? I can't remember. Naomi's smile sparkles perfect and white. The kind of smile that could stop a sacred holiday in its tracks.

My hand is on the knob. I hold my breath. It's unlocked and my heart stops beating in my chest for the whole clockwise turn. The light of her room fills the hallway. There she is, in bed, with her hands to her mouth, eyes bright and open in surprised delight. She's in a nightie with blue flowers, and wearing a thin gray robe over the top. A totally involuntary, sudden, instantaneous smile springs up to my face, without my even thinking to give it to her. Instant happiness as soon as I see her.

Oh my God! she mouths.

I slip inside her room.

Quietly as I can, I close the door and lock it, even being quiet with the lock itself. Rotating it so slowly, I can bolt sliding through the frame. Slow. Fucking forbidden. And then locked tight. Just us apart from the world.

Her eyes are frozen on mine. She scoots to the far edge of her bed and lifts the comforters. To welcome me home.

I turn off the lamp on my way to her. Everything becomes dark and still. My shirt and baseball cap come off in one yank. I sink down on top of her, and she wraps her body around me. I pull her robe off and bring the straps of her nightie down off her shoulders.

"Not a sound," I whisper into her ear.

She doesn't answer out loud, but instead shakes her head against my cheek. I pull my face back from her and find I can see her in the dim, strange light of the snowy sky outside.

I pull her to me, my cock rock solid as I press into her. She tenses, and in place of a groan, she gives me a long, beautiful exhale.

I feel the cheap spring of the mattress dig into my knee as I feed her every inch of me. I slide her nightie up her stomach, and my hand finds its way to the narrow of her waist.

Her hips rise. Her hand leaves the back of my neck to grip the metal headboard.

Fuck. Fuck me.

Fuck. Fuck.

Fuck.

25
Naomi

I wake up to a note tucked under my pillow.

Beautiful —

Thank you for last night. You are pure magic.

Yesterday afternoon I had a close call with You Know Who. So I researched a few things. Download an app called Signal. It's secure. My screen name is The4Loves. I'll write you there.

I grab my phone from my desk and jump back under the covers. I download Signal. It asks me for a screen name. I'm tempted to type in a;sldfk;ajkadlfkj or 12345 but I decide on ErosEros. And then comes a message:

There she is.

Room spins briefly.

oh my God. are you sure this is safe?

Yeah. As safe as it can be.
I hope you know what you're doing to me.

you're doing the same thing to me.
i wish you were here

No shit.
I want you again. Soon.

Grip sheets.

so do i.
i can smell you everywhere.
i wil l never wash these sheets again.

I'm a broken man, Naomi Costa. All your fault.

Toe curl.

are you going to breakfast?

Thought you'd never ask.

Over the somewhat sad serving tray of pre-scrambled eggs, we brush past one another. I linger by the bacon, and he touches my hand by the sliced oranges. I see him sit down next to Osgood, and I pretend to listen to Lucy tell me something about a guy she met. I barely listen. I'm pretty sure I hear the words *foot fetish*, but it really doesn't hit my radar. Back in my room, I report back:

lucy says I'm glowing.

Osgood is a piece of work.

btw id din't tell you.
i had a chance to rescue the hairpiece
i declined.

Oh shit. You did him a favor.

Snort.

did you shower?
No. Did you?

Lewd as it is, I'd savored walking up to feeling his cum on my lips. Slightly sticky, slightly dry. So fleeting and yet so, unbelievably, wonderful.

nope.

Hang tight a few days. I have something special in mind.

I'm not sure what that means, but okay…sure. I'll hold off on a shower for a few days. I'm all for a little water conservation.

I mean, you can shower. Sorry. Lol.
Hang tight for our next date.

Which means there is definitely going to be a next time, yes, yes, yes.

i can stand a few days I think.

I can't. But I'll have to.

Hard swallow.

First time we were together, did you like the tie around your wrists…

you know I did.

The spanks…

i begged for more.

And my hand around your throat.

Full body flutter.

that's when I came.

I remember. I fucking remember.
Do you trust me?

Sweet Jesus.

i do.

Good girl.

I should go. Duty calls. Bastard.

I don't know how to say goodbye. I don't want to say goodbye.

thank you for last night. i need to feel you inside me again.

Fuck you for being so perfect.

God, coming from anybody else, that'd be offensive. From him, I get it. We're at the limit of words. Fuck you for turning my life upside down, fuck you for ruining what I understand. I get that down to the very last letter.

fuck you right back.

The week goes by with more texts. Most often, we run into each other in the dining hall at lunch. Osgood eats near where he teaches, so lunch is ours. We have, by silent mutual consent, abandoned the dessert area because it's too damned busy. Usually we happen to meet at the cooked vegetable island, which doesn't get a whole lot of traffic. One particularly quiet lunch hour, I see him standing there considering steamed broccoli like it's some philosophical quandary. I know he's waiting for me. I immediately abort my plans to make a salad and feign a pressing interest in steamed baby carrots. Placing my tray next to him, I stay outside that imaginary but definite bubble of appropriate personal space.

I'm pretty sure it's just the heating lamps, but part of me wants to believe that searing warmth on my arm is him. That he lights me up that way.

He says, "Broccoli, I love it."

In my head I interpret this as, *I want to rip your clothes off.*

"Me too," I say, by which I mean, *Right here, Master Beck. Right here.*

"I'm pretty passionate about cauliflower too." Obviously, that translates to, *Your nipples need to be in my mouth.*

"Especially if it's raw." *Please, please, please.*

And a slow, almost silent groan escapes from his throat.

Once I get my carrots and my mysteriously cod-like baked tilapia, I sit down alone. It's not unusual for me. I pull out my book for Medieval History. I can just see him over the top of the cover. What he doesn't know is I have his book hidden in here. I've read it over and over. Next to my glass of water, my phone buzzes. I flip it over and open up Signal.

Fellows' dinner canceled tonight.

> whoa! really?

Yeah. Something went really wrong with the dishwasher.

> you didn't...

Plumbing sabotage is surprisingly easy.

> holy shit!

So you're free tonight.

I freeze with my broccoli on my fork.

> do I get to see you?

Eat your broccoli.

I put my broccoli in my mouth.

8pm. Be at the Starbucks on Chapel, window table.

Crunch goes an undercooked stem.

that sounds like a date.

Possibly.

I don't hear from him for the rest of the day and I don't reply either. Instead, I work furiously, as fast as I can, thrusting myself into a godforsaken paper about a mostly unknown Revolutionary War hero with one eye and who seemed to divide his time between writing semi-belligerent letters to Washington and "getting in small skirmishes" on roadsides. I have no idea what I'm writing. No thesis. No outline. Just words, words, words.

Paragraphs.

Pages.

They might be good? I mean, good enough?

Yeah. Fine. Good enough for today.

With a crick in my neck, I finish the draft and save it to Dropbox, lest my computer spontaneously implode. I bite into an apple—Lucy is always stealing them from the dining hall, and her room is starting to look like a Vermont orchard, so I get the overflow. I look out my window, and the snow and ice have changed back to rain. It pounds down into the mud on the edges of the grassy quad.

There's another paper to do, this one a two-page reading response. I look at the clock. 3:00 pm. I give myself a limit of two hours and pound it out. Who knew love could make a person so freaking efficient?

Then at five, I jump in the shower. I slather myself with a little extra body wash. I take some time with my hair, actually finger-combing it and using extra conditioner. In the little shower stall, behind the pale blue curtain, I dry off and make sure to get every inch of myself covered in lotion. Back in my room, I lock the door behind me and put on NoMBe's "California Girls."

"*Oh how I love the smell of West Coast pheromones.*"

"No kidding," I say to my computer.

I need you this way, he'd said, when I showed up at the Guest Suite in my leggings and sweatshirt. So now it just doesn't feel right to go ask Lucy for something flashy. *I need you this way.* God.

So I pick out another pair of leggings—these are what you might call my "dress leggings," no stains, not faded—and a high-necked tunic sweater. It's dark blue and everybody always compliments my eyes when I wear it. As for shoes? It's warmed up and the snow has melted because of the pouring rain. So there's just one option.

My busted old yellow galoshes.

26
ben

The garage attached to the Master's House is roughly the width of a horse and carriage. It also, thanks to the absolute insistence of the Yale Relocation Office, now contains my trusty old Jeep Wagoneer. 1987, wood panels, and leather seats that same oxblood red as that sofa that I'd leaned Naomi over in the guest suite. I feel a ripple of need rush downwards, and my cock hardens.

Focus, Beck. Focus. The Wagoneer. Focus on the Wagoneer. You can't be getting a hard-on in your garage, for Christ's sake.

But I am. Yeah, I am.

I get inside the Jeep. The engine turns over immediately with a satisfying roar. Coming from the radio is NPR at full blast—it used to be 90s hits back in LA. I laugh a little to myself, because of course, and turn down the volume.

The last week without her has been agony. Every day I think about how to get to her. I've had to seriously fight the urge to sneak back up to her room and fuck her silent and senseless again and again. But I haven't, because it's just too damned risky. I haven't even gone up that stairwell. I know that if I run up it again, I'll never want to come back down. So instead we met over the vegetables and gave each other secret glances in class. It had been enough to live off of, just barely, because at least I had tonight to look forward to. The plumbing sabotage had been a stroke of genius, if I do say so myself.

It's 7:55 pm. I'm damned nervous because I know that, practically, this is a terrible idea. This is one of those ideas that if you had a buddy, he'd say, "Dude. Hold up. Let's walk that back…"

But I don't have a buddy. I have her. I want her. I need her. She's all I can think about, the air I'm breathing, the world I'm rushing through. She's it. She's there. And I'm going to take her out. On a genuine date.

Slowly, I nose the Jeep out onto Elm. Some students pass in the rain, and I'm careful not to nudge anybody by accident. Talk about a scandal, me knocking over some poor international student. God.

With the Jeep halfway into the street and blocking the sidewalk, I hurry to sling myself in the driver's seat, using the roof rack for leverage.

And then a familiar voice is behind me. "Where are you headed?" says Osgood. "At eight on a Thursday?"

He's lost the alpaca and is trying out a kind of tweed cap with a bill. He looks a whole hell of a lot like Elmer Fudd.

"IKEA," I tell him. I'm standing on the running boards, so I'm about a foot taller than he is. I'm tempted to stay like this just to make a point, but I don't. I step back down onto the wet pavement and face him. "I've got to buy a chair. And some meatballs."

I can tell he finds this suspicious, not only because he's narrowing his eyes to say *that's suspicious,* but also because there are literally a million chairs in my house, and every meal I eat is served in the cafeteria. But what else was I going to say? Bookshelves? Dishes? Curtains?

"That wingback just isn't cutting it. I need something that I can get comfortable in. You know? Put my feet up? Do some grading? Write some helpful emails?"

It occurs to me then that IKEA is probably not the right choice for comfortable chairs—idiot—but now I'm in the mud, I've got to sling it.

"How's work been?" he asks. He's wearing this beat-up old rain jacket with the hood cinched tight over his face. He's almost sausage-like.

"Good. Class is good, I'm settling in." Settling in? Fuck. I'm on Mercury.

"Staying out of trouble?"

I just smile and zip up my coat. The rain shifts to a dreadful, heavy, slapping, frozen drizzle. "No trouble. So I'll see you around."

And then he does the eyes-to-fingers thing *again.*

I'm tempted to do it right back at him, but I don't. Instead I say, "Need anything? Ottoman? Drapes?"

He shakes his head and shuffles off into the rain.

Heading down High Street, I'm reassured. He hasn't picked up on us or he would have said so. I can say that much for Dean Osgood. He may be pursuing scandal like his rare moth, but he can't keep his feelings to himself for shit.

I park just on this side of Chapel. I'm a few minutes early, but so is she: From behind the squeaky wipers, I see her sitting in the window of Starbucks with her phone. Wearing those damn cute, sad galoshes again. I hammer out a text to her.

Walk down High, towards Crown, cross Crown, and then right. Don't hurry. I'm in an old Jeep. CA plates. Can't miss me.

Her face lights up into the most overwhelming smile. She replies with simply:

!!!

The light turns green, and I join traffic. I go down two blocks and take a right, parking in a loading zone in front of one of the infinite pizza places in New Haven. All the while, I'm watching for her in the rearview mirror. She comes into focus from behind, and I see she's glancing at herself in shop windows. But not boldly. Subtly, gently. Like a girl who knows she's beautiful, but is a little too damaged to flaunt it.

I don't know what it is about her. I've been with a lot of women but never, not ever, have I chased one like this. I'm chasing her even though I have her. I'm chasing her even though she's mine. It's the endless pursuit of this perfect thing. She's turned me into Plato himself.

Calmly and elegantly, she crosses the street and gets right in the passenger's seat, without saying anything as she slams the door. She turns to face me sweetly as she buckles up.

"What are we doing?" she asks. Her voice is breathy and happy. "And please tell me that back seat folds down."

I put the Jeep in drive, and get a little farther away from campus. The world feels unclear, like I'm in a tunnel. We pass under traffic lights, every one of them green. Finally, when we've gotten on CT-15, I put my hand on her thigh. My thumb is on the seam of her leggings. I feel her muscles right under my palm. Those muscles I've grabbed, those muscles I want

133

to mark. "So, I thought it might be nice to do a few errands…"

She turns to me. "Finish that sentence."

"…and do something romantic…"

"Keep going."

"…before I show you how much I missed you."

Her head lands softly on the headrest, and then she knits her hand over mine.

∴

As I drive away from New Haven, her fingers inch up my leg and every mile feels like a hundred. Romance is going to have to wait.

The first chance I get, I pull off the highway and find an empty warehouse parking lot. I put the Jeep in park and grab her.

I'm growling into her mouth. *Get me inside that body right fucking now.* She reaches down and takes my cock in her hand, rubbing it on the underside, from base to tip through my pants, like we're teenagers out for the night. We're not teenagers, but we are *this close* to having sex at a stoplight in Madison Goddamned Connecticut. Sex with her, it's like that. Like a rebellion, or like getting ripped off a surfboard by a wave from behind.

A car honks behind us. She is ceaseless, and she draws it right out of me into her, through her mouth and lips, saying *Everything, give me everything.*

"Fuck!" she says, in a whisper. "Why are you so good? Why, why, why?"

Popping open the door, I see her face under the dome light, reddened from my scruff, the edge of her lips a little less clear. She looks vulnerable, and I love it. "Hold that thought."

In the pouring rain, I open the back door and fold down the seat. With a giggle, she sneaks through between the front row and lies down.

Slamming the door and climbing on top of her happen in one movement almost. For a moment, we are a swishing mess of jackets and squeaking boots. She unzips mine, I unzip hers. Our boots come off in a pile between the seats. Now she's all softness under me. Her sweater has trapped her perfume, and I press my nose down past the turtleneck, against her throat, kissing her hard, and halfway hoping I'll leave a mark so she has to wear this sweater for the rest of the week.

This time, with the hard seatbacks below us, there is no mattress to sink into. I can explore her just exactly as she is. The smooth angle of the small of her back, the gap between her neck and the seatback are all new spaces that I need to touch. Soft and delicate. I pull her sweater slowly off her body, peeling it away so I can see what's underneath. What's underneath, of course, is another shirt because it's freezing, so I peel that off too. As I suck on those nipples, teasing them and biting them, she fumbles for my belt with one hand, the other around the back of my head. I slide one hand down past her leggings.

"No underwear," I say, letting her nipple go. It keeps the shape of my bite, slightly upturned and compressed.

"I ran out. You soak them through."

"What, all your underwear?" My stubble just grazes her hipbone.

"I mean, all the sexy ones. I only want to wear sexy when I think of you."

Her leggings have absorbed that smell so much more strongly than just her panties

had. With one hand parting her pussy lips, I massage that clit on the outside of the leggings with the other. I know I'm making her insane. I know I'm pissing her off. I know what she wants me to do, but I'm not going to do it, not yet.

"Take off that bra," I say.

She sits up, shifting the back of her bra to the front. She slings it from her finger towards the front seat, and it catches on the headrest. "Take off that shirt," she says back.

I'm powerless with her. Every other woman I've ever been with, I set the terms. I take off the bras. I kiss first. I say what's what, and they listen. Until I collided with Naomi Costa, at least I knew who I was in the bedroom. But not anymore. She's brought out the switch I didn't know I had. I want to pull and push and fight for control forever. I pull down her leggings, and she falls back onto the carpeted surface with a moan. I want to own her, I want to rule her.

But I also want her to do the very same fucking things to me.

I dip my tongue down into that outrageous wetness. I stay there for three long plunges.

With two fingers, nearly three, I reach inside her. Her body comes right up off the carpet. "Oh, God. Whoa."

"Too much?" I want to hurt her, but just enough.

"No," she says through a gasp. "Not… Shit." That last word, it's long and tremulous, guttural. Coarse. *Shiiiiiiit.*

I pull against the weight of her pelvis, drawing her up a few inches more. Her legs help me out. Slipping that third finger all the way in, I leverage her body against her G-spot.

The sound that comes from her mouth, it's an inhalation under her tongue flicking against her own teeth. "Oh my God, what is…"

Still I hang on to her, putting my tongue to her clit now. I feel her start to seize my fingers from inside. Her thighs begin to come together and give her away, she's that close. I don't give her any mercy. I keep her that way, hooked on my hand, and bring that orgasm right out of her. As she comes, she grips my bicep with her tiny hand, her fingers spread out and pale against my shoulder. Her strength is tremendous, the rolling waves tearing through her. When she finally releases her hand, I know I'm going to have a bruise of her fingers on my arm.

When her body begins to go slack, I let her go. She's got her hands to her face now, saying, "*Shit…shit!*" on a loop.

Wherever she is, that's exactly where I want her. Yanking her leggings down even more, I pull my dick out of my pants, and she takes it quickly in her hands. She reaches inside her own pussy to moisten her palms, and rubs herself all over me.

With her other hand, she massages my balls, just gently, cupping them in her palm. "Please, Ben. Please get inside me. Please."

As if I had any other thought in my head.

I push into her, and with my other hand support her back. Her body rises up as she gets used to how I feel inside again, her hips rise slightly, and I feel a second wave of wetness draw me further into her.

In the confined box of the back of the Jeep, I have leverage that I'd never had with her before. I can feel her pussy in a way I never did in bed. I can feel her pelvis, her cervix like an impassable dam that I'd like to blow up with a hundred raging orgasms. She's got my head spinning so that some deep, reptile part of my brain starts talking. Put that seed in her, Beck. Get it inside her. That's where it belongs.

"You feel so fucking incredible," I tell her, pulling her to me with my fingers gripping both sides of her waist. She grabs one of my arms, hanging on tight.

"I'm close."

On top of everything else, she's fucking insatiable. Two orgasms, back to back. That's what I'm talking about.

Pinning her other arm with my hand above her head, I drive in harder and whisper, "Do it. Let me feel you again."

Out here, in the middle of nowhere, she screams out like she hasn't been able to before. Her cries tear through the air, half sadness and half bliss, tumbling from yes to no, and then my name, "No, no, no, Ben, Ben, Ben," and then she screams out, *"I love you, I love you, I love you, fuuuuuuck,"* and she pulls me in so deep, I don't have a chance of hanging on.

Does she realize what she just said? I don't know. But what I do know is we are ten thousand couples, fucking in back seats on dark rainy nights. But nobody is falling as hard as I am right now.

Her eyes wide and honest, she looks right at me. "Tell me this is real."

"Real as fuck."

"How real?"

I come hard and strong inside her in three massive bursts, her name getting diced up into three furious syllables, "Na-oh-mi, *fuck.*"

Again, I collapse on top of her. Whimper on the in, moan on the out. Over and over. I could listen to that until the day I die.

A tap at the side window startles us both, along with a light shining in. I throw my jacket over her and then lean over to wipe the fog from the window with my forearm. Outside stands a cop. I roll down the window an inch.

"Evening, Officer," I say. I feel her toes curl against my thighs.

Even through the high beam in my eyes, I can see he's got a smile on his face. "Time to keep moving, folks."

∴

"This isn't romantic," she says, as I pull up in front of shoe store in Madison. It's the heart of suburbia out here. All strip malls and family minivans, not a Yale professor in sight.

She's peering through the now rain-blurred windshield.

"Come on," I say. "I need boots. I can't shop online for boots."

"Is this what you call romantic? Shoe shopping? Ben!'

It's all I can do not to burst out laughing. "Miss Costa. Don't be a brat."

She purses her lips. There's that smile. "I'm hungry."

"My feet are wet. I don't want wet feet. So," I shrug. Keeping it nonchalant.

She has exactly zero idea why I'm doing this. Good. If she did, she'd never agree. Ever.

So then I go around to the other side of the Jeep and open the door for her, keeping her dry with my umbrella, and shaking it off outside the door before we go inside.

The shoe store feels like a blown-out photograph, so bright and shiny with those fluorescent bulbs against the darkness outside. As we enter, we separate. She heads down one aisle of men's shoes. I head parallel down another. All the time I'm watching her. Her fingers trail over the shelves, but she's locked on me.

With her help, we settle fast on a pair of good, solid rain boots. They're made by Bogs, and they have a sweet handle built right in. I ask the lady for a 13, and she gives me an efficient nod before heading into the stock room.

"You've got big feet," Naomi says.

"Is it true what they say?"

"Yep. Totally true. In your case."

A half-laugh jumps out of my mouth. "Now, about those," I say, nodding down at Naomi's yellow galoshes.

She wiggles her feet, and the toes come up off the floor. "These? They're great."

Actually, the rubber is cracked, and I'm almost positive I can see her socks. "Sit down," I tell her. "Right there." I point to one of those weird benches with the diagonal mirrors at the end of a row of dress shoes. Of course, she doesn't sit down. I didn't expect her to. She's a lot feistier than that.

All the girls on campus wear Hunter boots. I've seen them in every shade. Leopard, rainbows, shiny silver. I don't care at all about what they look like. What I want is for them to be watertight, to keep those pretty feet warm and dry.

"What size?" I ask, pressing gently on her shoulder, the tips of my fingers on the fine edge of her collarbone.

"I don't need new boots," she says. She's playing with the sleeves of her jacket.

Again, I'm on my knees in front of her. I like it down here. A lot. A

138

lot more than I'd ever admit out loud. I slip off her boot but don't see a size inside. What I do see is what I suspected: a wet blotch on her sock.

"Size," I say again.

"My booths are are totally fine. I mean, you should see my dad's …"

I scratch my face with the tip of my thumb and wait for her.

"Tell me."

Embarrassed, she stares off at some half-priced sandals. "Nope."

Time to up the ante. "Tell me, or I take you home right now."

Now she looks like she's all fire and hot spun sugar inside. Sweet but a little too hot. Boiling over. "Oh, yeah? Dad?"

"I'm serious. I'll take you right back home. No dinner. No nothing."

Her face reddens. Now I'm biting my fucking cheek to keep from laughing, but I'm not kidding either. I don't know how a person can bring out the fight and laughter in me, but she does it. Without fail.

"Miss Costa. Shoe size. Right now." I stand up, towering over her.

The laughter spills right out of her, somewhere between happy and slightly ashamed. She shoves me a little but leaves her hand on my stomach as she looks up at me. "Eight, okay? Eight."

So when the shop lady comes out with my boots, I say, "And a pair of Hunter boots for her. Size eight, and I have no idea what that is in European."

The lady looks tickled and crosses her arms over her chest. "What color, honey?" she asks.

Naomi is staring straight at me, defiant, furious, but also with that undercurrent of tickled joy that I find so fucking addictive.

But then she softens in a way I really haven't seen her. Not like this. Gratitude, a glimmer of being overwhelmed. That sheen comes back up into her eyes.

"Pick your color, beautiful," I say. The shoe lady, behind Naomi, with her arms crossed and her apron too tight, smiles at the two of us. Her eyes shift back and forth, back and forth.

"Red," Naomi says finally. "I'd like them in red."

∙∙
∙

Instead of the fancy dinner I'd planned to take her to, we stop for burgers, fries, and shakes. Between the parking lot and the shoe store, we've missed our reservation.

She sticks a fry in her mouth. "I like this better."

God. See. Exactly what I was thinking. "I never know what fork to use."

She sucks on her shake, and I see the lovely hollows of her cheeks. It's a long minute that passes with her sucking vanilla through the straw and watching me. Finally, she says, "I didn't either. I can help you out with that."

As I unwrap my burger, she hands me a napkin before I even know I need it.

That's when it hits me.

It's not the napkin. It's not the salad forks. Not red galoshes or thumbhole hoodies or eyes with a navy-blue edge. It's not philosophy or laughter or that sizzle that she puts all through me.

It feels like tear gas.

I don't just want her. I don't just like her.

I *need* her.

I've never needed anything. Ever. I've never felt this deep, sinking desire inside me. I've never felt so exposed and wide open and fucking freaked out. Nothing is so consequential as to be *needed*. Nothing is so important as to be *loved*.

Until now.

With a bare semblance of sanity, because, you know, my entire worldview is crumbling, I keep my shit together. I don't pinch my fingers to my nose, I don't drive 90 miles an hour back to campus after we eat. Instead, through the foggy, dreamy streak of the nighttime drive, I keep my hand on her thigh, only moving it to shift gears when absolutely necessary.

But there's a weight in my stomach. *Tell me this is real. How real?*

I love you, I love you, I love you.

What if love isn't a construct? What if it isn't something soft-hearted humans made up to feel better about the world as they hurtle meaninglessly through the sky?

What if I've been utterly fucking wrong all along?

27
ben

I get us to campus. I'm grateful that the two of us can be quiet together because I have no idea what to say. None. Anything that comes out of my mouth now is going to be a hard-core profession of love, and I am *not* ready for that. I don't know how to do it. I don't know how to handle this.

As we part a block away from college, I kiss her. I don't know if she can tell I'm distracted.

Back inside my house, I stand in the kitchen over the sink in the dark like a beaten man. A man who's lost control.

She's let loose this great passion in me, this thing I never knew existed, this roiling angry volcano that wants to create and destroy, to take over and make new. To need and want and believe. She's leveled me, and in this new wave of Ben Beck, he's hanging on so tight, it's fucking terrifying. Fighting against the need to not be alone anymore.

I'm the atheist who's seen God and wants to run from church forever. The unbeliever in the light.

Being alone, it's easy. It's fine. It's good.

She's my student. She's a junior. I'm falling in love with a girl twenty years younger than me. I think this is love. It must be love. It feels like getting mugged. It's fear. It's helplessness. It's all of me right in her hands.

Her scholarship. My job. There are ten thousand reasons that this is the worst idea in the world. Ten thousand little reasons, ten thousand big ones. I look up at her window. After a while, I see the light go out.

I feel sick, I feel wrecked.

I cannot do this.

No way. I cannot. I cannot open up my heart. I don't know how.

I take my phone from my pocket and straighten up. I'm an asshole. I've spent my life being the asshole that believes in nothing and who keeps everybody away. I can be that guy again. I am that guy.

Signal opens up. I stare at the blank message field for a second. And write,

We can't. I can't. I'm so fucking sorry, Naomi.

Before I can grasp what I just said, I close the app and put my thumb on the Signal icon. I press the tiny x to delete it.

It's too much. It's too fucking terrifying.

And then I go to my messages and delete her number too.

It's a little after eleven at night when I decide to go for a jog in the needling rain. My lungs burn with the cold, but I breathe harder and make it burn more. My skin stings, my body aches. I have to get Naomi out of my mind. I don't need her. I don't need anything. I'm *fine*.

God *damn* it.

The truth is, I hate running. I'd rather sit on my ass. But running is the best kind of self-punishment I've found.

Behind me, I hear footfalls in the rain. Slap, slap. I turn to look. Just my luck I'm going to get murdered out here.

But it's Naomi in a drenched hoodie and jogging pants. Her hair is wet against her head, and she's got this *look* on her face. Like a panther. I can see her by the light of a faraway street lamp.

"Oh, Jesus," I moan to myself.

She is coming right for me. She's not stopping.

"I'm sorry," I say, holding out my arms.

No response. She tackles me, straight on, like some untrained housecat. She makes contact and latches on to me with all fours. I go tumbling and land with a smack in the leaves.

"You're an asshole."

"I know that," I say.

She lets loose a tiny-fisted punch and it lands almost comically on my chest. I grab her wrist. Her hair is coming down over her face and she's got her teeth set close and mean.

"A real asshole."

"Naomi," I say, rolling over onto her in the wet leaves. My knees grind into the ground on either side of her body.

"Let me go, you bastard," she says, squirming underneath me. There's all manner of kicking and punching going on besides. I've got my hands wrapped around her wrists, but she's a fighter.

"Stop trying to hit me," I say. Hanging on to her is like hanging on to my brother's toddler right now. So tiny but *so* difficult to pin down, not to mention she's all wet and she's determined to beat me as hard as she can with those tight little fists. *What* goes one into my abdomen, and I involuntarily clench up, roaring into the dark.

"Holy fuck," I groan. "Calm down," She does not. She even gets my jaw with a glancing hook.

Trying to contain her is like putting a tornado in a box, or a raven in a cage. Totally impossible. She squirms and she pounds. I hear her tennis shoes scratching like mad on the ground. I try to get a little bit of purchase with my own shoes on the wet, gravelly path, but I just can't. She won't let me. She's too angry to hold. Finally, I get her by the shoulders by wrapping my arms entirely around her body in a bear hug.

This quiets the tornado, barely. "Thanks for that message. Super job, Professor."

"I'm fucking sorry," I say, sounding angrier than I intended. "You just don't understand, Naomi."

She grips my shirt so tight, I hear threads breaking. "Actually I do. I do fucking understand. I know what it's like to be so independent you don't want to say the word *feelings*. I know what it's like to be on your own. But I also know that when you see something you want, and need, and love, you *have to grab it*," she says. She punctuates these last words, pounding on my chest, driving her elbow into my body

She's a shitload stronger than she looks. Inside and outside. And everything she's saying, it's so fucking true. All true.

143

"You and me," I say, grinding my knees into the ground now, "It's impossible."

Just when I think I have a handle on the situation, she hooks her legs over the backs of my thighs, and she manages to flip me. *Unbelievable.* Right over onto my back, where I land with a cold, mucky *thunk*.

She growls at me. "A guy who says nothing matters, and fucking me like you do." She gives me a shove. "And an illiterate fisherman's daughter at Yale. A girl who doesn't fucking belong here, who is terrified forever, and then finally finds you, *you,* you nihilist asshole!"

"Calm *down*," I say, totally unconvincingly, my voice shaking.

"No, I will not. You don't get to tell me what to do. Not now, not ever."

She struggles a little harder but now we're nose to nose. Now her chin is trembling. I see it thanks to the faint far-off light of a blue police telephone by the side of the path.

I cannot help myself and put my thumb to stop the trembling. But she swats my hand away. "Don't you dare. Don't you dare do that. I'm not yours to care for, not unless you stop acting like such an insufferable asshole. So fuck you, Master Beck. Fuck you and all your *nothingness*."

My vision starts to funnel in on her, just her, not the rain, not the night, not the wet leaves, not even my fucking thoughts. Just her. Her. Her. Her

"You want me to show you how I feel?"

She blinks just once, still fuming. "Do you want to send it to me via secret text? Stick it between some stones? Whisper it on the stupid wind?"

Now it's my turn to flip her, and I do, face down into a pile of soft wet leaves. I rip her running pants down. I push my palms into her ass, and then press my cock inside her from behind. I part that ass and let the rain come down on it.

"Show me," she seethes over her shoulder. "If you can't tell me you love me, *show me.* Or go, go back to your bullshit solitary life."

God, it's so insane. She shouldn't have one bit of power from down there below me, but instead she's got all of it. She's got me by the balls. Always has, always will.

"Shut..." I reach up and hold her down by her neck.

"The fuck..." I position myself at the opening of her pussy.

"Up." And thrust deep, deep inside her.

She snarls out this long, furious *Yeahhhhh* into the ground. Her fingers are digging deep into the dirt.

We are beasts in the forest. I am rutting her raw. We get rude and ferocious, tearing through the leaves with our hands. I see her fingernails encrusted in dirt as I fuck her into the mud. I fuck her into the rocks. I fuck her until I can't see straight. Until there is nothing but Naomi, alone in the goddamned universe.

"I'm going to mark you," I say low into her ear.

She starts squirming again, but hanging on to my hands too. "Do it, Master. Mark me. Do it."

I pull out and pump my cum all over her back, all over her hair, all over her ass. She's the one. Right now in the filth and the mud, it's all so simple.

Coming out of this dark haze, I finally snap to. I look around. I'm fucking Naomi Costa on in the ground in East Rock Park.

Seriously?

How does she do this? How does she make me lose my logic, my common sense, my decency?

I've got no idea. But she most definitely does. How can any living person do this to another?

Flipping her over under my bent legs, still with my orgasm ripping through my body, I get down low over her face, rain dripping from my hair onto hers. Half her face is smeared with mud, like some little warrior. An assassin of hearts.

"You know I fucking love you. You know I do."

And she takes my face in her filthy hands and kisses the hell out of me, teeth-to-teeth, smiling at me against that kiss as the rain begins to slow.

I reach down between my legs to get to hers and start working her clit, I let the rain fall, washing the dirt away. I use my own spit to get it perfect again. Then I hook three fingers into her like I did in the Jeep. I bring that screaming orgasm right out of her. With my free palm, I cover her mouth while she grips my shirt in her hands, shaking me at the height of the climax, like it feels so good she hates me.

I know that feeling.

I'm in love with that fucking feeling.

Eventually, I don't know how long it is—she does that to me, warps time—I stand up and help her from the ground, offering my hand and then hoisting her up. In every way, we'd battled it out, and now here I am, neither the victor nor the loser, helping up from the ground the one who'd given me a knock-out punch. I wipe the mud off her face a little.

Shit has gotten more serious than ever. I need her and I admit it. I accept it and let it boil up and stay there, all through my body.

"What are we going to do?" she says.

"I have no idea. Something."

She sighs, hard and worn out, and then she presses her head to my shoulder as we emerge from the forest, back into the real world.

"We better split up," she says.

Fucking A. I'd like to scoop her up into my arms and carry her into college, Beauty-and-the-Beast style. But she's right. Of course she is.

"Sorry I tackled you," she says under the streetlight.

I push a little hair back from her forehead. "I'm so glad you did."

Without a goodbye, she lets me go, and takes off jogging back to Durham. Leaving me without her. All alone in the rain.

28
Naomi

By the time I get back to my room, it's almost 1:30 in the morning. Everybody's still wide awake because it's just before midterms. This is not exactly optimal. While I can't see myself, I can feel the mud caked on every single part of my body, and I'm pretty sure I smell like really, really fabulous sex.

But there's nothing for it. I can't hide; I've got to go up the stairs. As I walk, little bits of mud fall onto the steps, and I look back behind me. I've left a trail like Pig-Pen.

What we did in the forest, it got a little violent. It got a little raw. I just loved it. I needed it. We are not missionary position people. We are Naomi Costa and Benjamin Beck. Catalyst and reaction.

I peek into Lucy's room, and there she is, furiously doing the readings she hasn't done all term. I've seen this rodeo before. She stockpiles her ADD meds for just such occasions.

"Proust, who the hell is Proust?" she squeals and lifts her eyes. "Holy *shit,* what happened to you?"

Now I try to elegantly smooth my mud-crusted jogging pants, like, *It's nothing.* I do realize, of course, that I look like I just got done with

Tough Mudder or one of those horrible game shows where everybody gets hit by big foam hammers into a frothy moat. I try to shrug it off. "Took a spill on my jog."

She's sort of plucking her way towards me with her hands out. "Don't come in here. You'll ruin my rug."

I have this momentary flash of myself rubbing my body all over that white shag. It'd be like a Rorschach. It'd be hysterical. But she'd never forgive me. "I'm going to shower. Look up the number for facilities in case I clog the drains."

Lucy nods slowly and puts a lollipop in her mouth.

The shower is long and hot. Everything aches. My skin stings. My muscles burn. Even my ass hurts from when he pulled apart the cheeks so ruthlessly there, with my face in the leaves.

And I love every single pain he gave me. I see I've got scrapes all over my knees from when he had me on my stomach. God. So fucking bestial, so animal, so *hot*. Growling in my ear that he loves me.

The very last thing I wanted to do was leave him. I want to keep my hand in his always. I want to have adventures and make mischief. So as I give myself another once-over with my body wash and check for remnants of dirt in my hair, I try to ignore the sinking feeling inside that says that we are ineffably, uncomfortably, impossibly doomed. I try to tell myself that this could be forever. Forever, forever, forever, Naomi. It exists. This feeling inside me could last always.

The squeeze bottle of shower gel sputters sadly.

And I try not to analyze the shit out of that metaphor.

Back in my room, still in my robe, I look at the calendar. Brutal. A million shades of events, day after day. I have been starting to fall behind, my mind has been so distracted by Ben. And now? God.

All of philosophy seems utterly trivial compared to Benjamin Beck.

Just before I'm going to crawl in bed, my email pings. It's from Professor Beck to the class, reminding us of our midterm paper. The prompt asks us to apply the philosophy of mysticism to *The Four Loves*.

Under the covers, I open up Signal.

nice prompt, professor.

Right?

> i'm glad you like the book though.
> i may be obsessed.

That last line. I realize he might think I'm talking about him. Am I?

It's too late for me. I'm there already.

> Me too. Me too. Me too.

••

The next morning, I wake up to a light rain tapping on the window. Minimal seepage through the gaps in the frame, and happily, no wet leaves either thanks to the packing tape. Still in my sleepy dreamy half-wakefulness, I know that what I really need to do, of course, is get things done for classes. Like make outlines and do some complex color-coded highlighting maneuvers. But instead I'm slated for an extra shift at the Beinecke, doing grunt work.

I don't even have time for breakfast, I realize, throwing on my clothes and grabbing an apple. I look outside. With a sort of flipping delight in my heart, I realized the old yellow galoshes are out and the new red Hunters are *in*. For a moment, a moment I don't have to spare, I admire them and me in the full-length mirror. I feel almost guiltily glad wearing them. Never in my life have I gotten anything so nice. Maybe it's just one gift, but never have I felt so spoiled by anybody. Not even Lucy. And that's saying something.

Today in the library, I'm in a new room in the basement that smells like carpet glue. One of the lights above me flickers, and the heating system whistles in the vents. The shift begins with moving small, ancient, paper-bound books to do entirely with butterflies into archival acid-free storage boxes. I have a strong suspicion these archival boxes are just regular boxes and the powers-that-be pay $50 each just to feel righteous, but I don't say that. I just do my job, arranging them carefully in each box with my white gloves and my paper hat.

This utterly simple task is overseen by a man with enormous glasses and a mass of curly white hair, who points at everything I'm doing. He is the world's authority on butterfly pamphlets. His name is Professor

Hammerwell, and he smells a lot like Rice-A-Roni.

Pamphlet. Box. Pamphlets, box. Occasionally he will sort of whisper something, "Oh yes, good! Capital!" when he looks at one of them.

"Yes! Miss Costa! Look! The monarch!"

"Wonderful!" Pamphlet. Box.

One of the librarians comes and interrupts us. She's very nice, really. A little odd, but nice. Her name is Lillian, and she's forever telling me things are "highly irregular."

"Miss Costa," she says.

Pamphlet. Box. "Everything okay?" I ask.

She looks at Professor Hammerwell and gives him a pair of nitrile gloves.

"Fine. How's progress?" She peers down her nose at me.

"Perfectly regular."

This pleases her *immensely,* and once she's recovered from the delight she says, "I'm wondering if you can help a professor get something from the stacks."

I'm flabbergasted. I freeze with a pamphlet semi-clutched between a thumb and forefinger, which Professor Hammerwell unwedges carefully from my grip. The thing is, I'm like stage management at the Beinecke. Neither seen nor heard and always behind the curtain. So this? This is *highly* irregular. "Sure, if you'd like me to."

She looks equally flabbergasted as I feel, in fact. "He did request you specifically," she says, as we leave Professor Hammerwell to delight over his pamphlets. We march through the floor-to-ceiling cabinets. She lets me out a fireproof door and shuts it behind us.

I'm thinking that the professor in question has to be Professor Sarka. I get all kinds of images of rare manuscripts of sea creatures in my head. Krakens eating boats, that kind of thing.

But it's not Professor Sarka at the bottom of the steps. It's Ben.

I yank the paper cap off my head and stuff it into my pocket.

Lillian, always very nice and demure and quiet, whispers, "Here she is, Professor Beck."

"Thanks, Lillian," he says. He isn't looking at me. I, meanwhile, am gazing up at him the way people look at statues of ancient Roman generals.

Lillian walks away, and that's when I whisper, "What are you doing here!"

My voice, though just an airy gasp, echoes all over the lobby, bouncing from marble surface to marble surface forever.

He's got his serious professor face on. "I need help in the stacks, Miss Costa. I told them you're a student of mine, majoring in Philosophy. I said it would be very educational."

Completely against protocol! How he does things, I just don't know. It could be those eyes. Those eyes could rob a bank. "And they just let you?"

"Lillian said it was *highly irregular.*"

I snort.

And he gives me this look like, *Good morning, sexy.*

I make like my heart is not parting my ribs and walk up the steps next to him. We pass the Gutenberg Bible. I don't give it a glance since I've seen the thing more times than I've seen a regular Bible, but Ben stops dead in his tracks. "Holy shit."

Seeing it through his eyes, I realize it *is* amazing. And it's amazingly easy, I also realize, to take magic for granted. "One time they let me turn the page. I had to use a special little page turning thing and had to hold my breath."

"This place." He shakes his head.

"They've got the Declaration of Independence somewhere," I whisper. "But never mind that, Professor."

He's towering over me now. Everything in me says *unzip his jacket!* But I just jam my hands further in my hoodie. "What are we after?"

"I don't fucking know," he says. His voice is lower, and the carpet here on the second floor dampens it.

"You just wanted to see me?"

He nods.

"At work?"

Nod again.

"We have to do *something.*" I gaze up at him, unblinking and warm all over for about three whole seconds. "What about Aristotle?"

"Perfect."

So I lead him into the viewing room, which looks just like a police interrogation room. Before we go in, I turn to him and say, "I have to search you."

A low growl sneaks out. His eyebrow answers, *Search away.*

"For writing implements, sticky notes, gum, lotions, chapstick."

His face softens in a kind of amused wave. He hands over a pen and a mechanical pencil that he had in his jacket. Burt's Bees. A small tube of sunscreen. "Habit," he explains. And his phone. I place everything in a small Tupperware bin in the hallway, then place it in a small locker, like they have at gyms, and hand him the key.

"You're very efficient."

I let my fingers linger in his palm before I drop the key. "I do try."

The viewing room has white walls and a white table, with blue industrial carpet. There's a computer station in the corner, but other than that the place is just a big table and two chairs.

When the door clicks shut, I turn around and he's right in front of me.

"Hello, beautiful."

The flush is immediate and wonderful. "I love that you made this happen."

"How are your knees?"

The answer is *battered*. But I just shrug. "They're...okay?"

He winces. "Mine look like I just learned to rollerblade," he smiles, and his eyes shift side to side, on the lookout for lookouts, and he reaches out to take me in his arms.

The blood whooshes in my ears. I know I'm not supposed to be doing this. I know it's dangerous, but I cannot help it. I actually cannot help it. His arms open, and I step into them, unzipping his jacket to get close to his body. Gore-Tex is not for lovers.

For a moment, I just keep my cheek to his chest and then slip my arms around him, beneath his jacket, feeling the warmth of his skin and the dampness of a freshly taken shower.

"What are we going to do?" I ask. Same as I asked last night.

He brings his hand up to my cheek, and his lips press gently on the top of my head. "We'll figure it out."

Groaning, I drop a little of my weight on his chest. "This is impossible."

"A lot of things seem impossible," he says, pulling me away a bit so he can put his eyes on mine. "But that doesn't mean they are."

"What happened to my nihilist? What happened to the guy who doesn't believe in anything, not even love?"

His blinks become a little faster, and I'm just floored. I know that feeling so exactly, when something gets you so far to the quick that the world gets blurry.

"You happened, you philosophy wrecker."

He kisses me then, deeply, tenderly, the kind of kiss I'd like to wake up to forever.

And that's when the door squeaks open. We part immediately, suddenly acting like strangers, muttering weirdly to ourselves like we've been so busy thinking we haven't had time to talk. It's Lillian.

"Just wanted to see what you needed access to," she says. But I can see from her eyes obviously going back and forth that she's putting it together. She's no idiot. And you'd have to be an idiot not to feel the energy in this room.

Ben blurts, "Socrates."

I say, "Aristotle!"

She eyes me particularly. "Let me know when you have a box number you'd like me to retrieve.

"Definitely," says Ben, raking his hands through his hair. "We'll let you know."

And then the door closes, I put my hands to my face and laugh softly and painfully into my palms.

29
ben

One thing I know for sure: Librarians miss nothing. Ever. They're like all-seeing spirit owls of the damned universe.

As the door shuts, I grab Naomi and kiss her as hard as I can. I don't care what the stupid librarian saw. I'm so hard, so pent up, I feel like I haven't been inside her in years. In fact, it's been less than twelve goddamned hours. So with my next kiss, I say, I hate you, I love you, I need you, and *I'll rock your world.* But she pulls away like she's been punched.

"Ben!" She wipes her mouth, still smiling but also watching the door. "God," she whispers. She's not kidding around. "You'll get me fired!"

She's right. It's like this lemon haze overcomes me.

"Do you have any idea what these hoodies of yours do to me? The thumbholes?" I make a noise that sounds more herd-animal than person

She makes this *I can't help it* face, and I want to rip those leggings down and take her right here over this ridiculously huge library table. She's also wearing my boots, the boots I bought her. The boots that make me feel like I own a little piece of the perfection that is Naomi.

I kiss her again. This time fast, just a press of my lips to hers.

I'm a wildman. My inner Hyde has been unleashed.

She starts smiling now. Her frustration has faded a bit. "You're unquenchable."

"Not my fault," I say. I'm possessed by this seam on her leggings again. These leggings are old ones, and soft. A little grayed from so much wash and wear. I feel all my resolve disappearing and take a step closer.

"Stop, stop, stop," she says, through whispers and giggles, and pushes me away.

"I need you to clear your schedule. Pretend you're sick. I'll write you a note," I say. "Masters, they can do that right?"

Her eyes flash in the most mischievous way. "I have to write papers. One of them is for you!"

"Screw the goddamned paper. I'll inflate your grade until it soars above the sky like a weather balloon. I gotta go," I say, moving away from her out of sheer necessity to keep myself from grabbing her again. "Keep your phone on you."

I leave her there, with her hands in the air. Outside the room, I smooth my rain jacket and squelch along in my boots. Escaping silently is impossible. Lillian is at the end of the hallway.

"Everything alright, Professor Beck?"

"Definitely," I say, "I just realized I've got office hours."

"On a Saturday?"

"Work never stops!" I say, and jog down the steps.

I'm noticing a pattern here. *Let that shit go* has, because of Naomi Costa, been replaced by *Keep your shit together.*

As I'm jogging past the Gutenberg Bible, I hear her whisper fill the huge marble cube of the Beinecke. "Professor Beck!"

I turn around in a circle. This is what people say when they hear the voice of God, I think. Completely disorienting, completely overwhelming, fucking transcendental.

"Up here!"

Now I see her. And she's holding all my stuff in the little Tupperware bin.

So I walk-jog up the stairs. What I'd really like to do is sweep her off her feet, press her up against the wall of the Rare Medieval Alchemy Manuscript section and kiss the shit out of her again, but I do not. I put my chapstick and everything else in my pocket, and say, "You make a mess out of me."

"Tell me about it."

I'm off again. I push out of the revolving doors, nearly maiming an old lady with a walker. Jesus. I can't decide if I like this new feeling. It's a sea change. Like when Beck (not me, the other one) recorded that album *Seachange* and everybody said, "What the hell happened to him!" Exactly like that. It's like a different planet that I have no desire to leave at all.

Standing out in the courtyard in the gloomy New England rain, I feel this wave of hope, this wave of the future. The light looks different, the world looks different. That girl.

She's given me something to believe in. She's taken me out of my own head.

So I head towards the Commons, thinking. Plotting. Scheming.

The work of every philosopher since the beginning of time.

30
Naomi

I'm working on the paper for Ben's class. Had it been any other professor and any other time, of course, I like to think I could have pounded it out with all the efficiency of a philosophy-analyzing machine—thank you, color-coded highlighters and Post-it flags! But now? Between Ben and C.S. Lewis and my lovebrain, I've got nothing. It's a confusing morass of utter B.S. that will probably read like word salad.

Skimming my eyes over the words, it's confirmed: Jello word salad. I've got dangling modifiers and sentences that end with, "???"

I cannot take my mind off that kiss in the viewing room. That kiss was different than any of them before. Kissing isn't fucking. Kissing is speaking without words. And today, in the viewing room, he was saying everything that he hasn't yet said out loud.

I stare at my screen. Wait. I'm making him lose control.

Me!

I try to focus. I have exactly zero idea what I'm writing, but I have four hours to write it. What I'm not going to do is skip this paper because God forbid anybody ever accuses him of giving me preferential treatment.

Midway through the second body paragraph, my phone buzzes

NICOLA RENDELL

under my leg. I freeze.

I have been able to focus through hurricanes. I have been able to study through drunken fishermen screaming insults at one another. I have been able to keep my focus with moderate sustained difficulty through two years at Yale. And yet now my phone buzzes and someone might as well have detonated a bomb in the quad.

There's no point in resisting. And I give in, opening up Signal. It's a hyperlink. My heart begins thumping wildly in my chest again. The first part of the URL says:

http://www.Airbnb...

Even though I live alone, I live in the constant threat of Lucy wandering in babbling while eating almonds, so I stand up and lock my door. Then I take a deep breath and open it up.

Romantic Private Seaside Cottage.

Mystic, Connecticut.

"This cottage, all by itself on rugged Mystic shoreline, has been completely renovated…"

The little thumbnail is beautiful. Sun-bleached shingle siding, pitched roof, balcony, beautiful garden…so beautiful and mystical, in fact, that it takes me a few seconds to figure out what's happening. I scroll down. He's booked the place for tonight. *For the two of us.*

Yeah?

yes yes yes

I love when you talk dirty.

you haven't heard anything yet.

Jesus.

I try to think of something double-dirty to say, but again I've got nothing. Not right now. I've got to get my hands on him to know just what to say.

158

Problem: Us leaving together is so suspicious.
Osgood will figure us out.

My wheels start spinning. Think, Naomi. Think. I have no car. And Mystic, an hour and a half away, isn't exactly somewhere that public transportation will take me. I click my tongue at my phone thinking, thinking…

Can you get there? I'll pay.

I feel my face flush hot and a little mad. Just him buying the boots and burgers made me ache, never mind the surely astronomical nightly rate of this beautiful cottage. I'm still independent, even if I'm dead broke.

i've got it covered.
when?

Naomi. Seriously.

ben. seriously!

Fine.
Be there at 6.

i cannot wait.
thank you.
so much.

Beautiful. It's nothing.
I can't wait either.

Staring at the thread, I let my mind start whirring even faster. Uber isn't happening. Zipcar maybe?
I've never rented one. I look it up, and no, no, no. It'll break me. Spring tuition is due soon. Meal plan. The panic of all the untold things, books and bills and the ordinary everyday stuff of just living starts to swell up around me. I shove it back down. Now is not the time to worry

about all that. Now is the time to enjoy this amazing thing that is about to happen to me.

So I stand up and swallow my pride. I go next door and knock on Lucy's door.

"Open!" she says. She looks a little like an 80s pop star with a slowly advancing coke problem; three days of double-dosed Adderall will do that to a person. Not to mention she's got her hair on her head in an actual scrunchie and is wearing tiny pink shorts with tube socks.

"It might happen this term, Naim. They might give me the ax," Lucy says. "Have you ever paid anybody to write a paper for you? There's a company in Singapore…"

I bear my teeth. "Don't you dare. Do the work. You know you can. Don't make me call you a wuss."

"I'm not a wuss! I may have a *small* problem with historical chronology. Why they insist on me taking history classes, I just don't even…"

"Wuss!"

Ooooh, she doesn't like that. Her eyes are flaring and her nostrils flashing, all the mixed emotions. "You got it? Do the paper yourself. You're not getting kicked out of here for something so stupid. Right?"

We have this same conversation twice a year. Singapore-wuss-art major-historical dates-wuss!-fine-fine! Like clockwork.

"Fine!"

The biannual academic ethics confrontation abating (oh my God, the irony), I flop down on her bed. She's got matching Marimekko sheets that are so pretty I used to be afraid to sit on them. Until I found out she has three sets.

"Here's the thing. I need some money."

She snaps her face towards me and then cups one hand to her ear. "That's it. *That* is the sound of hell freezing over…"

I lower my eyes and fuss with the buttoned edge of her duvet. She's offered to help me with everything all the damned time since I've known her. At every turn, I have resoundingly rejected every penny.

But this is different. This is for love. For hope, for Ben. For us. *Us!* "It's an emergency. And I'll pay you back with compounded interest."

"Don't tell me your dad fell overboard."

She's got this handle on the macabre that's almost superhuman. "No, but nice try. It's something else. I need to leave town."

Her nose starts shifting. "I'll give you whatever you need if you tell me his name."

160

"I always knew you'd end up a blackmailer. Remember when we saw that movie on Lifetime and I said you could totally play that part?"

She eats an almond. "You learn a thing or two in Greenwich. So… What's his name? Spill it."

The thing is, for the first time in my life I've got a secret from her, and I just cannot tell her. Even Lillian spotting Ben and me at opposite ends of the room was terrifying, never mind Osgood leering around corners everywhere. "I just can't tell you his name, Luce. I can't. I don't want to get you involved in it."

She looks surprisingly wounded by this. Not faking it. Just a big, sad frown. "I want to know. I've never seen you like this. I want to know who's got all the dynamite."

A prickle rolls up my back. "I want to tell you. I want to tell you everything, but I can't."

Even just in telling her that, I feel like I've pretty much told her everything. I've told her all my secrets right between the lines.

Finally, she gives a sort of final nod. "You're smart. And even if it's who I suspect, I won't tell." And she zips her fingers across her lips. "How much do you need?"

I lower my voice. "If you could spare $100, I'd be so unbelievably grateful."

She picks up her purse from the floor and pulls out her Burberry wallet. From the zipper compartment she takes two crisp hundreds and holds them in the air.

I stare at them as she rubs them against one another out there in front of me, making papery noises between us. "No. I can't. I'll never be able to pay you back ever."

"Stop," she says, pressing them into my hand. "It's not a loan."

"Lucy." I have no idea what to say. "Really…"

She jams her wallet back in her purse. "I'm only just paying it forward for when you have to come bail me out of jail one day."

As ever, my eyes begin to moisten and I feel that sting in my nose.

"Now get the hell out of here," Lucy says, kissing my cheek. "I have classes to fail."

31
ben

It's a day of firsts. First time I ever felt the desire to take a woman away on a romantic weekend, first time I ever booked an Airbnb, and the first time I've ever gone on a true, bona fide shopping spree, the planned contents of which show me just how much fun life with Naomi could be. Life. With. Naomi. Could. Be.

Don't drive off the road, Ben. Don't be that guy.

First things first, on my way out of New Haven, I stop at Home Depot for some utilitarian items. Nylon rope, zip ties, and a handful of assorted-width Sharpie markers: fine tip, regular, magnum, and king-size. Mercifully, the self-checkout lines are open, so I don't have to explain— "It's all consensual!"—or my outrageous hard-on.

Leaving Home Depot, I spot a thoroughly shady-looking establishment across the way called Kinx Adult Emporium. I drive over to it, not sure if I feel like it's Mecca or Chernobyl. She's so classy, so gorgeous. I don't want to debase her, I just want to make her squirm a little. To make her pant and writhe and slip that perfect tongue out over those lips. Or maybe it's me I'm making squirm.

Inside, I find it to be incongruously like a craft store. I don't know what I was expecting. Furtive men behind curtains? Porn sounds? That's not this place. I wish she was here with me so damned much it hurts. I want to walk down every aisle with her and ask a thousand questions about what she might like or might not like. Because honestly, I'd buy every fucking thing in this place if she wanted it. Feathers, harnesses, cock rings. Every lube for every purpose. Or none of it, if she didn't like it. But I don't want to make any decisions for her, for us. Not unless they're absolutely necessary. So, keeping my make-Naomi-happy mission in mind, I go to the vibrators. The array is *astounding*. I'm pleased, as a deep abiding feminist, to see that significant research-and-development money has been spent on the vibrator industry. As for what she'd like? God. Talk about personal. Briefly, I consider texting her to ask if she owns one or if she'd like one or what kind of things she might conceivably dig—gyrating penis with pearl beads, ten-speed battery-operated golf ball? Anything is great with me, provided it makes her feel exactly what she wants. But then I don't want to put a bunch of pressure on her. I want this to be just right.

So I go for the Hunter rain boots of vibrators: the Hitachi Magic Wand. Even if she owns one, she could always use another. To keep in my house, maybe.

Jesus, man. Pull yourself together.

Second thing, a blindfold. The choice is easy. Top shelf, nicest one, soft black satin—just like her dress that first night. And then on my way out the door, I grab a nice bottle of massage oil. Because you just never can tell.

When I get closer to Mystic, I start looking out for local groceries. Not because I'm *that guy that shops local,* but because I like the idea of finding things a world apart and the very best quality.

In the bags next to me in the Jeep, I now have assorted goodies. Fresh eggs from a local dairy I passed, fresh half-and-half. Tea for her, coffee for me. Strawberries, bananas, and the apples. Cheeses. Bread. Wine, both kinds, and champagne, just in case. I know she's not 21. Of all the rules we're breaking, that's the one that worries me least.

But there's one last thing:

Before I get to the house, I drive around Stonington looking for just the place. MARIE'S BOUQUETS catches my eye.

Flowers for Naomi. It's a bit of a gamble. Lilies? Roses? When the florist sees me walk in, looking no doubt disheveled and holding my old wallet patched with duct tape, her eyes slide over to a half-price bouquet of blue carnations.

"Alright. So. I want to buy flowers for a woman," I say.

The florist seems like she was expecting this. Of course.

"I love this woman," I said. When I say it I feel my nervous system bounce once, really hard, on the floor. "Love her, love her." The subsequent bounces prove no less jarring, and not in a bad way.

The florist said, "Anniversary?"

Holy shit, the possibilities of *anniversaries* sprinkle into the future like so many splatters of bright paint. How fucking amazing. But no, no. "We just started…"

Started what? Dating? That's not the word.

The florist narrows her deep-set eyes. "What's she like, this woman you love?"

Smart, pretty. Black hair, blue eyes," gulp, "freckles. Her birthday is in April. She studies philosophy. She makes me feel like I'm dreaming."

I smooth my hair and stop talking. Aside from everything else, she's turned me into an out-and-out babbler.

The florist smiles. "Have a poke around. See if there's anything that strikes your fancy."

I open up a few refrigerators and think that she kind of reminds me of sunflowers, but I can't go walking in there with a bundle of sunflowers, can I? No. I want *romantic,* not farmhouse.

But then I see them. I don't know what they're called. "Those," I tell the florist. "Wrap up all of those in the shop."

"That's more than a hundred stems, sir."

"Sold!"

And so, with my arms full of these flowers I can't even pronounce, I thunder down the old roads to the *Romantic Private Seaside Cottage.*

The place is beautiful from the outside. There are still a few leaves dangling from gnarled old elms outside. There's a gravelly path that goes around from the parking places to the front. The ocean is right there at the edge of the yard. Right. There.

Inside, it's also beautiful. Possibly a *little* nautical for my tastes—so many embroidered lobsters on the cushions, Christ almighty—but clean, and quiet, and ours. Just ours, that's what matters. I unpack the groceries and put my duffel upstairs. I come back down to the kitchen. I put my hands in my pockets. I look at the time.

Of course.

Only four freaking hours to go.

32
Naomi

The Zipcar is parked in front of a place called Alpha Delta Pizza, which will make anything from souvlaki to rice pudding to potato skins to eggplant parm. All the delivery guys are standing around in front of the door, surrounded by a fog-machine-like cloud of smoke. They wave to me, I wave back, and hop in the car. It's a white Prius with an audio cable waiting for my phone. Perfect, absolutely perfect.

I turn on the ignition, the engine makes no noise whatever, and I'm off.

As I drive, I feel myself letting go of campus and my life there. The pressure of deadlines and the archways lessens, and I let myself think, for just a second, about what would happen if circumstances changed. What would happen, say, if we weren't professor and student? What would happen if one of us did something to change things around? What if I took the pressure off myself and us? Us. Is there an us? I think there might just be an us. Early days, yes, but still. I'll never know if I never find out. So it's worth thinking about. Carefully, calmly, logically.

Which I can do. I think. If my heart would stop fluttering.

About twenty minutes into my thinking, though, it hits me—or

Google Maps hits me—with the news that I'm going to be *two hours* early.

Oh man. There's punctual and then there's waiting around, obsessively checking Facebook with your heart pounding in your chest for the love of your life to appear.

Gotta slow down, Naomi. Take it slow. No need to go full steam ahead. Illogically for the time of year, I get a craving for something cold and sweet. So I stop for a Slurpee at a 7-Eleven, and treat myself to some Good & Plentys, which make me think of absinthe on Ben's lips. The Slurpee, in turn, gives me a brain freeze, which I have to grit my teeth through with my head against the steering wheel right there in the parking lot for a while. I look at the clock. That ate up all of ten minutes.

Looking at the map, I see there's a non-highway scenic route. Being from Maine, I know that's Department of Tourism double-speak for *very slow road*. So that's perfect. It's Route 1, the original colonial Route 1. I see old historical marker signs that say it's the old King's Highway, established 1751. It feels like that, snaking between the gorgeous fall trees and pressed on one side up against big blocks of Connecticut granite. The drive becomes so slow and quiet that my mind keeps driving to different possibilities again. About how the world brings two seemingly opposite people together, who then can't imagine what they did before.

And about what in the world to do next.

I'm always doing that—pre-worrying my way through things that haven't happened or might never happen. For this, with him, I want to stay right here in the moment. For just this little while, I promise myself, I won't worry. I won't overthink. I will stay right here. With him.

The whole drive, my phone doesn't buzz. I don't know if this is because he knows I'm driving and is keeping me from being distracted, or because he's up to something. Or both. The thought of that, it gives me shivers and makes me feel like I've had way, way too much tea.

As I continue west, the sun begins to set. I roll down the window a little, to feel the warm autumn breeze. Imagine Dragons plays through the speakers and I feel like I'm back in high school. Life, in other words, is awesome.

Finding the cottage, on the other hand, is a bit complicated. On the Airbnb reservation, the owner said there'd be no cell service, and Google Maps would be no help. He wasn't kidding. As I turn down the tiny road on the far, far edge of Mystic, everything feels just like the 1770s.

Unchanged.

I pull over and look at the screenshot of the directions, and then wind my way through stranger and stranger tiny lanes and farm roads, no bigger than a horse cart across. Finally, I see it, CT Route 2. It's at a plain intersection, with massive stone farm walls on all four sides. I'm still a little early—fifteen minutes. So I pull over and sit in the dark car, counting back from 60. Fifteen times.

33
ben

After pacing around so much my shoes actually feel hot, I see headlights. With my knees on the window seat, I stare out and down the driveway. Holy hell, that's her.

Right, because who else is going to be, Ben? UPS? Pull yourself together, man!

I have no idea how she got a car, and I feel guilty for making her figure it out, but it had to be that way. Safety first, me figuring out a way to pay for the car later.

I hear her car door close, and then the trunk. The lights go off when the locks beep. I'm completely possessed by the noise of her feet on the gravel. Soft and light and beautiful. Nothing like my clomping around like a yeti. Her steps circle the house, and I creep towards the front door, not wanting to interrupt that noise. How I love that noise. Her coming to me. Her here with me. And then there she is in the doorway.

I don't move towards her. I just take her in. She's wearing this beautiful dark-brown sweater. It fits her curves just right. She's got her purse on her arm, her rolling suitcase behind her, and her red boots in her free hand. Her sweater is long in the sleeves, and comes down to her palms.

I'm a goner.

This is entirely different than anything before. This isn't the guest suite, this isn't the Jeep. This is a whole world, just for us.

"Hi," she says.

"Hi," I echo back.

"I can't believe this is happening," she says. She sets her stuff down. I pull my head out of asshole-land and take her suitcase. I carry it upstairs and put it on a luggage rack I found in the storage closet. I wipe my palms off on my pants, and then come back down to see her.

She's looking in the fridge, and she turns to me. "You've been busy."

"But wait!" I say, and go around to the dining area. I bring her the bouquet. It's absurdly, ridiculously huge, but looks even bigger in her arms.

"Ranunculus! How did you know?" she asks

I grin so hard my face hurts. "I didn't know. They just seemed like you."

She sticks her nose into them. I love that. I know they have no smell. But I love that she sniffs them anyway.

Here's what I thought was going to happen: I thought she was going to walk in, and I was going to kiss her like I kissed her at the library, and walk her backwards to the couch while tearing off her clothes in a frenzy. There'd be jeans flying and shoes clattering to the floor. Underwear hanging on lamps. I'd take her hard and aggressive and tell her I fucking love her and it's making me actually ache, it actually hurts my muscles and bones.

That is not how it goes.

Because I'm really nervous. Awkward and clumsy and tongue-tied. I look around for vases—that's how big the bouquet is, vases plural—and find a few, one under the sink, one on the shelf. All of them painfully nautical. Lots of anchors and flounders and sand dollars. At the sink, we divide the flowers up. She fills the vases, I arrange the flowers. Try to anyway. I have no idea what I'm doing. Do I put them in one by one? In clumps?

"That's…." She glances at me as she turns off the faucet.

The word is *sad*. "Here, I'll fill. You arrange."

"I had no idea you were so definite about gender roles," she says, with a tiny, sparkling giggle. And then picks up her left foot and tips towards me, balancing on her right. She presses the side of her head to my shoulder.

She makes me too weak to ravish her. All I can do is fill this vase and hope I don't make an ass out of myself.

The flowers distributed, she begins exploring while I get to work with the wine and cheese. I'm marginally better at arranging cheese on a plate than I was putting flowers in order, and within a mere five minutes, I join her on the couch. "Red or white, madam?"

"White," she smiles. "Red gives me headaches."

"Or champagne?" I add.

"Oh, yes *please*. That's perfect."

All those things. Headaches and quirks and preferences, that's what I want to know. That's what I need to know. The tiny minutiae of Naomi Costa. But also the big heart-filling dreams, and the little ideas that make life so damn much fun.

"Thank you, Ben. For all of this," She glances around. "I've never had anybody…"

I tuck her hair behind her ear. I see she's wearing pearl earrings again.

She puts brie on a cracker and hands it to me. She makes one for herself, and we sit there chewing for a second. She straightens out *Ships of the Royal Navy* on the coffee table.

"They didn't mention the nautical theme in the description," I say. I adjust a pillow shaped like a starfish that is presently jabbing me in the kidneys.

She frees one of the starfish legs. I think it was caught on my belt. Were her freckles always so pretty? "I like it. Reminds me of home. I'm from Maine, do you know that?"

Oh shit. What do I do, feign innocence? I memorized everything about her from the registrars' portal. "I did actually know that."

Crunch goes the cracker in her mouth. "You snooped!"

"I'm in charge of your well-being, Miss Costa," I say, putting on my best Yale voice. "It's my job to know these things."

She wrinkles up her nose. "I don't even know where you're from. I've told you I love you and I don't know where you grew up."

"Vegas," I say, making another brie cracker. "Charming place. View of the dumpsters, plenty of cockroaches."

"Oh God," she moans, one hand to her mouth and chewing.

"But it was near the library. So." I shrug. What I'm hoping is she can tell I grew up without the proverbial bean too. "What brought you to Yale, anyway?" I ask her. As soon as the words are out of my mouth, I realize it sounds like I'm asking *How did a girl like* you *end up here?* But she doesn't take it that way, thankfully.

"The scholarship gods."

"And you, obviously."

She rolls her eyes. "Maybe. I don't know."

That's not false modesty there. That's a girl who doesn't know that she deserves what she has. Who doesn't belong. And boy, do I know that feeling too.

"So, this thing with you and me..." She trails off.

No, no way. Don't tell me she's going to break up with me here. I freeze with my cheese halfway to my cracker.

"What, what's wrong?" she asks. "Why do you look like that?"

"If you tell me we're splitsville, I'll drink this whole bottle and probably fall asleep in the shower." I set down my cracker.

She adjusts her body to point towards mine and tosses the pillow over the back of the couch. She takes my hand in hers. "That is *not* what I was going to say."

"Jesus," I gasp.

"What I was going to say, Mr. Worrier, is that I've never felt this way. I realize I'm not even 21, but you know. Still..."

Now's the time to profess my love, except that I, who can fill three volumes with a whole lot of words about nothingness? No words. Sliding down to my knees, I'm in front of her, at her feet. My back presses the coffee table away, and I take her hands. "Me neither."

A little blush comes instantly up into her cheeks. As she leans forward to set down her glass, I stay put and am awash with the soft curtain her hair and the hollow of her neck. She doesn't pull back. Instead, she traces the tip of her tongue around the edge of my ear so gently, so effortlessly. My cock is instantly hard, and I slide back up over her body and pin her down lengthwise on the couch.

"We always end up like teenagers," I tell her, one knee in the cushions, before I lean in for a kiss. It occurs to me that wasn't all that long ago for her. But time, it's relative. Old souls are a real thing. I feel the laugh in her breath as she presses her leg against my erection, making me groan. I run my hands down her hips, gripping those sexy little jeans with my fingers spread. I hook a finger into her pocket and press. She tightens her legs around me, like a vise. Just like that, we get lost a while. The wind and the waves pick up outside, or maybe it's just the way she's kissing me.

"Do you know what I'm going to do to you tonight?" I say when we part finally. My voice is so dark, I don't even sound like myself. But being this close to her, I just can't help it. Without unbuttoning her jeans, I move my fingers down past her panties with my palm to that tight stomach. Then my fingers find their way to that magnificent wetness.

She moans a distracted, "Nun-hun," and leans her head back, bracing it against the armrest.

I work her clit gently for a while, just barely reaching inside her. With my tongue, I trace the ripples of her throat, all the way down to her collarbone. Every time I'm with her, I know her better. I learn her shudders and her moans. There's a particular one, a kind of surprised, delighted gasp that I've learned, a jagged breath, that tells me she's getting close.

I hear that and back off. Not yet. Not yet. I want to make this last and last.

"What's your feeling on rope?" I ask.

Her purr says, *Strong to very strong.*

Her hand is gripping the back of my neck and keeping me close. Her other hand is working its way down my zipper.

"Not yet. Not yet, beautiful. Not fucking yet."

Her hand moves away.

With that, I hoist her up on my shoulder and slap her ass as I carry her up the stairs. Halfway up, I lift her sweater from her stomach and begin giving her an epic hickey on that perfect, lovely curve between rib cage and abdomen, and she erupts into giggles and squirming kicks. I surprise even myself with the broad, wide smile I see on my face as I pass the bathroom mirror.

34
ben

She lands with a squeaky thump on the mattress, her hair a mess. Immediately she tries to put herself back together, but I don't give her the chance. I draw her up off the bed into my arms.

"I'll go slow," I whisper to her. Gently, I pull her sweater off.

"Now you," she says, reaching for my sweater.

I stop her hands. "No you don't. You've owned my ass long enough."

Her dark lashes part all the way, and I see the white of her eye around her irises. Now, God. That lip bite. Fucking A.

She looks amazed. "Have I?"

"Oh yeah. I used to be a fucking tiger in bed until you came along."

Her hands move up my abs and land on my nipples. "I think you're still pretty much a tiger, Tiger."

"You haven't seen anything yet." Now I'm unbuttoning her jeans and yanking them down off her ass. They peel off her inside out, and she's left in her panties and bra on the bed. I stay fully clothed. If she even touches my belt, I'm done for, I'll never be able to keep my cool.

"What are you going to do to me?" Her voice, it shivers with excitement.

"Nothing you don't want," I say, feeling the gentle ridges between her ribs through her skin. Everything about her, her rib cage, this little scar under her right breast, the bigger scar off to the left. Every last thing is perfect. Real. Honest. Beautiful.

This bra is especially nice.

Which is a shame.

It's plain white with a pink bow right in the middle between her breasts.

Lowering my body over hers, I run my tongue around the edge of her belly button, thinking about when it had overflowed with whiskey. I lay my ear down on her breastbone and can actually hear her heart thumping.

After a handful of perfect heartbeats, I turn my head, placing it between her tits. That's when I look up at her. She's craning her neck to see me, because I have her flat on the bed.

"I love this bra," she says, like she's warning me.

Shame, like I said. I take that little pink bow in my front teeth and yank it off. She lights up with the sound of ripping thread. It's part surprise, part exhilaration. Exactly how I want her.

Greedily, I pull her left breast out of her bra and feel her areola tighten under my tongue. Her hands grip my body whenever I bear down, and then continue on when I ease up a little. Her skin is so milky white, and so fucking soft against my lips.

Pawing at my face a little now, she's trying to get me to come up to kiss her. Hungry and desperate, trying to rush. But there is no rush, not here.

When I release her breast, I lick a little circle around one nipple and then the other. "Put your head on the pillow, Miss Costa."

She scoots up, hands to the mattress and never taking her eyes off me.

"Bra," I say.

She sits up, so perfectly obedient now. Off comes the bra, and her breasts swing loose. It's all I can do not to just take her right here, right now, and make the missionaries fucking weep. But she does that to me. She makes me take my eyes off the prize.

And I hate her for it. Okay, not exactly. Between hate and love, right there. Equidistant.

Now, at least, I've got a plan. I did think this part out because I knew she'd get me lost, just like she has.

Standing at the side of the mattress, I take a length of rope from under the bed. I'd stashed it there, because to do what I want to do, I'm going to need a lot of it.

"What are you…"

"Do you trust me?"

Her nod is so big, even her hair swishing against the pillows sounds enthusiastic.

"Good girl. Give me your left wrist."

With the rope in my hands, I stare down at her. My cock presses through my boxers and right into the teeth of my zipper.

Binding her left wrist first, I check and double-check that the knot is tight but not too tight. But the nylon rope is slippery. "Here. Let me. What you need is a non-slip loop knot," she whispers.

The sailor's daughter, of course, she knows her knots. Never was there anything hotter than a woman tying herself up.

That wrist done, I loop the rope around the brass bed frame but I don't knot it. I bring it back to her body, to her left ankle this time. I circle her ankle twice. Now to the footboard. She's trembling there in front of me. But I keep it together. Step by step, because there's work to be done.

The rope presses into her skin as I bring it diagonally across her until finally she's laid out in front of me, not just tied to the bed frame by wrists and ankles, but underneath a tight X of rope that will only hold her tighter if she fights me.

When I set to tying the finishing knot, she turns her head, smiling a little. "Yeah. Over, under. Right."

I see that her fingers are shaking, and she brings her palm closed into a fist. Her head is up off the pillows, tense and curious.

"That okay?" I ask. I pull on the rope. "Are you good?"

She nods.

"So relax, beautiful," I place my hand behind her head, and she lets me take its weight. "Don't fight me." Then I lower her head down onto the pillows and whisper for her to close her eyes.

Her smell is everywhere. Again, it takes all my willpower not to enter that pussy however I fucking can. Cock, fingers, lips.

I slip it over her head. "Can you see?"

Wordlessly, she shakes her head.

"Don't lie, beautiful."

She snickers. "Pull it down just a little."

So I do, until she nods. "We're going to need a safe word."

She swallows. Her head is deep in the pillows, her hair spilling out from every direction. "What do I say?"

I could let her pick it, but that's not how it's going to be. "Dominus. You say that, everything stops."

"Dominus," she says, trying it out.

"Latin for Master. Got it?"

Her swallow fills the room. I'm taking that as a yes.

35
Naomi

The next thing that happens is a familiar smell. At first, I can't place it. It's chemical and yet sweet…

Marker. He's got a marker. My whole body gives a sudden, excited shake. I think he's going to write on me. Somewhere, something, his handwriting in ink on my skin.

God, yes, yes, yes. Is that a thing? Writing on skin? Because that's so hot.

He's hovering over me. I can feel the mattress depressing on either side of my body, under his knees. "What are you going to write?"

There's an airy breath. I know he must be smiling. He smiles so much. I love that about him.

"What I want to write is *mine* on every inch of your skin," he says. I feel a touch on my arm, and at first I think it's the marker, but it's warm and soft. His fingertip. He trails it up my forearm, lingering on the shallow depression above my elbow. "Mine, mine, mine," he says. "All over you. A thousand times."

I can see it in my head. Mine everywhere. Big and little. Sloppy and neat. "Please. I'd love that," I whisper.

"I want to get a jar of ink," he says. Now his palm is flat on my stomach.

"And put my prints all over here." When he says *here,* which he says slowly, he slides his fingertips down my abdomen.

All I can do is nod. I have no way to tell him how much I want that.

The mattress squeaks a little as he lowers himself down on me. His weight is heavenly on my legs. The feel of his chinos pressing into my bare skin. The agony of knowing his beautiful cock is right there, not six inches from pressing into me. It drives me right out of my mind.

"But there's really one word that needs writing first. Before all the rest."

The words line up in my head like flashcards. Trying to guess. But then I just let it go. Let him do it. Let him take control.

The tip of the marker is cold on my skin. It begins on my right side with a downward stroke.

I, is what I think at first, but then there's a curve at the top. And a kick-out. *R.*

Another downwards stroke. *I* again? Nope. Three right-to-left lines. *E.*

Oh God, I think I know. Diagonal stroke, and a second. He makes the crossbar just over my belly button with agonizing slowness. *A.*

I know the word. But I just want to savor every last drop of this. Downward stroke, half circle. *D.*

Small check mark on my left abdomen, small downward stroke. *Y.* Already I'm nodding.

"Are you?" he asks.

And I tell him a long stream of *Yesses* straight through the squiggle and point of a *?*

READY?

My hands are in tight fists, my nails pressing into my palms. Whatever he's going to do to me, if it hurts or teases or pulls or pinches, I want him to do it. All of it. "Ready," I whisper back.

The next thing I hear is a snapping. Rattling of markers. Another uncapping. Now he's closer to me. I feel his forearm over the soft skin of mine. This is harder to make out, it's on my wrist and small. "What does it say?"

He doesn't answer at first. The little marks continue on my wrist. I hold very still, trying to get a sense of what it could be. "Ben," I whisper, "Tell me."

"It'll drive you crazy not knowing, I'll bet," he says when he's done. I hear him cap the marker shut.

God, yes it will. "You don't want me distracted."

His laugh is quiet and smug. I love it. "It says *Property of Master Beck*."

Annnnnnd toe curl! Everything curl. I try to reach up to touch him, but the ropes hold me tight. "I want you."

Now I hear his zipper coming down, tooth by tooth. Everything is so exaggerated because I can't see. He's not touching me though. He's off to my right. I hear his footsteps on the carpet. "You're gonna get me." I hear his belt clatter on the ground, and I moan right out loud, just at that sound.

There's nothing for a while. Perhaps he's just standing there watching. But then the mattress squeaks, I hear the gentle crack of his knee, and I feel the soft skin of his erection on my belly. He presses into me with just the tip, but not gently. Enough to make me feel fire in my muscles. I realize I'm clenching my fists in anticipation, and I stretch them out. God, to touch him right now.

As if he read my thoughts, his jaw is under my fingers. He glides his stubble back and forth. I lengthen out my fingertips as far as I can to touch as much of his cheek as possible. My pad of my thumb rests on his jaw, and then he turns and kisses my palm. "That's exactly what I wanted."

But then he pulls away, and I feel so helpless, so needy, so anxious for him to come back. His weight leaves the mattress. I surprise myself with a long stream of, "*Please, please, please, please,*" on my exhalation.

Suddenly he's on the other side of me, whispering in my other ear. "Do you know why this is so important to me?" he says, his breath warm against my cheek. "Why I need you tied down?"

This is all so disorienting, not being able to see him or touch him or read his expression in those dimples. I shake my head and whimper a "*No.*"

He's gone again.

The mattress creaks, and I'm relieved to feel his skin against mine again. Thigh to thigh. His hips part my legs a little further. I feel a small cramp in my ass as he positions me to take him. "To take back the power you steal from me."

That's when he presses into me. No hesitation, no waiting, no gentleness, just a smooth, forceful press of his body parting mine. My back comes right up off the mattress, and I feel the ropes bind me even tighter.

"Don't fight it, beautiful. Just let go."

Let go. I'd never let go for anybody, except for him. Just for him.

He's hitting my cervix, he's pulling my G-spot up and over with the tip. His balls meet my ass with every thrust. I don't try to squeeze him, I don't try to take over.

I'm his. I show him how much I'm utterly his.

There is nothing I can do, there is nothing I want to do. But I do, so fucking much, want his cum inside me. "Please, Ben, just…"

He's doing this thing to me, where I'm all half sentences and guttural groans.

"Why are you so fucking beautiful?" he asks.

I've never come during sex. I've never come from the inside out. But he's getting me really, really close.

"Answer me."

What was the damned question? "I don't know why. I don't know."

"Answer me."

He's looking for something. He doesn't understand that when he drives…into…me…like that, I can't even think. But why am I so beautiful? Why?

"For you," I groan out. "I'm so fucking beautiful for you."

His next thrust is more urgent, more desperate. "Good *girl*."

He goes and he goes. Without being able to see him and touch him, all my senses are between my legs. He feels huge inside me, and my lips feel swollen and sensitive. He goes harder and longer than he ever has before. With every thrust, our grunts couple up. His low, and mine almost a whine. And then just when I feel exhausted, when I stop focusing on coming?

I start to come "Oh shit, Ben. Shit, that's it."

My calves cramp hard against my curling toes. My biceps ache. I feel the rope on my nipples. And I'm gone.

As I'm going, it's like a switch flips in my head. I don't just want his cum inside me. I want to have forgotten my fucking birth control. I want to have fucked up and have us make a mistake that ties us up together. I want all the things that I know, I *know*, I'm not supposed to want. But I do want it. He fucks me harder, and the headboard bangs. The idea of his cum inside me makes me want to blow up my five-year plan with dynamite. And so what spills out of my mouth? What outrageous thing do I say before I can stop it?

"I want your baby."

He snarls out a gasp, but he doesn't slow at all. Instead, he says, "Did you take your pill? Are you good?" Another deep thrust.

"What if I didn't?" I did, but the primal idea of *not* having taken it? Holy shit. That makes me so incredibly wet for him, he has to feel it too.

He grips my waist with his hands and drives in again. "You don't know what that idea does to me, Naomi. You can't understand…"

I do know. Because I feel it too. Profoundly, irrationally, way down in my inner core. I scoot my head down a little so I can just barely see him through the edge of my blindfold. He's as serious as I've ever seen him. He's not pissed, he's not worried. He's *driven*. Driven and focused like he hasn't let me see him. Between gasps and drives, I whisper, "Get me pregnant. Do it."

And then *he's* gone, roaring against the ceiling, with the headboard thumping into the drywall as he growls out my name and says over and over, "How the fuck did you know…"

36
ben

I don't know what time we fell asleep, but I wake up early and feeling like a brand new man. For a while, I just lie there next to her, watching her sleep. Scooting down my pillow a bit, I get a tiny bit closer to her to listen to her breathing. I love the way she sleeps, with the covers tightly bound up to her chest. I watch her for a while, get the rhythm of her breath. I enjoy the quiet. College is nice, but also noisy. Kids yelling, music thumping, weird plumbing sounds. The silence between us out here, this is heaven.

I get up and head towards the bathroom, but I realize it's chilly in here—it feels like winter. I don't know what winter feels like, exactly, because I've never lived through one, but the fact that I'm covered in goose bumps and my balls recede into my abdomen is a pretty good tip-off. I take an extra blanket from the closet, this one amazingly non-nautical, and drape it over her body.

I brush my teeth, quietly as I can, and then I turn on the floor heater so everything is nice and warm when she comes into the bathroom. I also make sure I don't leave a mess in the sink with my toothpaste. I want it all perfect, just perfect.

The way she was tied down, the filthy things she said, I have this sudden urge to get the rope out again and wake her up ensnared. But letting that brain and body rest, that's fuel for me too.

I slip on my sweats and my sweater and make my way downstairs to the kitchen. It's even colder down here, open and a little bit drafty. I turn the coffee on and put some water to boil on the stove. She likes tea. I don't think she's noticed me watching her so close at the dining hall. Black tea in the morning. Iced tea at lunch. Chamomile with dinner, with a little drizzle of honey.

Rubbing my arms a little, I look around, and I think, *Beck. It's time you figured your shit out. Time you manned up.*

Time you built a fire.

It can't be that hard, I think, as I put on my boots and head outside to get some wood. I mean, people have been doing it forever, right?

Right.

I pick some good-sized logs and carry them in. I get down on my knees in front of the fire. Looks straightforward enough. Fireplace. Matches. Some kind of composite blocks or something, which I assume are fire starters. I make a sort of a pyramid out of the logs. Seems logical. Possibly.

Once, in some movie, I saw someone twist some newspaper up into a kind of roll. So I do that, trying not to make too much racket. Then I put the match to the paper and put it on top of the logs.

I light one of the fire starters and throw it underneath.

There, I think, standing up. Not so hard at all. It starts crackling satisfyingly. I dust off my hands and head back to the kitchen. Well done, man. Well done.

Back in the kitchen, I take out some of the fruit I bought for her and cut it up. Then I turn on the oven and open up my secret weapon: Pillsbury Cinnamon Rolls. The canister pops open with a doughy thump. I arrange them in a pan that I find in the cupboard and get to work on making her a tray for breakfast in bed.

There's a warm smoky smell in the air. I'd call it a burning smell, except of course it's not. Just the fire, or possibly some kind of something in the oven itself.

I tend to the coffee. That's one thing I can do, at least, is make coffee. I bought some tea for her too. Never in my life have I spent so much on groceries. And I realize, standing there trying to figure out how to open the Twining's English Breakfast box without tearing it in half, that I really love this feeling. Doing things for her, learning things for her, fussing over her.

Still though, that damned burning smell. And a sort of haze in the air. I turn around.

Thick, black smoke is pouring from the front of the fire. We're not talking a small fire situation here. The thing is growing and licking the edges of the mantle already.

And that's when the fucking smoke detector goes off. *Screeeeeeech* above my head.

For the love of all that is unsacred on earth, if the Mystic fire department comes, I'm going to die. What kind of man can't light a fire? What kind of man lights a newspaper and sets the house on fire?

I grab the near-boiling kettle of water from the stove and toss it on the smoke. This doesn't help. It just makes it so much worse. Then I hear thumps upstairs, her footsteps. "What's happening!" she yells.

"We're good! Go back to bed!"

Actually, we are not good. Not good at all. I take one of the vases and pull the flowers out and pour it on the smoke. The flames lick up towards a commemorative ship in a bottle on the mantle.

Her incredible, intoxicating laugh trails down the steps in front of her. Full speed, and naked, she dashes into the kitchen. "Just going to stand there, boy scout?"

It's like I'm paralyzed. All I can do is watch the mantle begin to smolder. I may or may not have my hands on my cheeks.

She's still giggling. She's searching the kitchen, and now fire extinguisher in hand, and like an absolute Smokey the Bear protégée, she pulls the pin on the thing and moves me aside.

"Open a door!" she tells me, heading into the smoke.

I manage to shake myself out of my low-oxygen fog and open the windows and doors. She sprays the fireplace all over with the retardant foam, which looks oddly like whipped cream. The whole emergency becomes nothing but a black sizzling mess.

"Well, good morning!" she says, turning around.

There she is. Naked, holding a fire extinguisher and smiling at me.

She smells like a cookout and looks like heaven. I don't think I've ever been happier in my life.

••

"I could get used to this," she says, padding around the bathroom tiles. She is aligning her toes with the grout lines, and comes up on the balls of her feet every so often before luxuriously lowering herself down onto the heated floor. Meanwhile, I've got one hand in the shower testing the water, and the other wrapped around her. The shower itself is like a showroom display of seahorse tiles. So many fucking seahorses everywhere. On the upside, it's enormous *and* it has a bench. On the downside, there is obviously something wrong with the water heater. Something very, very wrong.

"When you review this place," she says, "I really think you should suggest that they consider a nautical theme." She's examining a sand dollar on a display shelf. Utterly, profoundly deadpan. She turns to look at me in the mirror, which is made out of a fake life preserver, painted red and white.

I nod. "I'll mention it." The water becomes roughly the temperature of lava on my hand.

"Do you think they bought it all at once, like at some special Marshall's, or is it a collection?"

"Believe me, it's a collection. I mean, did you see the mugs?" Now the shower goes back to ice water.

"No...don't tell me...clams?"

"Whales, clams, flounders, some sort of regatta mug from 1997. It's a long-term effort."

Then she bursts into that mischievous smile. "How's it going there, Tiger?" She rubs her bare arms with her hands.

"Variable," I say. That's not the word. Insane is the word. I can't even really feel my hand anymore. Is it hot, is it cold? Are we going to have to go to Urgent Care for third-degree burns? Are we going to freeze to death?

She slips in alongside my chest and puts her hand next to mine under the water. "Oh my God," she says as it immediately starts steaming and then drops to something near sub-zero.

She toggles the knob herself. It's shaped like an octopus. Of course it is.

The temperature goes back to boiling oil. "Holy shit," she says, starting to laugh.

Back to ice.

And what ensues is possible the most delightful, contagious fit of laughter I've ever seen in my life. As it gets cold she starts giggling, as it gets hot, she pulls her hand away and cackles. "Maybe we should just use the beach shower outside. Or the garden hose."

Now I try toggling the octopus a little harder. It's wonky and loose on the bolt.

"There's a YMCA in Stonington," I say, peering up at the showerhead like *that* could be the culprit.

"Screw it," she says, and yanks me under the water.

She leans her head back into the now-icy rain shower, her shoulders lifted up towards her ears and hissing in the cold. She begins shivering, and I grip her hard. I'm shivering too. "Live together, die alone," I chatter into her freezing hair. Briefly, it gets hot, and we have to both step back. Holding hands. Then, miraculously, things do reach an equilibrium. Like us being under the water balanced everything out.

We are hesitant. I'm waiting to get scalded and snatch her away. It seems fine for now. I think.

"Every time I look at you I think of new things I want to put on you." With my finger I write new words all over her in the water. Want. Goddess. Minx. Beautiful.

She turns and takes me by the shoulders. "My turn."

With her first finger, she starts high on my chest, working down. I. LOVE. YOU. When she finishes, she looks proud of herself and smiles up at me, blinking away the water from her eyes.

I pull her close. "Really. I never knew what it was."

"I'll bet you didn't think it existed. Nihilist."

"True, actually. I thought it was..."

"A construct?"

I dig my fingers into her ribs. She tries to fight me off, but only a little.

"But it's not, is it?" she says, looking up at me. "It's real."

"God, is it ever real. So real I can feel it, taste it," I say. "So real, it's changed the very way I think."

I watch her press her lips to my chest and push some of her wet curls away from her shoulders.

She lowers herself down to her knees in front of me, that perfect flesh of her body touching the tile floor. She curls her feet under her body, one foot over the other, toes slightly bent.

"Show me what you like," she says, sliding her hands up my ass and looking up at me with the most devious innocence that ever was.

She just traces the tip of my cock with her tongue. I can feel my blood throbbing through my erection, and I take myself in my fist, keeping my left hand on her shoulder, my right hand on my dick. I begin working my length for her. She's watching so closely, studying everything.

"You look at me just like that in class," I tell her.

"This is what I'm thinking about in class."

She cups my balls in her hands, just sliding one finger along my perineum. I have to brace myself against the shower when she does. Her eyebrows rise like she had no idea that was going to happen.

"You know what you do to me. You fucking know," I say.

"Maybe," she says, and leans down, licking my balls.

Gripping myself hard, I move up and down, from head to balls, pulling the skin up and back again.

"You're ruthless," she says. "I could never be that rough with you."

"This is how I fuck you," I say, stroking faster and more urgently. I let go of her hair and lean my hand on the shower wall.

A small, sexy, *"Jesus,"* slips from her lips as I stroke base to tip.

It gets me so high, watching her like this, watching her watch me. It feels so fucking good, I know I'm close. That worshiping position she's in, it's killing me. She's got my balls in her hands, and she positions herself right at the end of my length, but she doesn't take me in her mouth. Instead, she opens her mouth and stays right in front of me, with her tongue on my frenulum. Waiting for my cum.

There are few things that make a man come harder than an open mouth, begging for his cock.

37
Naomi

As I towel off my hair, I admire the way his waist narrows, and that six-pack besides. Eight-pack. Is that a thing? I trail my fingers up his arm. "Who are you? Where did you come from?"

He smiles down at me, his strong hand on my back, "My question exactly."

From the counter, he hands me my lotion. "Lemon sugar." He shakes his head.

"What?" I ask.

"First time I met you, I couldn't stop thinking about the way you smelled. Like lemonade." With one hand he moves my hair away from my back and turns me around so I'm facing the mirror. He fills his hand with lotion and begins massaging it into my skin. My eyes close instantly, and I brace myself on the sink. My sort of helpless *"yes please"* moans fill the bathroom.

He gets seriously to work on my body, staring with my shoulders. And this isn't some amateur shoulder rub. This is serious. This is *amazing*.

"You're tight up here," he says.

I mutter a *"lots...of.... papers"* in between the rubs. He moves down, on to my scarred side.

It's not that it hurts, but I'm sensitive that it's there. I'd damn near forgotten it, except now in the slowly un-fogging mirror, it's impossible to ignore. I forget how ugly it is because I so seldom look at it myself. Gently, he puts lotion on that side. "When did that happen?"

This isn't really a story I want to tell. But it's one of those things I want him to know. One of those horrible things that someone who loves you should know. The things that shape us are sometimes hard to say. "Thanksgiving Day, five years ago. I was on the boat with my dad."

He moves away from the scar, rubbing lotion now into my hip. "You fell in."

"I was knocked overboard by a wave." Even just saying it, I can feel the fear come back up into me. My boots filling with water, my body getting heavy, feeling the foam and gasping for air. "The propeller was going full-bore."

His hand doesn't move further, frozen on my hip but gripping me a little tighter. "Jesus."

I glance at him. I feel the cold run through me even though everything is warm right now. I feel the water going up my nose. I place my hand on the scar, on the three big diagonal cuts. "When it happened, when I was in the hospital, I remember them saying they'd never seen anything like it. That they couldn't believe I was alive. They didn't realize I could hear them."

He presses his fingers to his nose. His eyes are worried and focused right on me. "You're so lucky."

"Three pints of blood lucky," I say, nodding.

He begins massaging me gently on the shoulders again, as if he's tongue-tied maybe, because what's a person supposed to say when they learn about a near-death story? That's why I never talk about it, partly. His hands travel down my back, and the heel of his palm stops on my ass. He begins pressing into my left cheek nice and hard, placing his knee between my leg and his other palm on my chest for leverage. It's almost not sexual—I mean, it is, he's massaging my ass with his huge hands and I'm outrageously turned on—but it also just feels *amazing*. "You're..." I stutter. It feels *so damn* good. "...Really amazing at this. You could moonlight...as...a masseur."

He squirts more cold lotion on me. "Actually, I'll have you know, that's how I put myself through grad school."

I open my eyes and look at him in the mirror. "Seriously?"

He's smiling while he's working on my neck a bit. I feel it in the soles of my feet and all through my skull, somehow. "Nobody knows that. They wouldn't hire me as TA, so," he kneads into my back with his thumbs, "I did this instead."

But then he stops.

My pathetic, spoiled groan surprises even me. "Noooo. Please, no, don't stop."

Lowering his head to kiss my shoulder, he smiles into my skin. "I'm not going to stop. I'm going to do it right."

And so upstairs, on our messy unmade bed, he lays me out flat. He produces a bottle of actual massage oil and proceeds to give me an absolutely, astoundingly, mind-bendingly good massage. I'm fairly sure I'm drooling into the pillows, and I don't even care. He pinches my skin a little, up and down my spine, he does that thing with the sides of his hands, making little hatchet moves back and forth. He tells me to breathe through knots. It's absolute unmitigated heaven. This man, who I adore, working out every last knot in my body. With every touch, I feel myself getting more and more turned on, and yet I'm helpless to do anything about it. I feel myself getting wetter and more relaxed, more pliable and softer with every slip of his fingers.

He's straddling me, and I can feel him growing harder and harder against my ass. "I feel you," I tell him, muffled by the pillow.

"75% of massages end in sex, you know," he says, laughing a little.

Into the pillows, I say, "Really?"

"I made that up," he says, and then flips me over. I'm expecting things to get instantly steamy. But they don't. He's rock hard, and I can see that. I can feel it on my flesh, but he massages the rest of my body with that same tender, incredibly strong and authoritative touch. He touches my breasts, and they perk up for him instantly, but then he begins massaging the muscles beneath. "Holy *shit*," I say. I can feel that one in my ass, amazing. Everything is a web.

"I need to do this for you more often."

"Like, every day," I say at the ceiling. He does a gentle pattering down my stomach. He works my thighs, even delicately massaging my face. His thumbs run softly over my cheeks, pressing down with just the right weight. Then to my temples. Then to my ears. I am utterly, powerfully, painfully turned on by this point. "I need you. Inside me.

Please."

"What, is this torture?"

Of the positively worst kind. "Please, please. Ben. Please."

He's right over me. I'm near paralyzed with pleasure as he presses into me. He leans over to the bedside table and takes out a thick zip tie. In one hand he pins my wrists together and then zips the tie closed, making sure he doesn't pinch my wrist bones.

And then I hear a buzzing. "I want to make you come hard," he says. "On me. Just like this."

I press my nails into my palms and feel a rush of extra-thick wetness. That's a Hitachi. A magic wand.

"Do you have one of these?" he says.

"Nun-huh," I tell him. I've seen them□who hasn't?□but I've never had the money to buy one. "Never."

"No vibrator ever?" he asks.

By way of answer, I slip my fingers down towards my clit. "These have always served me really well."

His dimple appears. "I think you may be in for a treat. I bought this for you. Yesterday. When I got the blindfold."

Honestly, the buzzing is almost scary. I have no idea what to expect. He presses it to my thigh to let me feel it. It's almost warm, deliciously warm and soothing. The head bends back just right. "Just for me," I say.

"Oh yeah. All for you."

He gives me a few good thrusts, and I squeeze him tight. "Damn it, Naomi. Why? You and your fucking Kegels."

I laugh at the ceiling and give him another good squeeze.

"It's not gonna work this time," he says, shaking his head in a no-you-don't way. "You wore me out in the shower."

And then he presses the wand to my clit. I'm unable to keep squeezing him because instantly, *instantly,* I start coming. Coming in a totally different way than I ever have before. An electrified, whirring rush.

"Whoa, whoa, whoa," I tell him, pressing my bound hands to his chest. He's got this look on his face, utter satisfaction and nodding like he's made something delicious for me and he's watching me eat it. "Oh my *God*, what is *happening?*" The feeling, it's not just an orgasm. It's a whole roller coaster of delight. I feel like I'm coming out of it, and I start squirming under him, but he doesn't take it away.

He keeps the vibrator right on me, and I dissolve into him, into it, into myself. Again. And then again.

"Enough, enough," I pant, wrenching it away from my body. "I want *you* now."

But he just shakes his head. "That was for you. And right now," he says with a lick of my ear, "I'm taking you on a picnic."

38
ben

I help her out of bed because she looks weak in the knees. "You're beautiful when you're wrecked."

"A picnic. A *picnic?* I want to stay here and eat grapes off your chest." She flops back down on the bed, drawing up the covers over her face. From under the sheets, she says, "Can't we just stay in bed forever?"

I help her out of bed again, this time both her hands in mine, and walk her towards her suitcase. "Promise. You'll love this."

She blinks hard. Her brows lower. "When do we have to check out?"

"Two."

I can feel her disappointment in the way she slumps against me. "Please. Come on. The bed is so warm. You're so warm. That vibrator is so warm."

"We have to eat. And this'll be worth it," I say, running my thumb down the thin, sharp bone of her jaw.

"Alright. I trust you," she says. As she does, she presses her head down towards my hand, so I'm cupping her cheek in my palm.

And I feel a wave of — God, what is it? Happiness, it has to be happiness—run through me.

"What should I wear for this junket?" she asks. She's already putting on red panties and so I'm completely unable to speak. She snaps the elastic, and I snap to. "Whatever you want. Thumbholes are a major plus."

"You do love them," she smiles as she pulls on black leggings.

I nod. "I don't understand what they're for, but goddamn, if they aren't the cutest things in the world."

So, after eyeing me a second like she's deciding what weapon to use, she takes out a red bra and snaps it on. She adjusts her breasts slightly, drawing them up with her fingers to make them look just a little more perfect, and I have to hang on to the banister. Then she picks out a white, long-sleeved thermal shirt with buttons down the front that fits her absolutely like a glove, and finally a navy-blue hoodie. With thumbholes.

"When you're dressed up, you've got power," I tell her, zipping up her sweatshirt, "But seriously, when you're like this. You could get me to do anything."

"Anything?"

"Anything."

"Like, maybe, make me some tea while I'm getting ready?"

"Done and done," I say, and throw on my clothes, trotting downstairs. I find two mugs, whale-themed, and get coffee and tea started. Bonus, the oven is preheated, and I put in the rolls.

This floor smells like fire, and I wonder what'll happen to my security deposit, but I'm not worried. Even if I have to pay for ServiceMaster to come clean this place up, it's worth it.

So I get to work. I assemble everything for the picnic. The baguette, unfortunately, has taken on the texture of an aluminum baseball bat. "We have to stop for bread," I yell up to her.

"Muffins. We should get muffins," she says back.

Cheese, fruit. Chocolates. An avocado that is now, miraculously, ripe. It all goes into the shopping bag on the counter. Two bottles of water, some paper towels. The wine. I find myself grinning almost stupidly as I do all this. Who knew falling in love would be so much fun?

When she comes down, I realize I'm probably looking like her prom date, waiting for her to come down in her dress. Screw it. That's exactly how I feel. She steps into her Hunters, I step into my own boots. And after a few more minutes, with hot cinnamon rolls in hand, we're off.

At the Jeep, I open her door for her.

She says, "I can do this part myself, you know. I'm not that girl that needs doors opened."

Yeah, but she just doesn't get it. "Never again. I'm opening them always."

Shaking her head at me, she smiles.

"What?" I wipe my fingers down my lips. She's looking at me like that, like I have something on my face.

"You make me melt."

God. Ditto.

We head east, listening to Wye Oak and then Bear's Den. My first New England fall. Blood red, bright and eerie. On the way, we stop at a bakery, and she insists, absolutely insists, on buying the baguette and the muffins. I relent.

East we go from there, into Rhode Island. The day is beautiful, and just riding in my Jeep with her, I feel peaceful for the first time in as long as I can remember. Believing in nothing, it was taking its toll.

"You're nailing it on the sweater hunt," she says. She reaches over and adjusts the fold on the wooly turtleneck I'm wearing.

"I mean, I just kind of let L.L. Bean guide the way," I say. "But I could use your help picking things out."

She beams. "You want me to help you pick out your clothes."

"I'm good on the warm weather stuff. And I know what pants I like..."

"I know what pants *I* like," she says, and grips my thigh.

"But sweaters. I don't even know where to start. However," I reach into my jacket and grab a beanie, sticking it on my head, "I feel like this works, right?"

She gives a sort of a delighted moan. "Yummy. You're so yummy. I've seen that before, you know."

I think back. "Oh fuck. On the ice."

She nods, grinning and facing the road. "Spectacular. You need to get a pair of Yaktrax."

The what? "New England, even just being at Yale, it's like coming to a different planet. It *is* a different planet."

"I remember that feeling. I still have that feeling. I still think they're going to discover me as a total fraud," she says. She's eating her muffin, berry by berry.

Those words. *They're going to discover me as a total fraud.* Whoa. "*You* think they're going to discover you?" I say, taking my eyes off the road for a little longer than is probably advisable. "You do? You were admitted.

You had grades."

"They make mistakes in admissions," she says.

Holy fuck. Does she really think that? "No, they don't."

She rolls her eyes. Embarrassed. Ashamed.

"Department of professors, that's who make mistakes," I tell her. Because that, I believe, is most assuredly, unequivocally true. "I wrote a book that ended up on a jacket that ended up on a music video. And then they gave me a job? Talk about a fraud."

"Oh come on," she says. "You don't really think that's why they hired you."

"Are you kidding? I *know* that's why they hired me," I say. From the dashboard, Google tells me to take the exit for Westerly, Rhode Island. I haven't put in the *exact* place, but close enough to get to where we need to go.

"Haven't you ever looked at your Rate My Professor stats?" she asks. She looks utterly incredulous.

"Haven't *you* ever looked at your grades?" I say it with just the same tone she's using on me.

We sit in sort of a mutual, incensed huff for a minute.

"Grades don't matter," she says finally.

"Neither does Rate My Professor."

She shakes her head. "You deserve your job. Everybody loves you. Not just me."

I cannot even handle that logic. "I'll tell you a secret I'm not supposed to tell you but fuck it. At the last faculty meeting, Phelps and Davidson were *fighting* to get you to do your senior thesis with them. I mean, a full-on debate."

Her eyes show me she's relented a little. And I hear her mutter, "If I even make it that far."

"What?" I ask, gripping the wheel. "What was that?"

"Nothing," she says, quickly looking away.

I want to press her on that. But I don't. I can see she's rattled by the way the color comes up into her face. And the last thing I want to do— that I ever want to do—is upset her.

After a few miles she says, "I never thought of you as an outsider, but I can see how you'd feel that way. I think that's why you're so..." she stares out of the windshield, "...special."

Whether or not she's right about me doesn't matter. I've got twenty years on her. I can see this with way more clarity that she can. But she doesn't get it. She can't see it. So I lean over, and pull down the visor in front of her eyes, and flick the mirror.

"What..."

"You might as well be talking about yourself."

Her gaze is searching and suspicious. But I know I'm right. And she knows I'm right. If she believes it or not, that's up to me to prove it to her.

∴

I pull up in front of the beach. It's a beautiful, rugged swath of sandy dunes, studded everywhere with clumps of beach grass blowing in the wind. It's perfect.

Except it's on private land.

I hadn't counted on that. Nope. Hadn't seen that part coming.

So we stand together in front of the fence, with a big sign that says:

NAOMI BEACH
NO TRESPASSING

Her eyes are moist as she looks from me to the sign and back again. It's not the wind, I don't think. I love making her get a little misty-eyed. My new favorite thing.

But the wind, incidentally, un*real*. Sand stings my face in little needle-like pinches.

"I didn't know this existed," she says. "How did you find it?"

It was chance, actually. Incredibly circumstantial chance. Something that I really never credited before. But when I was looking for the Airbnb, I zoomed in on Block Island at first, and to the west her name caught my eye. I thought I was seeing things, but I wasn't.

She's so freaking adorable there in front of the sign. I grab my phone from my pocket. "Smile," I tell her.

"No, no," she says, grabbing my hand. "Us together."

And I snap a selfie of the two of us, with her name right behind our heads.

"Why is it so insane here?" I ask, hanging on to my hat and gripping the picnic bag.

She laughs, but the sound gets sucked away into the wind. "There's no Sound to protect us." She points. "This is the *ocean* ocean. The real deal." She pulls her hat down a little further. "This is how it is at home. The Atlantic is savage. Isn't it amazing?"

That blush, that delight. Emergency exits. Private land. Codes of ethics. Burn that shit to the *ground*. I'll do anything to see that smile.

I climb over the fence, put down the bag, and hoist her over with my hands to her waist.

"You're such a romantic," she says into my shoulder as I set her down.

"Pfffft. All your fault."

Hand in hand, we walk towards the ocean, down a path slightly overgrown with sea grass, and dusted every which way with snakes of sand. The waves smash against the beach, in big gray furious snarls. We pick a place up a little ways, past the farthest edge of the waves.

I unfold the plaid blanket I borrowed from the house. It's got an eighteenth-century Man o' War on it. She trots off and comes back with four good-sized rocks, which she places on the corners.

"Brilliant."

'Thank you, sir," she says, and the sun catches the blue of her eyes, and I find myself crinkling the grocery bag in my hands.

We take our places on the picnic blanket. Side by side, her in a little ball and me cross-legged, we just enjoy for a second. I put my arm around her, and she lets her body drop against mine.

From the bag, I pull out a strawberry from the little plastic box and say, "Close your eyes. Open your mouth." Yep. That's me. Feeding strawberries to a woman on a beach. I am the cliché. I am done for. "I never thought I'd be this guy."

She chews and smiles, finally opening her eyes. "I like you as this guy."

God. I jam a strawberry in my mouth, because so do I, and I just don't know how to say it.

So together we sit. I make a sandwich of brie and avocado, with a dusting of sand. We talk and talk about all sorts of things. I learn her birthdate (July 20), her favorite color (pale yellow). She likes salty more than sweet, and has a thing for buffalo wings.

"Favorite book?"

"I have twenty of them," she says, wrinkling up her nose. "The Patrick O'Brien books. Do you know those?"

Do I know them? "'*What a fellow you are, Stephen!*'" I quote back to her. And she laughs and laughs, falling down on the blanket.

We drink the remaining white wine from last night straight from the bottle, passing it back and forth. Sharing all sorts of secrets.

Finally, over chocolates, when we're both a little quiet and the wind too, I tell her, "I want you to know, I also lost my mom when I was really young."

Her eyes widen and search my face. "Did you really?"

"Yes. And my brother," I tell her. My voice gets jagged just saying the word. "So, I get it. Kind of. As much as I can," I say. "And that, I think, is all I need to say. Until you want to say more."

She places her head on her knee. "Thank you."

Pressing a kiss to her temple, I want her to know that I get it. Completely. All the stupid questions, all the sad looks? None of that is needed. It's all understood.

Then she does what I don't have to the courage to do: She addresses the elephant. I honestly didn't have the balls to look him in the eye myself. But she does. Of course. "But, Ben. What the hell are we going to do?"

I play with the cork a while. The vintner, if that's the word, is The Divining Rod. Something about that feels just right.

"We'll find a way," I say. What I don't say is, *I hope.* Which is how I feel.

"You think?" There's a storm coming in, and the sky is dark behind her beautiful face. The ocean, that face, all this. God damn it. This cannot last forever. Happiness like this, it's got to be fleeting. But I'm going to hang on to it as tight as I can.

"We have to," I say, pulling her close. "Because I don't know what I'm going to do without you."

39
Naomi

After our picnic, with frozen fingers, we return to the Jeep. It's desolate out here, nobody anywhere at all, and a storm is coming. "Thank you," I say. "For everything."

"That sounds like a goodbye," he says.

"Oh no," I tell him. "Just the opposite." I carefully maneuver myself on top of him in the driver's seat. It's a tight squeeze, and my new boots squeak like crazy. But I do manage it, and lower myself down onto him.

"Here?" he says, holding on to my hips a little bit tentatively.

"Here," I say, and unbuckle his belt with my numb fingers. The skin under his sweater, so deliciously warm, and I feel him shudder as I warm my hands up against his body.

With my back wedged against the steering wheel, there's just enough room. He's that tall, the Jeep is that big, that we don't even need to slide the seat back. I make slow, small, purposeful circles with my hips and feel him harden beneath me.

"I need to get this off you," he says, and with one hand he lifts me towards him as if in a tight embrace, pulling my pants halfway down my ass with the other. I free his cock from his jeans and slide it into me.

His groan fills the space, louder than the wind outside by far.

I slide my sweater away from my body. I pull and tease at my skin, sliding my hands up and down my torso, pinching my nipples. I reach over to my purse and grab the markers from the house. I offer them up to him in a row.

"Good girl."

"I knew we might need them."

He picks the regular old Sharpie. Still inside me, he presses me back against the steering wheel. On my left breast he writes, *Need*. On the right one, right over my nipple, *Want*.

Taking him deep into me, I touch my clit with my palm and let my fingers slide down around his cock. That finest feather-light touch. I bind myself to him, gripping his neck as a ballast.

"Come with me," I whisper. I feel his hips tense up immediately beneath me. Our eyes locked, I nod a little. Getting closer. He keeps me tight with his hand, reaching up behind my back and pulling me down by my shoulder.

He's watching me so intensely, I know he's looking at my pupils. That's how he focuses on me. Down to the very flutter of my nervous system, made real in my eyes.

"There, there you are," he says, glancing from my left eye to the right one and back again.

He's right. I start to cry out, and his thrusts take over from under me. "Please. Don't let me go alone."

With arms hooked under mine, his fingers pulling down on my shoulders, he pulls my face to his. "Never. Never fucking ever again."

And so we come together, utter perfection, as the sand starts battering the windshield.

40
ben

It's time to go. For so long, I had a wall against all the emotions—sadness, happiness, love, joy, worry—but she's broken those walls down. And so sadness, he hits me like a motherfucking cage fighter. It's a brutal, worried, empty feeling, like a kick to the stomach when I'm down already, already heartbroken that we have to say goodbye.

We pack up our things in silence. I have no idea what to say or do, really, except, "We'll figure it out."

But I can see she's sad too, and I'm not sure she believes me.

"If I lose that scholarship," she says.

"You won't."

"Or you have to leave…"

"I won't."

What the hell am I saying, talking like this? As if I have any idea what's going to happen. But the thing is, I need to reassure her. I have a desperate urge to tell her it's going to be okay. The irony. My whole life I've been telling everybody it's *not* okay. Now here I am, trying to tell both her and myself that faith is real. Faith in things working out, suddenly, is something I *need* to believe.

At the door of her Zipcar, I wrap my arms around her waist. She raises both hands and places them around my neck. "Thank you," she smiles up. "I'll see you in the dining hall later today, maybe?"

It's like an arrow. That's not enough. That'll never be enough. Not now, after this time away together. "Of course you will. Over lemon bars. Or cauliflower."

It lightens the mood just enough for her to get up on her tiptoes to kiss me goodbye. I make sure she has her seat buckled and tell her not to be an idiot and text while she's driving.

"I won't," she says. "Promise." She smiles up at me, past the roof of the Prius.

I thump the roof with my fist. "I want the receipt for this, Miss Costa."

"It's okay," she says, "I have it covered."

"Please," I say.

She lowers her eyes and reaches out to hug my body. It's awkward and beautiful. "Okay. That's a deal."

I watch her pull out of the driveway. There is a knot in my throat and a hole in my stomach. It's like an aching, throbbing, dark nostalgia for something I knew once but might never know again.

I hope so fucking hard that this isn't the end for us. With all my heart, I love her. But I know, as she disappears down the way, that we might be doomed. That we are star-crossed. That our love is impossible. And for the first time in as long as I can remember, I wipe tears from my own eyes.

41
Naomi

Back at Durham, the dream over, it takes only a few showers for his words to wash off my body. Of all of them, *Lover,* written boldly above my ass is the very last to fade.

During the following week, in class, I watch him closer than I've ever watched anybody in my life. He utterly possesses me. I watch him with the intensity of a lover while still acting like his student. I always dawdle after class, messing with my phone, hoping for a chance to be alone with him, but that moment never comes. Students love him and ask a thousand questions, until the next professor enters the lecture hall. So that we have to part with just a glance and the barest smile.

He doesn't come to my room—that was pure madness. We are careful in public. At fellows' dinners, I stay on the other side the room, only occasionally passing by him with a plate of cut-veggie nonsense. At Master's teas, I stay by the door while he stays by the fireplace. If we need to, we make cordial talk and don't hold our stares too long. When I get close to him, I can actually feel my body tense up. It takes all my willpower not to reach out and put a hand on his chest. Osgood seems placated, but I notice him keeping a close watch on the butler's pantry.

November barrels on. We text, trying to find another way to meet. One night, he does pick me up way past campus on Crown, and we drive to an abandoned parking lot and make love in the back of the Jeep. Every night I fall asleep like some lovesick schoolgirl, clutching my phone, thinking of him four stories away, alone in his bed, hopefully doing the same.

Life itself becomes fuzzy and distant. I go through the motions, but I forget ordinary things. My laundry piles up, my to-do list for classes gets longer and longer. For the first time ever, I'm late handing in a paper. My thoughts are all with him, not with the world. Until one day, I realize all of a sudden what I would have ordinarily seen coming a mile away:

Tuition is due, and I'm short.

It's not that I haven't been careful enough with my money, it's just that there's not enough money to go around, not enough hours in the day to work.

I do the math again and again. I'm short. A thousand dollars short.

I know why it's happened, and it's not because I'm lovesick or in the clouds. It's because every term, I dip a little ways into my savings—the tiny bit my mom left me—and finally the little dips have added up to a big one.

Right on cue, my dad calls.

"It's a glut. You have to come back," he says. No hello. Just an update on the situation on the boat.

I stare at my bank account. "Dad. Listen…"

The seagulls fill the silence on his end and the rain hitting my windows on mine.

"I need some help. I'm short on money for room and board."

Oh, the satisfaction that must be on his face. I'm sure even the stupid lobsters notice it.

"I told you this was going to happen," he says.

I'm filled with a rage so profound, I can't even reply at first. Sometimes I wonder what my mom must have seen in him. That cockiness must've been attractive once. When it was totally inconsequential. But now? Now, he's just an arrogant, distant thorn in my side. If she were alive, she'd probably have dumped him out to sea herself. "My grades are fine. It's the money."

"Lobster's down to five a pound. Five a fucking pound. For lobster. I can't haul it in fast enough, and I make shit when I do. It's hardly worth my doing," he says.

205

That little pang of desperation just kills me. That big bear of a man, so crude and rough, brought low. "If I come back for Thanksgiving and work the glut," I say, "Would that help?"

He inhales deeply. "You know it would."

"Can you help me with money, just this once?"

He just lets the chains clank a while. "Pay depends on the haul. Or have you been gone too long to remember that?"

"Alright," I agree. "Deal."

"You helping will make a little cash to spare," he says softly. "So we'll see what we can work out."

As I hang up, though, the situation keeps eating away me. Working a lobster glut to pay for spring tuition? It's unsustainable. There is absolutely no way I'll make it through senior year. It's piling up on me. Ben aside, this place is burying me, and I can't see a way out. Three more semesters. Even if I went to the loan office, then what? Then I have to bury myself in debt to stay here, and *not* be with Ben?

The answer is actually profoundly simple. It fills my head with a warm, calm obviousness. The solution was there all along. All I had to do was look for it, and I realize just the thought of it makes my shoulders loosen up.

So with a deep breath, I open up Signal. The thought that has been bothering me since I first started falling for him begins to make utter sense: That I could make this so much easier, that I could make life so much smoother with just one decision and a little paperwork. If I asked my dad about this, he'd tell me *I told you so* again. If I ask Lucy, she'll tell me her parents would pay my way. Or she would herself. And I'm not doing that.

Ben's life hasn't been altogether different from mine. He might be the only person around here who will understand. And it's for us, too, besides.

hi.

Well hello.

i need to see you. i have something to run by you.

I like the sound of that. I'm in my office on campus.

oh. shit. never mind.

Come see me, beautiful.
You're my student after all.

His office is in Connecticut Hall, on Old Campus. I've never been to his office, but I know where it is. Right around the corner, second floor. It still doesn't have his business card or even his name on the door. Being a Master's Aide, I realize I should probably order him some business cards; surely he will never, ever think of doing it for himself. At first I'd have mistaken that for some nihilist cocky B.S., but now I know he's just the same as me. He doesn't feel worthy. Simple as that.

But he's worthy. He's everything. And I have this impulse just to take care of him, to do everything he needs, to love him senseless in every single way.

Except I can't do that if I'm a student at Yale.

With a deep breath, I knock on his door. There's a fire in his eyes I haven't seen in ages.

He pulls me in and locks it behind him. "I think Osgood is onto us."

"How? Where?"

He opens up an email and reads, *"Beck. I need to see you about Miss Costa. – Osgood."*

My heart drops right to the floor. "What does that mean?"

"I have no fucking idea," Ben says, staring at his phone worriedly before putting it in his pocket.

"I should go," I say. I don't know why, but I'm suddenly smoothing my hair. As if we'd been caught.

He nods. "Did you have something you need to ask me?"

I did, but I don't anymore. "It'll wait," I tell him.

"Come to the house in an hour. I'll tell you what he says."

On my tiptoes I give him a brief kiss on the cheek, my body already aching for more. For everything. For every cell in his body to be openly, proudly, admittedly mine.

Heading down Prospect, I tighten my scarf and clench my gloves to my body against the coming blizzard. Osgood suspecting, that seals it. Decision made.

A spray of ice comes up from below and also, somehow, above. Not even the god-awful New England winter can deter me now. I turn left, brace myself, and head into the Admissions Office.

42
ben

My mind is full of Naomi as I walk up Science Hill in the wind and falling snow. A blizzard, they're saying. Nobody can stop talking about it, and the damn thing even has a name, Winter Storm Veronica. Even the wind makes me think of her, on being on that beach together. I'm not even really thinking of Osgood now. Just clinging hard onto what she is and how I love her, as if this is the last moment I'll have with her alone in my head.

That first night I saw her, fuck if I knew what I was doing. I wanted her, and I took her, but then by slow slips and starts she unfolded me, piece by piece. Or maybe it wasn't so slow. Maybe it was all at once and it took this long for my head to catch up to my heart. Never in my life did I think that those panties on that perfect body would become an obsession. Whiskey in the belly button, a million proof. Never in my life did I think I'd write on every inch of that skin, and what didn't have ink I covered in kisses. Never in my life did I think that the smell of lemons would make me weak. Never in my life did I think I'd become a tea drinker, head-over-ass in love and just wanting to know what she tastes, to think of what she likes and how. To be bound to those things, to hold them so fucking dear, to cherish them. To cherish *anything*, let alone everything, that is her.

I never thought I'd fall in love, because I didn't believe in it. I never had hope for love, because I didn't believe it. I needed nothing. I needed nobody. But it's her I need now.

She's an addiction. One I never want to quit. Not unless someone takes her away from me.

Which Osgood very well may.

His office is stuffy and a little dark. There are those damned box frames on the walls, filled with butterflies and beetles and bugs.

"Beck," he says. "Shut the door."

I do. At first, I don't sit. I'm feeling hostile and angry before he's even started talking. That email put me in a fighting mood. "What do you want?" I ask, forcing myself to take a seat at last.

"Are you having a relationship with Miss Costa?"

"Not this again," I say. I have this urge to put my feet up on the table, on his padded desk, and cross my arms. But I don't.

He looks off towards some box of butterflies. "Facilities cleaned the Guest Suite."

For a second, I hear nothing but a high-pitched roar in my ears. But then I remember the obvious. We cleaned up. We were super fucking careful.

"And?"

From his top drawer, he pulls a pair of red lace panties, holding them squeamishly with two fingers.

Those panties.

Her panties.

The ones I peeled from her skin? Are in his hands.

"What are those?" I ask. When in doubt, play dumb. Always play fucking dumb.

He drops them back in his top drawer. "I think you know. Between the sofa cushions."

That goddamned button-tufted oxblood sofa. She probably thought I kept them, I realize. I'd said I wanted to do that before. I thought she had them all along.

What I want to say is *Prove it, you bastard*, but I don't. Because I say that word *proof*, I'm implying guilt. "Strange," I say.

"I told you, Beck, that any whiff of scandal would get you kicked out of Durham. All I need to do is start this rumor before the Provost throws you to the wolves. One of the janitors—under the merest of pressure!—said he heard furniture banging against a wall and a man veritably *panting* Miss Costa's name."

Now I'm just seeing red. Now I'm plain furious and thinking how much I'd like to punch those tortoiseshell glasses right off his fat face. "*Bullshit.*"

He smiles. Victorious. "So maybe he didn't."

The motherfucker.

Standing, I give nothing away, nothing more than I have, or try not to anyway. My hands are fucking shaking, so I stick them in my jacket pockets. "That's it?"

"Oh yes, Professor Beck. That's *it.*"

•••

I've told the staff to go home. They think it's because of the blizzard and Thanksgiving that I've let them go. Letty left looking pleased and talking about sausage stuffing. I tried to make nice conversation and said something about mashed potatoes, I don't even know. All bullshit. I just need to be alone. Completely alone with her in this house, just once before I lose her.

When she knocks on the door, I yank her inside and pull off her coat, dropping it on the floor. The zipper rattles on the marble. I say nothing. All I can do is want her. We're already fucked, and I'm the only one who knows it. I need to have her one more time before our universe blows apart. The cosmic shit hitting the fan.

I'm not worried about me. I'd give up the teaching and the books for her in an instant. It's her that I'm worried about. Her, her, her.

Furiously, I force her up against the door and pull down her pants.

"Not here," she says between my almost angry, deep kisses.

"Doesn't fucking matter," I growl at her, and dig my hands into that ass as hard as I can, so hard that she turns to look at me worried, panicked. "I just need you, Naomi. Don't even talk to me right now."

She whimpers. She gets it. She damned smart. One word, one look, she knows everything. She spins back around to face me. "He knows?"

"I need inside you."

Her eyes slide closed slowly as she inhales. But then she rebounds, and in two quick tugs she's got my pants down and then my boxers.

Almost violently, I spin her back around, bending her at the hips with my hand on her back. What I need is to release into her, to know all this danger has been worth it.

And yeah, it is. Love and lust and everything in between. Tangling her hair into my hand, I force my way into her, but she's ready for me.

I am not going to lose her. But I might have no choice.

"I need to take you hard," I say.

"Do it," she tells me, turning to face me over her shoulder.

"Really hard."

"I'm ready."

But goddamn, how times have changed. The last thing I want to do now, right now, right here, is hurt her. So I do slow down, as much as I can, but not relenting on the depth. Still inside her, I take her hips and guide her to the steps. Without any prompting, she takes hold of the banisters, and I fuck her even harder than before.

Within minutes, she gives me that low, sexy, ball-busting, "Shiiiiiiiit," of her orgasm.

Gritted teeth, I come into her, roaring as I spill my seed into her body.

Then there's the beep-beep-beep of the security system, saying the front door is open, followed by a cold blow of air.

We both spin, me still hanging on to her and buried deep. There he is. Osgood, not even looking at us but looking straight up at the ceiling.

"Don't mean to bother you," Osgood says, keeping his eyes off the outrageously X-rated situation in front of him. "But I'd say this is proof enough," he says, and then slithers out the door.

Neither of us moves for a moment. We just stay there, and then she slowly groans and falls to her knees on the steps.

I step away and wipe a sheen of sweat off my face. If he didn't know before, he's got his proof now. I rub my temples. Idiot, Beck. Such a fucking idiot, losing control. That's when I see her shoulder bag, on its side by the door, with papers spilling out. The top one?

TRANSFER APPLICATION.

The rage. I hear her voice suddenly, from that first day of class, *I'd like to have your job one day, Professor Beck.* She'd be brilliant at it, she should do it, she needs to do it. I want to see her follow that dream all the way to the end. And the desire to protect her and stop her from making idiotic life decisions because of me narrows my vision instantly. "Don't tell me," I say, snatching up the papers. They're a photocopy of an original. I see her signature and the date at the bottom. "Don't you dare fucking tell me you gave up this place for me."

I can see she's afraid. She's never seen me flat-out raging before. Not like this.

She doesn't stay in a ball though. She stands right up to me, still with her pants down past her ass. "This is the answer, Ben. You know it is."

Everything in my head makes a few solid revolutions. The consequences of this, the madness. It's not the fucking answer. It's giving up her future, for me. I can't stand it. I won't let it happen. She's come so far, and now she wants to give it all up for me? No fucking way am I letting that happen. I'm not worth it. She deserves *so much more than me.* "Thought a few fucks was worth blowing up your life for?"

Her eyes fill up with tears, and her chin starts trembling. "You don't mean that."

The continuous dream of the last three months finally falls apart, giving way to the eternal epic fucking-over of the real world. What the fuck have I done? What the fuck has happened? All I know it's a fucking nightmarish, epic, profound disaster.

The papers fisted in my hand, I ask again, "So what the hell is this?"

"Nothing," she says, all wide-eyed and flushed, coming to me and reaching out for my hands. "I was just trying to…"

The fact is so simple I cannot believe it hasn't hit her yet. I'm no good for her and I never will be. I'm blowing up her life and she can't even see it.

She makes a move to hang on to me, but I push her away. I don't even look at her as I say, "Get the hell out of here. Right now."

43
Naomi

Yanking my pants back up, I get right in his face. I've never seen another human being look so angry, so broken, so dangerous.

"What did you say?"

"You heard me, Miss Costa. Get out of my house right now."

He catches my slap midair, squeezing my wrist so tight I feel the bones shift.

I know what he's thinking. That I fucked everything up for him. I feel the tears flood up into my eyes again. No. No way. I am not letting him see me cry.

"What we did, we did together," I say.

"Get out."

"You can't just push me away like this," I say.

"I can and I will. This was a huge mistake, Naomi. You cannot imagine what can happen to you now. This has to stop. We have to stop. So get the fuck out of my house."

And there's something in the way he says it, something in the set of his jaw and the muscles clenched in his throat, that says he's not talking about this, not anymore.

I grab my stuff off the floor—my jacket, my bag—and take off through the blowing snow across the quad.

The trip up those 72 steps has never, ever been longer. Every ten, I have to stop, to catch my breath, to keep myself from falling into a heap of tears.

Most everybody has left for break, so I'm alone as I bolt for my room. My hands are trembling violently, and for one long moment, I just sit there in stunned silence. But then the tears do come in violent, jerking sobs, and I find myself with my cheek on the cold, wooden, slightly gritty floor.

Over and over again, I hear him saying it. *Thought a few fucks were worth blowing up your life for?*

It's a yanking, angry, cranking feeling, like my chest is being pulled open, like my ribs are breaking against my heart. That cannot be what he thinks.

I cry and cry until I can't even breathe through my nose. And that's when there's a knock at the door.

For a moment, everything goes into rewind. We didn't fight. He didn't kick me out. We weren't caught. He's standing outside my room, wanting to see me.

Only he isn't. Lucy is.

"Oh boy," she says, coming down on her knees next to me. "What happened?"

She takes my head in her hands and lays it gently in her lap. My cheek is jammed up against her Sorel boot, and I feel some tears spill from my eyes down onto the fur lining. I sniffle loudly and uncomfortably, but no air passes through my nose. It just puts pressure on my brain and makes me remember everything over and over and over again.

Lucy smooths my hair gently. She says nothing at all, except for quiet, soothing repetitions of, "It's okay. It's okay, Naomi. It's going to be okay."

But no. It is not. It most definitely is not. Osgood knows, Ben is angry, I don't even know what I am. Wrung out and horrified at the very least. At best, a scandalous embarrassment. This will surely follow me to wherever I end up next.

Eventually, I do pick myself up off the floor and face her. My eyes feel puffy and enormous, my face hot and raw.

She looks absolutely worried sick. "What happened?" she asks again.

Closing my eyes, I put my thoughts in order, and then in a flood of words, nasally and hard to form sometimes, I tell her everything.

Absolutely everything. The Lux et Veritas ball, the stairwell, the whiskey, the Master's welcome dinner. Guest suite, letters. It's my summary of the most heartbreaking story of my life.

"Well holy shit, Naomi," Lucy says. "I'll be *damned*."

"What?" I say, wiping my nose with my sleeve, "I thought you had it all sussed out."

She shakes her head. "I mean," she shrugs, "I thought you were with Osgood."

For two seconds, she keeps a straight face. My laugh comes out jagged and painful as I shove her to the ground.

"Weird old insect collectors are *such* a catch," she says, teasing me as we lie there on the floor of my room, looking up at the plastered ceiling like people look up at stars.

"Do you love him?" she asks.

I roll over and nod. I can't even say the words. I press my head into her arm.

Eventually, I wipe my eyes and finally realize it makes no sense, her being here. It's the day before Thanksgiving, and Lucy is sitting here with me, when what she should be doing is drinking dry martinis and eating cashews in Greenwich with her parents. "What are you still doing here?"

She looks oddly satisfied. "The storm has stopped the trains."

The trains. I'm supposed to get on a train myself in an hour. I gulp. Oh God. If I am stuck here for Thanksgiving break, I'll die. With Ben right downstairs, I cannot even handle that idea.

"Are they coming to get you?" I ask.

"Well, newsflash, I hate my family, so I was looking forward to a weekend of popcorn and wine. You, on the other hand, probably want to get out of here."

"You can't imagine," I say. "But I don't know how I'll get there now. *All* the trains are closed?"

"You know Amtrak and the MTA," she says. "They'll run the trains off the tracks on a sunny day. Storms? Pullleease."

Rubbing my face, I think that if only the damned storm had hit one day earlier, this could all have been postponed. I could have gotten stuck here. Maybe I'd have snuck into Ben's house. Maybe, maybe, maybe, if only.

If only.

Only no.

Just the thought of it all sends my whole world reeling again.

Lucy pulls her phone out of her pocket. "Roads are still open," she says, turning Google Maps to face me. It's all blurry under my swollen eyelids.

"It's not that far to Greenwich," I say. "Zipcar was great." I try to sound optimistic, but all the snot in my nose just makes me sound so, so sad.

She shakes her head and furrows her perfectly plucked brows. "How about you and me take a trip to Maine."

"In the blizzard?" I try to open my eyes a little wider and unsuccessfully sniffle again. A sort of sucking noise comes out instead.

She shows me her phone, now with the radar map flashing across it. "It's not that far north yet. What do you say, you and me? Outrun Winter Storm Veronica. Thelma-and-Louise style."

I swallow and I feel it in my ears. "I'm working the lobster glut with my dad."

"Ahoy, matey," Lucy says, and helps me up off the ground.

She has no conception of how horrible it's going to be. Lobster fishing for twelve hours straight. So cold and so god-awful, it's like the circle of Hell Dante cut out in edits.

"Are you sure?" I say. Because really, she cannot possibly be sure.

But she nods. "Four extra hands, they have to be better than two."

⋮

Lucy drives while we listen to Taylor Swift on full volume, so loud it makes the speakers in the doors buzz. The trip home is seven hours on a good day, but in the snow it'll takes us almost nine. I don't mind it at all. Being in the car with her, the world white and strange around us, and putting miles and miles between me and Ben feels like the only thing that will help me get over him.

If I even can.

I know I'm going to have to. He made that much crystal clear, and as much as I wanted to take him by the shirt and say, *You love me, I love you, that's the thing that makes everything worthwhile,* it's bad logic in the face of disaster. The whole idea, from the very first, was lunacy. We were in a haze. And now?

It seems he's seen his way out of the haze. While I, of course, haven't. Not at all.

Halfway home, just outside Kittery at the New Hampshire-Maine line, we get out to stretch our legs and fill up on gas. Lucy leaps out and swipes her card at the pump before I can even stop her.

We go inside together. While Lucy's in the bathroom, I make her a coffee with plenty of cream and sugar, and a tea for me. It's ancient gas station Lipton tea, but it's enough. The least I can do to repay Lucy, I figure, is shell out a few bucks for tea and some snacks. As I'm standing in line at the register, I feel my bag buzz against my body. My phone, more precisely, giving me that ominous single pulse of a notification.

All the way here, I haven't looked at my phone. I just couldn't bring myself to look, not with my head pounding from the crying and everything in me just wanting to get away. I'd even left my bag in the back seat so I wouldn't be tempted.

The knowledge that there's a notification makes me feel a little bit faint. I don't know what to do. Should I answer? Should I give us space? Should I throw my phone right in the garbage so I don't even have to think about this ever again?

The lady at the register coughs to get my attention, and I step forward.

"Some kind of weather," she says. "And you with a hole your gloves."

Weirdly, amazingly, I don't feel so ashamed of that here. I nod. "We came up from New Haven. It's worse down there."

Ringing up the tea and the bag of peach circles I grabbed on an impulse, she says, "Where you headed?"

I dig the requisite few bills from my wallet. "Down East."

And she smiles at me for the very first time. That smile of belonging, that smile of recognition. It hits me hard and fast. I haven't had anybody look at me like that in ages. That's the feeling of going home. "Be careful, honey," she says, "And Happy Thanksgiving," she adds, giving me my change.

That smile of your people welcoming you home? There's nothing like that on earth. For one second, I think, screw the transfer papers. What if I just threw it all in and came home to the boats? What if I became my mom?

Would that be so bad?

Life would be hard. I might be petrified to go back on the water at first, but at least I'd have gotten away from the mess that my life had

217

become at Yale. Surely, somehow, this disaster will follow me wherever I go. I'll get shamed to pieces and have to come home anyway. Osgood will tell someone and that someone will tell someone, and pretty soon I'll be the girl who screwed the Master of Durham. That'd follow me to UConn, to community college, everywhere. The slut who fucked the Master. I can hear it already.

It makes the lobster boats seem not so scary at all.

I steel myself and take my phone out of my bag as I step aside for a fisherman, there to buy tobacco. I slip my gloves off and put them on the counter. Then I open up my phone.

It wasn't him. It was the freaking weather app. *Again.* I open up Signal. The last message was earlier today, time stamped 9:32 am. Now, it's damn near three o'clock. He meant it. *Get out of my house,* was just another way to say, *Get out of my life.*

Part of me wants to write him, but what am I going to say? I'm not about to plead my case. I wouldn't know how anyway, not right now, and I know for sure I don't want to be where I'm not wanted. Where I don't belong.

And so as Lucy comes up beside me and takes her coffee, she says, "Ready, captain?"

I press the power button on my phone and swipe the screen to lock it. I zip it up in the side pocket and vow to myself I'm off the grid. Peace and quiet and no more notifications. And then I say, "I should probably explain a thing or two about lobsters."

44

Naomi

Sleeping next to Lucy in my childhood bed involves a lot of shin kicking, hair in my face, and periodic flirtatious moans of, "I didn't know, Officer!" and "Please do, search me!"

I kid you not.

And then, at 5:00 am, Dad pounds on my door with all the grace of a SWAT commander.

This jolts Lucy awake. "Officer?"

"Not real," I groan, rubbing my face. I don't think I slept at all. "Time to catch some fish."

"What should I wear?" She's stretched out like a cat in the warm spot where I was lying.

"Every single piece of clothing you brought."

But once we get ourselves dressed and head down to the docks, I am provided with possibly the best distraction that ever was: watching Lucy Burchett work a lobster boat in the middle of a bone-freezing storm, with so much icy spray that we have to take a hammer to the rails to break it off. And as an extra added bonus, there's no cellphone service that far out at sea, so I haven't brought my phone. I stayed strong through the night and didn't check. Didn't want to check. Didn't want to know. All of the above.

Being on the boat is terrifying, but not as bad as I'd thought. The fear of the fear was the very worst part of all, and enough time has passed since the accident for me to shake it off. At least Dad understood that and didn't start asking me to help until this year.

"She's coming in something fierce," Dad hollers over the spray.

I know he's talking about the weather, but it seems entirely possible that he's talking about Lucy. I don't know if it's because she's trying to make me laugh or what, but she is outrageously entertaining to work with. Like a little Tasmanian devil with top-of-the-line highlights. Her cheeks are bright pink and her eyes a particularly stunning shade of amber out here under the solid gray sky. At first, she's clearly kind of freaked out by the lobsters. Dad and I use the hauler to bring two traps on board, and I flip them open.

"Ohmigod," she says. "They're so...*weird*."

"They're angry," I tell her.

"I've only seen them in supermarkets. In tanks. At the Elm Street Oyster House. These are just so...*huge*."

"Careful not to get pinched there," I tell her, and open and close the pot, showing her the hinge, which shifts a little when opened, just enough to crush a pinkie.

The trap is nearly bursting and the lobsters are trying to tell us how unbelievably infuriating this whole experience has been by lashing out at our fingers with their claws. I set to work banding them. I show her how to sort them. I fling a female off the bow and Lucy shrieks. "Jesus!"

"She's fine. Totally fine. These ones," I show her, picking up a big one, "are marketers. The smaller ones are canners. Never mind, you'll catch on."

With a big male, I show her how to band the claws.

Before I can stop her, she's put her fingers on the edge of the pot as she's watching me. And that's when she gets pinched on the pinkie by a female covered in seaweed and eggs on her belly.

"You mean little fucker!" she says, sticking her finger in her mouth.

"Oh shit," I say, and pull her finger out of her mouth to take a look. It's not *that* bad. She's probably going to lose that nail, but God forbid I tell her so right now. "You're doing great. Lobsters are the assholes of the sea."

She snorts, and then picks up a male of her own. Awkwardly, she measures, and I give her the go ahead with two rubber bands. She's wearing one of my dad's coats, and she vanishes inside it. Also, a brown Carhartt beanie, slightly off to one side, with her long blonde braid a little damp on her rubbery yellow shoulder. She looks so stinking cute that if I had my phone with me, I'd snap a burst of photos and post every single one on Facebook.

Out of the corner of my eye, I see Dad watching us. What Lucy probably doesn't realize is she provides the best buffer ever between us. A mutual project. There's nothing like a greenhorn to bring the rest of the crew together.

"Naomi," he yells. "Pull the pots over to the portside. Don't want you to get caught up in the spray."

I nod at him and drag the pots across the deck. That was how it happened five years ago, in a storm just like this.

"Careful there," Dad says, now standing behind Lucy, "Or else..."

And he wiggles his fingers, showing nine instead of ten.

"No way," Lucy says. In her distraction, another lobster makes a grab for her. This one, though, he doesn't just pinch. He out-and-out hangs on.

She doesn't scream. I'm watching her with a sort of tickled amusement. She just grits her teeth and stares at me, wide-eyed and angry. "If I lose my finger, I'll never speak to you again...ever!"

My dad comes to the rescue, and uses his big old meaty hands to pry the claw off of her.

"Pretty tough for a city-girl," my dad says, and winks at me over her shoulder.

His coat is worn out, and he looks more tired than I've ever seen him. The traps have been mended, and there's a crack in the standing shelter. It hits me then that times have gotten *really* tough, and fast. All that pressure on me to come home, which felt like guilt, it was much simpler than that. It wasn't him rooting against me. He's broke, and lonely, and sad. He needs the help. I've misread everything. Or maybe I'm just wrecked inside and feeling like shit makes the world a whole lot clearer.

The day passes in a fury. We eat lunch on the fly in the bulkhead, grabbing halves of peanut butter sandwiches and swigs of water in the minuscule breaks between hauling more traps up from the deep. On and on. Lobster after lobster, rubber bands everywhere, freezing fingers.

Somewhere in the toil of it all, I do forget Ben. A little. Or at least he moves away from the center of my mind, in the background, just a touch.

By sundown, when we leave the deep water, we've made such a good haul that his boat is damn near overflowing. I know what he's thinking because I'm thinking it too: We might've hit the quota, the three of us. Maybe just.

Dad and I are in the bulkhead while Lucy is hanging her head over the side into the light spray that batters the hull at intervals.

"Thanks," he says. He's never been big on words, or gratitude. So that one means a lot. "Really, kiddo. Thank you."

I wipe the salt water and frozen sweat from my face with the sleeve of my sweatshirt. "Dad. I think you were right about me and Yale."

He doesn't answer, but his left eyebrow quivers a little. Then he takes the radio in his hand and guides us into the harbor.

We ride that way for a while, until he mutes the radio. He takes off his woolen cap and scratches his massive head, now much more salt than pepper. "If it's the money, I figure I've got five hundred to spare."

"It's not the money." My lips start trembling. "I'm just…" I look off towards the dark waters to the east before turning to face him again. "I just *can't* anymore."

But his face softens. The wrinkles around his eyes ease up, and it's like he finally understands something he hadn't seen before. "Your mom used to cry like that," he says.

"It happens all the time now," I say, trying to bite back the stupid tears. "It makes me crazy."

He laughs, kind of marveling at me. "Yeah, it was just like this. When she'd get happy or sad or overwhelmed or even if there was a good haul." He shakes his head. "Seems to me you're growing into her."

My eyes sting almost unbearably, still so swollen and red from yesterday and irritated from a day on the boat. When the tears do spill out, it's not really a relief, just almost a sizzling, searing pain. He puts a big wet arm around me, and for a minute we become a single squeaky yellow raincoat. He's never, *ever,* shown affection like this. "I'm sorry I've been so hard on you," he says at last. "I didn't understand. I don't understand. But I see her in you now."

I drop my body against him. The weight of the world seems to slide off me a little.

"I'll tell you something she always used to tell me," he says, squeezing me close again with one massive arm. "Never confuse running around with sinking."

I pull away to look up at him.

"You might be beached," he says, reaching for the radio, "But you're not sunk."

∴

We don't have turkey for Thanksgiving dinner, of course. Instead, we have lobster rolls, hot on Wonder Bread buns with plenty of mayonnaise. We have instant mashed potatoes, and Lucy raves over them in a way so genuine, it occurs to me she's probably never had potatoes from a box before.

"The texture!" she says, "So creamy!"

My dad smiles at his plate. "Where are you from again, Lucy?"

"Greenwich," she says, slapping a big pat of butter on the pile of fluffy white mush.

And dad smiles at his plate a little bit wider.

We eat clustered around the little dining table, under a too-bright kitchen light above. The weather warnings hum from the kitchen radio. Rain lashes the windows, and I clear the plates.

I'll have to face him some time, so after I serve up pound cake and ice cream, and Lucy begins asking my dad 1,001 questions about ground-dwelling crustaceans, I get up the courage to turn on my phone.

45
ben

Naomi. Please.
Please answer me.
Please.
I'm so fucking sorry.
Weds 3:42pm

You must have left college. I don't see a light on in your room.
Weds 5:34pm

I hope you're safe. The blizzard is awful.
I miss you.
Weds 6:01pm

I get why you don't want to talk to me. But I need to talk to
you. I am stuck here, alone, thinking of you on a loop in my
head. I asked you to leave because I thought it was best.
It's not best.

It's worse.
Please answer.
Weds 7:01pm

I have eaten an entire pack of Oreos in one sitting. I am a broken man.
Remember when I drank whiskey from your belly button? I need to do that again. I need your skin again.
Weds 9:56pm

Naomi. Come on. Please. Beautiful, please.
I love you. I'm going to bed soon. I am keeping my phone on.
Weds 11:58pm

Alright, so either you're not answering me because you hate me or because you aren't turning on your phone, which means you also hate me or are trying to forget me. I can't forget you. I could sit here and fight it but there's no reason. Me loving you. An accepted universal truth.
Thurs 1:13am

See what I did there? Groveling through philosophy? Eh?
No?
Please?
Thurs 1:19am

I've decided I hate this app. Seriously. What if you aren't even getting these messages, what if they're just getting scooped up into some secret server and some hacker is laughing while I talk about my broken heart?
Also, Happy Thanksgiving.
I miss you.
A shitload.
Thurs 7:20am

I broke down and called you just now. Your phone is off. I feel both good and bad about that.
Thurs 8:26am

I'm sure you're with your family. But I wish you could just come home.
Thurs 9:30am

They brought in the National Guard to shovel. Can you believe it? I hope it's okay in Maine. I checked and it seems fine. I hope you're safe.
I found the Sharpies just now.
I have never been happier than I am when I'm with you.
Thurs 1:57pm

I hope you are having something good for dinner tonight. I am going to have a sad turkey sandwich with no lettuce. I am out of Oreos. I don't even know if you like Oreos. I want to know that. I want to know everything.
Thurs 3:30pm

No whiskey tonight. I'm already too sad.
Thurs 5:01pm

I want you to know I ducking love you
I ducking hate autocorrect.
ducking.
I ducking miss you.
I ducking love you.
Thurs 7:46pm

https://docs.goo.gle.578sejvs
Open that. I need to write you a real letter.
Fri 8:55am

For a while, I just sit there staring at the cursor on the Google Doc with my laptop in my lap in bed. Just spill it, Beck. Just close your eyes and spill it. You love her. You want her to know everything. So tell her.

Dear Naomi –

This is marginally better than writing to you in tiny sentences. I'd rather you read me in paragraphs than sentences, because sentences aren't enough, let alone texts. I'm shit at texting. I've never really done it with anybody but you. That's not because I'm an old man but because I just don't have anybody else to text. I don't really talk to anybody but you. I do try, but I don't know how. With you, I know how. With you, things make sense. With you, I know what to say. Or you make me feel like I do, anyway.

I need to tell you just exactly how I feel, because no matter how hard I love you, you'll never know it unless I tell you. If love is real, which it is, I have to talk about it. About how it makes me feel like I'm two feet off the ground all the time and how I even see your face when I sleep. I'm sitting here reading the book you gave me and thinking how funny and true it is. C.S. Lewis, he's a little like you. He believes the shit out of everything until it lets him down. He lives big and bold and fully. I used to think that must be an awful way to live, but now I see it's the only way to live at all.

Let me tell you about not believing in anything. It's safe and sturdy, it's something to lean on. It's the atheist's salve, it's the opposite of God; it's just as comforting. When you believe in nothing, nothing can be unknown. Nothing can hurt you then. You've already seen the dark, and it can't get any darker than that. When I was little, everybody in my family left or died. I ended up in a group home for a while in high school. I learned to fight. I acted like you saw me the other day. God, how I fucking regret that. I learned to be angry and defend myself. I lost my way there too. I'm a slow reader, I bet you don't know that. Painfully slow. And dyslexic. Nobody knows that but you and me. I didn't even apply to college. The lady who ran the group home, she filled out an application for me to go to Clark County Community College. I got in. Then I kept on working and working at stuff nobody cared about but me. That was easy. Until you came along. Because now it's you I care about. I care what you think. You. Always you.

It's also easy not relying on anybody. It's easy to have one mug and one plate, which was how I used to live. It's easy to live off of Oreos and ramen and read books that make life seem meaningless. That's confirmation bias. When you feel like life is meaningless, and you read about meaninglessness, it makes more and more sense. It did make sense. It made a shitload of sense.

Until you.

You've made me believe in love. You made me need. You've made me see how things can be and are. You've made me understand why every decent song in the entire motherfucking world is about heartbreak. You've opened up the gates to feelings I've never let myself have because I was too scared to have them.

I threw you out of my house the other day because I felt you should stay away from me, because I don't know what happens when I love you like I want to forever. I don't know what happens when I tell you I know I've loved you for four months but I want to put a ring on your finger. I mean that. I want to hold you so close that we're breathing each other's air. I want you to forget that there are other men, because they'll never love you the way I do. I want to love you all the way into a Portishead, song, apparently, and I'm not even fucking ashamed of it.

I am willing to do anything to get you back. Please come home.

Ever-loving and heartbroken,
Ben

I sit in the wingbacked chair, staring at the screen. Everything hurts to think about, especially right now. My heroine with her fire extinguisher. But she's gone. In the pit of my stomach, I've got a feeling that's done. That I'll never be with her like I need to be again.

At first, this Google Doc seemed so brilliant, like maybe she'd log on and see me typing, maybe even add a sentence of her own, but she hasn't.

And writing it has shown me what matters and what I have to do to make it work. If that's even an option.

But I've got to try.

So I tie my shoes and zip up my sweater and look at the document one last time.

Suddenly, a little flag pops up in the corner.

"N" viewing.

Holy shit. The flag is pink. It's her, she's reading it.

I grip my temples. I don't know what I'm expecting, but what I see is her cursor moving down the document, line by line, blinking and taunting me. She's on the other end of this thing.

"Please answer. Please," I say. "Please. Just say something."

She types nothing in return, she says nothing back. And within a moment, the little flag with her initial disappears.

Everything inside me sinks. No reply.

Which leaves me with only one thing to do. I close the doc and open up a blank letter in Word. The words are hard to write, because in the process of falling in love with her, I've come to really like being here a lot. I love teaching these kids. I even love being the Master of Durham, weird as that is. But I love her more than I love any of it. So it's straightforward, just a few lines. I print it out and head out the door for Osgood's rooms.

With my resignation in my hand. I've made my choice, if she'll have me. If not, it's back to the desert, all alone.

When he answers, he's in his robe and slippers. "Beck."

I'm not angry anymore. I put the paper in his hand, folded up into thirds.

"What's this?"

"I'm resigning."

He looks surprised. He unfolds page, and I watch his eyes skim down the lines.

"So I'm out of your hair," I say. I don't even smirk. What a ridiculous joke that would be at a time like this.

He does touch his bald head though, like it was a jab.

"Sorry," I say.

"You'd do this for her?" he asks.

Would I do this for her? I'd do anything for her. I'd take this place apart stone by stone if that's what it took. "I don't think you've ever been in love like this."

I realize, of course, he's alone on Thanksgiving too. I hear a television in the background, so that was a totally asshole thing for me to say. It hits me how deeply lonely he must be too. "I hadn't either. I didn't know it existed."

Osgood puts the paper in the pocket of his robe. He looks like he's at a loss for what to say. I don't mind. I've got nothing to say either. I'm ruined. I put my hands into my pockets. "But you have to promise me you won't let her transfer. You have to stop that happening."

He rubs his beard. "If she wants to leave, that's her decision."

"Osgood. I'll personally go to Burma and find your moth and squish it if you let her leave this university. I don't fucking care if *I* have to pay her tuition. Do not…" I say, getting a little angry now, "…let her leave."

He stares at the floor. He thumbs the paper in his pocket. "Alright. I'll do everything I can to keep her here. I can promise that."

"Good," I say. I turn to go, but then I stop. "I'm sorry to let you down. I was never a fit for this place anyway."

I can feel myself getting overwhelmed with everything. Another totally unfamiliar feeling, another part of myself I never knew until she came along. "I need you to understand something. She's the thing I've always been looking for. She's the thing I dreamed about and never understood. I never knew what love was until I found her."

Osgood is watching me close.

"She's the rarest thing in the world, Dean." I feel my nose sting. "She's the thing I always needed."

And then he closes his door in my face.

That's that, I think, trotting down his stairs and out into the snow, back to my house. If she'll have me or not, at least I won't be her professor anymore. But I know she'll be angry, so it's not until well past midnight that I add to the document one last thing:

PS: I have handed in my resignation. You're safe to come back.

I lie down in bed. I feel responsible, I feel mature. I also feel sick, sad, and defeated.

46
Naomi

I see the PS first thing when I wake up. I try texting him on Signal, but it comes back with *not delivered.*

No, no, no, I think, pressing my face into the old worn pillowcase.

So I try to write him on the Google Doc. But he just sent me the link, didn't add me as an editor. There's no way I could reply even if I wanted to.

He cannot resign. He absolutely cannot.

I can't call, because I've never had his number. It was always blocked. I'd never needed it, and for a minute I think about emailing, but that's just not going to cut it. All this, it has to be done face to face.

Shaking Lucy awake, I drag her out of bed. It's like waking up a tiny sweaty kitten. "Why are we moving? What is happening?" she says. "Why does it smell like fish everywhere."

"Get a move on, matey," I tell her, and throw her sweatshirt across the room.

My dad is surprised to see us packing, and I make profuse apologies. "I have to get back to campus. There's a catastrophe in progress. Are you going to be okay without us?"

He smiles. "We rounded out my quota yesterday. So it's all okay."

I wrap him in a big hug. "Thank goodness."

"Thanks for your help," he tells me, and tries to hand me a few twenties.

I push them back into his hand. "Hang on to it. I don't need it yet."

When the truth is, I just know he can't spare it at all.

This time, I'm driving. My phone is dead, which is probably for the best. At least that way I'm not distracted. The winter morning is clear and harshly bright, so shimmery and white that it makes my pupils throb, even behind my sunglasses. Next to me, Lucy is on the lookout for cops because I am quite literally putting patches on the road.

"Shit, Thelma! We need to go away more often," Lucy squeals. "This is awesome!"

I accelerate to 90 miles an hour on 295. "Keep your eye out. Three more points and I lose my license."

"You're such a badass!"

"This cannot happen," I say, putting my foot down even harder. "He cannot resign."

"I think it's gallant," Lucy says, opening up a pack of crackers, "But I get what you mean."

I don't think it's gallant. I think it's utterly stupid, absolutely ridiculous. He *needs* to be there. He belongs there. I'm not letting him leave because of me. I'm the one that doesn't belong.

After about a half-hour of high-speed burning through the frosty morning, Lucy finally says, "Now, can we talk about money a second?"

"Way to get me when I'm down." We blow past a road sign that I can't even read we're moving so fast.

"How much does your dad make?"

"Is that how they start conversations in Greenwich?"

"All the time!" she giggles. "No, but seriously. How much? Thirty, twenty? Ten? I'm not judging."

I shrug, because honestly, I couldn't say. "He makes what the sea lets him make, really. Sometimes he earns a lot, sometimes nothing at all. You saw how it is. He hardly has anything. We've never had much, but now," I say, "it's really bad. Worse than ever."

Lucy begins unbraiding her hair and nods thoughtfully.

"Why?" I ask her. We zip past a tractor-trailer going 85, which is way, way too slow for right now.

"Well, I think you might not be taking advantage of Yale like you should be."

I don't know what that means. It sounds suspiciously like some kind of white-collar crime scheme. Lucy's dad may or may not have done some time for such a thing. "I'm not going to game my way through," I say. "Tuition is expensive. That's just the way it is."

In my periphery, I see her rabbit-shift her nose. "The year you came to Yale, did he make more money than he does now?"

That's an easy one. "He used to have a fleet of boats. So when I left, he must have been making...I don't know. At least a hundred thousand that year."

Lucy whistles.

"But," I clarify quickly, "that was to run the fleet. Relatively little of that came to him personally. It was all going back into the business. Then the year I left, they changed the groundfishing rules. He had to close down and go into business alone."

Lucy's eyes close slowly in a knowing kind of way. "And did you ever get your financial aid reassessed?"

"How the hell do you know so much about this?"

"Girl! When you've got money, you want to keep it. My dad is a legendary tightwad. I know all the ways to get cash from the system. It's an art."

"Not my art. And no, we didn't. Can you imagine me asking my dad for his W-2 tax forms? That's not a conversation we have in my house."

Lucy puts her sunglasses on. "I believe there's been a clerical error, my dear. We'll figure it out when the dust settles."

"It'll never settle."

"That pessimist nihilist whatever-he-is is rubbing off on you," she says as she turns up the volume on the stereo. "Just leave it to Lucy. I'm probably going to need your social security number."

"Don't get me arrested, that's the last thing I need."

She giggles. "Tell me about it!"

I focus on the road. Slush spews from either side of the Fiesta. Right now, I don't care about financial aid. I don't care about tuition or why she needs my social security number or my financial assessments or scholarships or *anything at all*. Right now, I just want to get back to campus and fix everything before Ben blows his life up. Because of me.

∴

We park on Elm. The plow drifts are higher than my head. I'm pretty sure there's an Emergency Warning Do Not Park order, but I can't be bothered with that. I've got a career to save. I leave Lucy on Elm with the luggage and hustle inside. There was a time when I'd have thought she couldn't handle it. But not anymore. I have never seen such a tiny person manhandle lobster traps like she could.

Through the quad I go and then through the door marked, DEAN'S SUITE. I run up the flight of stairs, with my red Hunters squeaking on the granite. As I go up, I think about exactly what I want to say and how. Truthfully I have exactly no idea whatsoever. The only way is to be honest. When in doubt, go straight at them.

Yep. I'm becoming my father. Or my mother. Either one, it's actually not so bad.

I rap on the Dean's door and then put my hands to my side. To steady myself, I focus hard on the fisheye of the peephole.

Within seconds, he opens the door, saying, "I was expecting you, Miss Costa."

"Can I come in?" I say. I notice that he's gotten a new toupee. He looks like himself again. Much less angry now, and a nicer hairstyle besides. "Please?"

I've never been inside his apartment. I don't know that anybody has.

But he opens the door wider, without hesitation, and lets me come through.

The room is sadly, painfully bare. There are no decorations, there are no photographs. It's empty, except for a few books on one of the far shelves. I hear a tinny radio playing in the kitchen. I realize he must have everything interesting in his office, because his work is his life and his life is his work. But here at home, he's just a rather lonely old man. Hardly the villain I'd made him in my head for the last eight hours, let alone the last four months.

"I think I know why you're here," he says, offering me a chair in front of the fireplace. Instead of a fire, he has a plug-in radiator in front of the grate.

"Dean." I bite my lip and get my words in order, focusing on the carpet for a moment before lifting my eyes to his. They're steadily on me, waiting. I say, "I cannot explain how embarrassed I am about what you saw."

He raises his fingers, like that's not something to talk about.

"But I'm not ashamed I did it," I say.

His eyes flicker at me. "Miss Costa. I think you should know that Professor Beck has resigned."

"I know. That's why I'm here. You can't accept that resignation."

"That was his choice, Miss Costa."

I scoot forward on my chair a bit. "He is the most wonderful thing that has happened to this college since I've been here. Haven't you noticed? Everybody's behaving, the seniors have stopped getting drunk upstairs. There are actually interesting people coming to speak, because they want to meet him. The fellows are donating more," I say. "That's all because of him. "

The Dean tips his head side to side, like *maybe, maybe not.*

"You know it's true. And not to mention what he's done for the Philosophy department. That class of his, it's the very best one I've ever taken."

"You may be biased."

That catches me off guard, not because it's exactly right, but because he said it with a kind of strange kindness. "I know I am. But Dean Osgood, you know I'm right. You know he's been so good for Durham. And you know me. He has made *me*," I point at myself, "feel like I belong. Like my brain isn't so strange. Like my story isn't so strange. I cannot be the only one who feels this way. Even if I am in love with him."

He winces. "That cannot go on. It just cannot."

But I'm on a roll now. I've got my wings on, somehow. All my courage is boiling up and over. "What has happened with me and Dr., Professor, Master…" Damn it, steady on, Naomi, "With Ben." I clear my throat. "What has happened with us had nothing at all to do with him. He didn't seduce me, he didn't trick me. We were strangers and now we're not. We had no idea what was going to happen when we first met."

Flashes of that ball run through my head. It's true. I really and truly couldn't have imagined it.

Osgood holds up his hand to stop me. "The fact remains that it did happen. It has happened. There have to be consequences. This is a college. This is a university. This kind of thing cannot go on without something happening in response. And the scandal, Miss Costa! Think of the scandal if the world learns that we've got some kind of playboy for a Master. Durham cannot handle it."

235

The anger rushes right up to my face, and I don't mind it at all. "He is *not* a playboy. You know that, Dean. Even if you don't like him, you do know him. Have you seen him talking to other girls? Has he been inappropriate, as you say, even once?"

Osgood shakes his head. "No, I haven't. That's true."

Deep down inside I feel a wave of possible relief. "I know you'd have preferred someone else, but he's incredible. Absolutely an incredible, kind, brilliant human being. With a huge heart." I'm making a gesture like I'm talking about some impossibly enormous trout I once caught. I slap my hands together and put them in my lap. "I think it says a lot about him that he's willing to resign to protect me."

Osgood sighs so hard that his shoulders drop. But he doesn't take his eyes off me. He doesn't give me some speech about conduct and ethics and all the rest.

"So please, tear up that letter. Just throw it away. I've submitted my transfer papers. I will be out of your hair…"

His eyes perk up, and he shakes his head at me, laughing.

"What? What did I say?"

"Professor Beck said that same thing. Exactly that same thing."

My heart pinches my ribs. "Don't let him resign, Dean. Please," I say. I realize I'm clasping my hands together, literally begging him. "There has to be something, *something* we can do."

Dean Osgood sighs heavily, blowing air past his inflated cheeks. "You're both willing to give up everything for the other, you know," Osgood says, standing to pour himself a brandy. "You're either exceedingly stupid or…"

I have a whole speech lined up in my head about love and humanity and this burning, wondrous feeling that floods through me every time I say his name.

"Or…?" I ask.

He doesn't answer.

It's then that my eyes light on the only picture in the room. A much-younger Osgood, with his arms wrapped around an even younger woman. He's smiling so wide, I barely recognize him, but those eyes are the same. It's definitely him. He's got a full head of hair, cut like one of the Beatles. The girl is beautiful and is kissing him on the cheek. She's young, really young. As young as me.

So maybe, just maybe, he knew this feeling himself.

I stop talking. I stop pleading. I put my hands in my lap.

The Dean gazes out his window a while. I sit quietly and listen to the heater tick. There are ten thousand things to say, but no matter what I do now, it's just words. It's not going to help my case. Silence is the very best friend I have.

"There are going to have to be sacrifices," the Dean says to the window.

Whatever that means, it's not a *no*. "I know that. And I'm ready to make them. Just don't punish him. Please, Dean Osgood. *Please.*"

Finally, the Dean turns around. His face is softer, and his smile is coming back. There are no words spoken, but the feeling in the room shifts. It's just possible, I realize, that I did it. That I convinced him.

And then he says, "Off you go, Miss Costa. Give me some time to see what can be done."

I nod. I stand up. I turn to leave. The ball is out of my court. Jury in session.

"One last thing, Miss Costa," he says, just as I'm putting my hand on the doorknob. I hold my breath and look back over my shoulder, meeting his eyes as he smiles, nods, and says, "In the meantime, be *discreet.*"

47
ben

I am in the bathroom about to brush my teeth when I lose heart for it. I haven't shaved in days, I've resorted to eating stale crackers from the pantry. I don't remember if I've even had any water, and there are bags under my eyes that make me look like a total lunatic. Whatever. Nothing matters anymore.

"Let that shit go," I tell myself in the mirror.

It sits in the air. Let that shit go?

Yeah. Right. Like that's happening.

Closing my eyes, I press my forehead to the frosted window next to the sink. I can't let her go. What have I done pushing her away? Did I really, for even one instant, think that was possible?

What an idiot.

Opening my eyes, through the blurry frosted pane, I see that it isn't empty like it's been for days on end. Now, I see a shape moving across the quad. It's like a living watercolor. It only takes me a minute to make sense of it. Long brown hair, red boots.

Naomi.

I tear out of the bathroom. I throw my sweater over my head and book it down the stairs, nearly killing myself on the bottom two but managing to sort of hand-over-hand my way down the railing while my ankles become totally useless.

Shoes. Where the fuck are my shoes? I search the foyer like a blind man with his hands out. The only thing I find are my flip-flops from the summer, stuck in the side closet, under an umbrella.

They'll have to do.

So in my flip-flops, I slog through the snow in the quad, mesmerized by the patterns of her footsteps, searching everywhere for that beautiful face.

She must have gone up to her room. Her footprints disappear at the shoveled walkway. I reach for my wallet to get my keycard. I pat myself down, left-hand pocket, right-hand pocket, back pockets. Repeat. But then I realize I've left it in my house. With my phone.

I am the Master of Durham, and I am locked in the quad. In sandals. In the snow.

And my sweater is on backwards.

This is the state of things. This is the truth.

Benjamin Beck is a disaster.

I make a snowball and hurl it at her window. I may be a pathetic sack of sad who can't feel his feet, but at least I can still throw a ball.

There is no answer. No beautiful face in the diamond windows.

"Naomi!" I yell.

"I'm right here."

I spin around. She's in the Zen garden, peeking out at me from over the gate.

All the things I wanted to say? They just vanish. She's got this huge smile on her face, a smile of hope, a smile of delight.

I stumble and try to get to her, but fall to my knees in a snow bank, helplessly stuck.

She makes her way through the bank towards me, the snow coming up past her boots, and then I'm in her arms. With my face pressed into the pockets of her hoodie, my cheek tight against her stomach, I say, "I'm so fucking sorry." I cling to her body and close my eyes. "I'm so glad you're here."

"Where are your boots?" she says. "You're going to freeze to death."

I couldn't care less. "Doesn't matter." I take my hands from her pockets and then rest them on the small of her back.

Her arms are wrapped around my head. So warm, gentle. So much like home.

"I think it's okay. I saw Osgood."

Staring up at her, I rest my chin on the zipper of her sweatshirt. "It's okay?"

She nods down at me and rubs the back of my head gently with her thumbs. Now she's smiling, her face a little red from the cold. "I think so. So let's get you out of the snow."

But I don't move. I just hang on to her. I smell lemons and winter. I cannot feel my legs. I am overcome by the shimmering fear of the unknown, in love.

For the very first time in my life.

48
ben

six weeks later.

I stand in the frigid January night, smoothing my tie. I feel as nervous as I ever have. I don't feel like the Master. I feel like I'm going on my very first date.

Her new apartment is on the corner of Crown and Howe. She lives on the second floor of a brick building with plaster gargoyles on the walls. I can see the lamplight coming from the windows, sparkling and warm. I check my jacket pocket and feel the invitation for the Lux et Veritas Winter Gala inside.

I press the buzzer, holding my finger on the button a second longer than is totally polite.

Waiting there, I put my hands in my pockets.

This was the fix. Osgood, Naomi, and I hashed it out. It is completely impolitic and risky. Osgood revealed himself to be a hopeless, devoted romantic, much to our utter surprise. Love, he said, isn't scandal. Not when it's sincere. So we sorted it out. Quietly, privately, discreetly.

Now, she lives off campus and we stay deeply under the radar. We tell nobody. Only Osgood and Lucy know our secret. If we go out, we go out of town. Like tonight, when we're finally going to go to the bistro we never made it to all those months ago.

I also know, as of today, that her tuition is covered. Completely covered, for the rest of her time here. That's sixteen months and three weeks, not that I'm counting. Financial Aid reassessed her dad's income. And it's 100%, no questions asked, covered through graduation.

So as potential life explosions go, this one turned out pretty damned well. I keep my job, she'll finish her degree, and we get each other, which is most important of all.

This is a new tux, the first real one I've ever owned, and it feels too nice. My shoes feel too fancy, my shirt feels too starchy. She's still got my black tie. She said it would be perfect. She's picked all this out for me, and she says it's just right. I believe her. I believe everything she says because she's got my heart, and I trust her with it completely.

A voice comes out of the speaker. "We're not interested," says Lucy, followed by an explosion of giggles. Contagious, smile-making giggles.

"Hi, handsome," comes Naomi's beautiful voice, lower than Lucy's, sexier by far.

The door buzzes and unlocks.

Inside, the place is a tumbledown old apartment house like every campus apartment in the world. Once a mansion, now diced up into little two-bedrooms with cheap doors and brass knockers. There are scuffs on the walls on the way up the staircase. But only fourteen steps to get to them, I count. A big change from 72.

Standing at the door, I hear soft music from inside.

Before I can knock, Lucy flings open the door. She's wearing her parka, carrying her book bag, and smiling at me wider than I've ever seen her smile.

"Don't you look nice," she says, giving me elevator eyes.

"Thanks," I say, holding the door open for her as she passes through under my arm.

"See you tomorrow," she whispers, and heads downstairs.

Inside, I don't see Naomi anywhere. What I do see are two glasses of champagne on the table. Leading down from them, tiny white chalk dots, down the table leg and across the floor.

I take both glasses and follow the dots to a door that's closed, but not completely shut. I open it with my shoulder. Inside, it's full of candles, with a bed in the middle. On the bed is the love of my life, in that black satin dress, lying on her stomach with her bare feet behind her, up in the air. Wearing the same mask she wore the first time I saw her.

As I come inside, she gets on her knees on the mattress. Her hair is off to one side, showing off the curve of her neck, leading down to those perfect breasts, just peeking out from the dress. Just right. Just fucking right, always.

She takes the champagne from my hands and sets it on the bedside table. Then she pulls me to her by my lapels. Hanging from her dresser is the gold half-mask I wore all those months ago, and my tie too.

"We're going to be late," I manage to say through a growl.

"Is that a problem?" she asks, blinking one slow blink. She slides her finger down my jawline.

"Definitely not."

She raises those big blue eyes to mine. She brings her lips to my ear and whispers, "Vos estis lux et veritas."

You are the light and the truth.

God*damn.* "So are you." I slowly unzip the side of her dress, taking my time, because we can do that now. We can take our time forever. The dress slips from her body, revealing WELCOME, MASTER written across her stomach in Sharpie.

Holy shit.

"Ready?" she whispers.

She's wrecked my theories. She's blown me apart. She's made me whole.

"Fuck yes," I say. "I'm ready."

The End.

Acknowledgements

First, thank you to my husband. My man. I have no idea what I did before you. You are an incredible, kind, brilliant human being. You have made me happier than I thought I could be. And also thank you for the term *preworry*. Nobody understands me like you do.

To my mom and dad, who don't know about this book but who'd get a kick out of it if they did. Thank you both for everything, absolutely everything, from perfectionism all the way down to a keen eye for the absurd. You taught me all I know about laughter and love.

To my beta readers: Roxane Crawford, you were my first reader. You provided exactly the right thoughts, encouragement, and nudges about kink at exactly the right time. To Delaney Foster, for being my girl and my cheerleader at every step.

To Samantha Stroh Bailey… I hope you know that without you, I would've thrown in the towel long ago. I am so unbelievably lucky to have you as a friend and band member. Go Rams.

To the team of professionals who helped me get this work in front of readers, I couldn't have done this without you. Jena Campbell at Indie Girl Promotions, you are infinitely patient and helpful in so many ways. I am so lucky to have found you. Jade Eby at the Write Assistants, I knew we were a match made in heaven from the very first conversation. Spirit animals forever. Najla Qamber, thank you for your artist's eye and for knowing what I needed before I did. To Eagle Featherstonehaugh at Aquila Editing, thank you for your meticulous eye, support, and patience with my crutch words. Besides, it's alright though. And to Alexis Durbin for her final edits.

To Professor Eugene Thacker at The New School, who provided the inspiration for Professor Benjamin Beck. *In The Dust of This Planet* deserves its place on Jay-Z's jacket and everywhere else. You may have written it for nobody, but I enjoyed the hell out of it.

To Helena Hunting for her interest in my work. To Alexa Riley for her encouragement along the way. And a special thank you to Alex Lucian who is such an inspiration to me and who was so very generous in supporting this manuscript.

Lastly, thank you to my readers. As I sit here and write this, I don't know any of you yet but I can't wait to meet you. Thank you so much for reading my work. I hope you enjoyed spending time with Ben and Naomi as much as I did.

Coming soon:
Confessed, starring Lucy. September 2016.
And many more in the works...

Made in the USA
San Bernardino, CA
03 October 2016